THERE IS A BOOK

THERE IS A BOOK

By Madelyn Galbraith

Copyright © 1971

Herald Publishing House, Independence, Missouri

Library of Congress Catalog Card No. 75-147021
ISBN 0-8309-0043-8

Printed in the U.S.A.

THERE IS A BOOK

Santiago stirred uneasily in his sleep. He tried to shut out all sound, but the voice continued persistently.

"I tell you, Edward, somewhere there is a book! Such civilizations don't spring up out of the dust, then crumble into it again without leaving some sort of record. I've been doing a lot of thinking while lying here, and I believe I know where it is."

"You're delirious, Scott. The Indian records were all destroyed when the people were converted to Christianity," another said.

"Christianity! The Indian's religion is exactly that of his ancestors!"

"You're talking too much and getting excited with it."

"Well, who wouldn't be? I was within reach of success I'm sure when I took this fever. Now I'm getting out of here and I'm going back to Mexico and find the key to the riddle. Someone has this sacred book.... " The voice faded, and Santiago roused with a feeling of frustration. He sat up and shook his head from side to side. There was no use trying to go back to sleep, for the dream would recur to remind him of that night of horror. He looked over to where his grandson, Romero, lay wrapped in his poncho. Santiago raked the remains of last night's fire into a little heap, added a few twigs, and fanned the coals into flames. A blaze sprang up and beat back the early morning fog. He leaned against a convenient tree and in the comfort of the campfire's warmth, he found memory washing over him like a flood.

They had been young then—he and Josephina—young and gay, rich and popular. She was beautiful, and people said that he was handsome. They had just completed furnishing their New York apartment, and he recalled how happy they had been when the door closed behind the decorators.

On this particular night they had gone to the nursery early and kissed the children good-night. Tony was seven and Marquita just six months. After getting himself dressed he had joined Josephina. She was sitting before her mirror and smiled when she saw his reflection in it.

"Ready to go?" he asked.

"Yes, almost." She arose, and as her full, white skirt billowed about her feet she paused to clasp a bracelet around her wrist. Santiago took a last look at their reflection and followed her from the room.

Santiago compared his appearance then with his present one. Tall, straight, and slim-hipped he had had waving black hair and flashing eyes. His clothes had been tailor-made, and he wore them well. Now he looked down at himself and smiled wryly at the contrast—white cotton pajama-like trousers and shirt, and on his feet a pair of sandals made in the village.

"Time changes everything," he mused. Then memory hurried him from the present to the past again.

There had been a party that night at the opening of an art exhibit, and after the showing of his pictures a friend insisted on another to celebrate the success of the first. Carlos Parmarez had spared no expense, and those fortunate enough to have been invited said it was the most elaborate event of the social season. Santiago drank far too much, and on the way home his reflexes failed when a car traveling the opposite direction materialized out of the fog. He fumbled for the brake but found it too late. There was a deafening crash, and he saw that Josephina's face was cut and bleeding. He tried to draw her to him but was pinned behind the wheel and couldn't reach her. When he called her name there was no reply. As he sat there, powerless to help, her beautiful body sagged, then fell forward. Mercifully, he lost consciousness.

During the weeks that followed he had only occasional lucid moments. Faces drifted in and out of his range of vision. At first, only his father and sister, Elodia, were allowed in his room. Later on, friends called to console and sympathize. But Santiago lay passive through it all. He never spoke except to answer a question. His father approached the doctor about his lack of interest in anything, even his children. He had not once mentioned them.

"Suppose we try putting him in the room with another convalescent," the doctor suggested. "I have someone in mind. He's an agreeable chap and an interesting conversationalist." So they moved him in with Dr. Prine, and that's how he happened to hear the conversation that had haunted him ever since.

This Dr. Prine was an elderly man, and from hearing him talk with his visitors Santiago learned that he was an archaeologist. While exploring ruins in Mexico he had developed an intermittent fever and had returned to his home to recuperate. He was improving now and chafing over the delay in his work.

Until then Santiago had never given a thought to the history of his people, but Dr. Prine's enthusiasm had aroused his interest. He had never spoken to the man and had insisted that a screen be kept between the two beds—but he had listened.

"Our experiment has not been successful, Doctor," his father said one day. "I want my son moved into a private room. I think he will be better satisfied alone." After he was moved and they were assured of his improvement, his father and sister took his children and returned to their home in Mexico.

As soon as he could sit up Santiago asked for books on American archaeology; he spent hours reading them and comparing their theories concerning the origin of the Indian. As soon as he was strong enough he joined other patients in the solarium. One day as he was reading he became conscious of being watched, closed the book, and looked up. The man beside him nodded.

"I believe we have the same interest. I see you're reading Spinden," he said.

"I can't say that I'm really interested, but I have become curious about the origin of the Indian."

"I've spent some time in Latin America studying the ruins, and the more I learn the greater my confusion. Have you seen Palenque, Monte Alban?"

Santiago nodded. "I was born in Mexico."

"You were?" He seemed shocked.

"I'm Indian. My name is Santiago Salazar."

"Dr. Scott Prine," the other said, extending his hand, "and I'm glad to know you. Tell me, have you ever heard of a written record of your people?"

"Nothing that you haven't read, I'm sure."

"No, no, it's a much older record than any that have come to light so far. I've been looking for it for more than twenty years. I'm almost convinced that someone has beat me to it and has it hidden away, perhaps in some native hut. I can imagine some tribal leader having it on his family altar along with his pagan gods. Doesn't the possibility intrigue you—the thought that in some hut, carefully wrapped in a straw mat, this priceless treasure is waiting to be found?" The doctor's voice vibrated with emotion.

"I never thought about it. I've spent most of my life in this country. What makes you think there is such a record?"

"Mr. Salazar, when the Americas were visited—or perhaps I should say invaded—by the outside world, the intruders found remnants of a civilization superior to their own. Archaeology has proved that the natives of these countries—and I am referring to both North and South America—had brought with them a fully developed culture. Where did they get it?"

"With all the research that's been done, surely someone has found the answer," Santiago said.

"Oh, we have copies of what are referred to as their 'sacred books,' but they are just legends that have been handed down from one generation to the next. Some of the stories tell of a people coming from the east, from some tower, crossing the waters in boats. These would appear to be fantasy. Somewhere, Mr. Salazar, there has to be a book written by the historians of that age. Each civilization has left some sort of record behind. This one did also, and only when this book is found will we have the real story of the Indian. You have seen the ruins of Mexico, I'm sure."

"Some of them," Santiago said.

"Then you'll agree that their builders were not savage tribes, but a people with a broad cultural background. Have you ever studied the carvings on the temple walls?"

"No," Santiago admitted, "I haven't."

"They're trying to tell us something, Mr. Salazar. What is it? There are few things more frustrating than to stand before a glyph-covered wall or stele and wonder who carved those strange figures and what he was recording. It's like trying to communicate with a deaf-mute when you don't understand sign language. I am especially interested in the frequent

11

appearance of the hand among the hieroglyphics. Sometimes it's shown from the back, sometimes closed or extended horizontally, and in one instance it is open with a cross etched across the palm. Now what conclusion do you draw from that?"

Santiago thought for a moment before replying. "I hardly know. The hand is a symbol of authority, assurance, power. Men shake hands to seal an agreement. A handshake is also a greeting. When a king is enthroned someone in authority places his hands on the candidate's head and invests him with the power of his office. The Pope extends his hands in blessing, and men speak of the hand of God." Santiago had difficulty putting his thoughts into words.

"I was wondering if you were going to leave out the last! Don't you see the significance, Mr. Salazar—the open hand and the cross?"

"I'm afraid I don't."

Dr. Prine was plainly disappointed. He took the book from Santiago's knee and turned its pages thoughtfully. "When I think what these people once were and then see their present condition I am ready to start a revolution."

"I don't know anything about that. I've been away since I was a small child, except for short visits with my family."

"I don't know how some of them exist. The government has tried to help, but from my observation only a small percentage of those in need have benefitted."

"I doubt that they know enough to profit by any aid given them."

"You share the idea many people have—that the Indian is stupid and lacks ambition. You're wrong. There's many a man who yearns to get above the grinding poverty he has always known. There's a chap down there who has been with me on every assignment. He wants so much to establish his family in better surroundings in a place where his children can get the education he lacks. His teen-age son is just as ambitious. He wants to become an architect. I have him in a school in Guadalajara. You'll hear of Mike Alazan some day."

"How did you become involved in all this? Why are you so interested?" Santiago asked.

"When I was young—just out of medical school—an uncle who was well established in Guatemala offered to make me his heir if I'd join his organization as its company doctor. It sounded good, so I went down. But after looking things over, I found the proposal wasn't so appealing. I was given three months to decide and a guide to show me the attractions of the job. On our tour I was taken past a partially uncovered mound. I had no idea of its archaeological value nor how our brief pause at the spot would change my entire life. I left it with reluctance but was back the next day, horrified at seeing a woman chase her chickens over the mound while a child tied a pig to a richly carved stone. And then I learned that similar stones had been used to build pens for the cattle. That was the beginning, although some might think it was the end. I suddenly realized that I could never settle down to doling out aspirin and quinine or treating septic sores. My uncle washed his hands of me. My younger brother went down and took over the management of the estate, which was really what Uncle Jim wanted. To sum it up, Johnny got all the money, but I've had all the fun."

"Did your mound produce anything to justify your sacrifice?"

"There is interest and value in every site. It was no Chichen Itza, but some of its artifacts are in the museum, I just wish I had started sooner. If only I had studied archaeology instead of medicine! At the rate we're moving, I'm afraid I won't live to see that book."

"You'll excuse me, Dr. Prine, but I can't understand your

obsession about a book that you don't even know exists," Santiago said.

"And I can't understand how you, Mr. Salazar, an Indian, can be anything else. It has become an obsession with me, I'll admit." Dr. Prine thumbed through his book absentmindedly. "Late one afternoon I climbed to the top of the Pyramid of the Sun in Teotihuacan to get a general view of the area. I'll never forget my feeling of frustration as I looked down on lesser pyramids, on acres of roofless walls. On one hand was the Pyramid of the Moon, on the other the magnificent, mysterious Temple of Quetzalcoatl. I, like Michaelangelo before his completed statue of Moses, could have cried 'Why don't you speak?' "

Santiago leaned back wearily, and Dr. Prine, seeing his evident fatigue, looked around for a nurse.

Santiago's attendant was coming down the corridor. "Ready to lie down?" he asked.

"I hope I haven't tired you too much," Dr. Prine said.

"Oh, no," Santiago roused himself to say, "I've enjoyed our conversation. I'd like to continue it tomorrow."

When he entered the solarium the next morning he looked around for the scientist. "I wonder where Dr. Prine is," he said.

"Haven't you heard?" a patient seated nearby asked. "He had a heart attack and died at four this morning."

Santiago looked at him in unbelief. "Oh! What a pity! All his work and research for nothing! Now the boy won't get his education . . . and Dr. Prine was so ambitious for him."

"What boy?"

"The doctor was sending an Indian boy to school. Now he'll have to go back to herding goats I suppose."

"Oh, maybe not. Perhaps someone else will see him through."

"But who will find him? What was his name? I remember

that he was studying architecture in Guadalajara." He closed his eyes in concentration. Suddenly he leaned forward. "I remember now! It may not be easy, but I'll find him!"

When Santiago returned to Mexico six months later he found Tony well adjusted to his new life and Marquita a miniature Josephina. It took time for them to accept him, but he finally won them over. Years passed, and the children were sent to the States to receive their education. Tony was married secretly while he was still in college, and a year later his wife died following the birth of their son Romero. Soon after that Tony entered military service, and Santiago and his sister, Elodia, brought Romero to Mexico. Then Tony was killed in an accident.

Seated by the fire, now, he thought of the boys and girls he had sent from the Valley to learn a profession or trade, with only a verbal agreement that they in turn would educate others in similar circumstances. Very few had kept that promise. Some had used him and his money to escape the dull surroundings of their homes, and once away, never returned. But those who did made him feel that the plan had been successful.

Now one of his protégés had him guessing. Luis Mendoza had left the Valley years before to study medicine but had never mentioned getting his degree. About the only time he wrote was to ask for an increase in his allowance, giving as a reason that he wanted to take special courses. Santiago had forwarded the money without question, but he was growing impatient.

He added another stick to the fire and leaned back to continue his musing. His thoughts turned to the members of his own family. Had he been fair in moving them into such humble surroundings? He tried to analyze himself. Why had he left his beautiful home near Mexico City? Did he, as the priest charged, feel guilty because of his wealth and was forcing his loved ones to share his penance? But they seemed happy—all but Romero. He was becoming more of a problem every day.

How about Marquita? She was a young lady now, and by Mexican standards should have been married long ago. She didn't lack suitors. The garden was filled with them—some from the city, others from Monterrey, San Luis, Los Mochis, and points between. And no wonder, for hadn't she been declared the most beautiful girl in school, and hadn't she grown even lovelier since?

He drew his knees up under his poncho and continued to study the fire. Pursuing his reflections he thought of his sister and the tragic death of her husband of three months. His own bereavement followed soon after and his father's death close behind. It was that that had brought him back from New York.

He recalled the dark days that had followed his homecoming when he had tried to take over the management of the estate. How many mistakes he had made and how it galled him to be forced into a role for which he was not fitted. He finally employed an experienced manager which left him free to wander over the mountains.

He remembered the day he came in from his roaming to find a letter from the school where Miguel Alazan was enrolled. The boy had to leave, he read, since with the death of his father he became the family's breadwinner. His teachers felt that it was a great tragedy, for the boy ranked as near-genius. Could he do anything to make it possible for him to continue his education? Santiago had gone immediately to the address given him. He was shocked at the poverty of the home and stood, rather than sit on the mat offered him, until Miguel came in from the field. Provisions for his return to school and the care of the family were soon made. Santiago was in a hurry to leave. Such paucity irritated him. As he stooped to pass through the low doorway his attention was drawn to a shelf displaying a number of clay objects. Human heads with animal bodies and the reverse. Human faces depicting anger, fear, hate, and triumph were grouped together.

"Whoever did these was a master of his craft," Santiago said.

"Dr. Prine gave them to me. I often helped him sort out these things," Miguel explained.

"Did the doctor ever mention finding a book? A history of the Indian?"

"Oh, yes, and he wanted to so badly. Someday someone will find it, but it's too late for Dr. Prine."

"Did you enjoy working for him?"

"Very much. He often took me with him. Once we went to El Castillo."

"That's in Chichen Itza?"

The boy nodded. "You're going there?" There was excitement in his voice.

"I may."

"Then go with God, señor, go with God!"

"Are you leaving again this morning?" Elodia asked at breakfast.

"Yes," Santiago replied briefly.

"I wish you'd tell me where you're going and when to expect your return."

"I don't know where I'm going or when I'll return. I simply can't be content here."

"What you need is to get busy again. You haven't unpacked your easels since you came home."

"I don't need them. I'll never paint again."

"Why? To me it's unforgivable not to use such talent as you have. Few men are so gifted," Elodia argued.

"I know my work is good, but my pride in it was responsible for my tragedy. You know, Elodia, the flattering articles the newspapers and magazines carried . . ." He toyed with a spoon, his eyes downcast.

"I know, Santos, I read them and they are not over-praise."

"Such adulation isn't good for anyone. It's more intoxicating than liquor. All the flattery that night went to my head and I drank with everyone who praised me until I was seeing double. I killed my wife!"

"You did not kill Josephina. It was an accident!"

"An accident that wouldn't have happened if I'd been sober."

He arose and turned to leave the room when Elodia asked, "Did you take care of the young student?"

"Yes, and his family. They were actually in need! I didn't know there was that degree of poverty anywhere. Certainly none of our people are in that condition."

"I doubt it. I think Father provided for all of ours."

"I hope so. I would be ashamed for anyone connected with the estate to be in such straits." Elodia followed him to the door and watched him ride away.

His restlessness had driven him far that day, and he had ridden for hours without purpose until he came to the Valley. He paused on the rim of the ledge above and measured it from the point below until it lost itself in a canyon miles away.

It was like a basin filled with gold, so profuse were the esperanza blossoms. The river reflected the flowers that bordered its banks as it rippled its golden length through the Valley. The surrounding mountains were hung with a silvery mist, and through this haze the blooming jacaranda trees dotted the slopes with purple. The peacefulness seemed to call to him, and he directed his horse down the incline into the Valley.

The closer view was not so inviting, and a feeling of disgust for the place momentarily possessed him. He had failed to see the village from the ledge. Now he noted that the natives lived in squalor, their homes little better than pigsties. There had been at one time a lovely fountain in the plaza, and although the water still flowed the basin was choked with dirt and leaves.

The few men he saw seemed apathetic; the women looked careworn and hopeless. Children of all ages with fly-tormented eyes paused in their joyless play to watch him as he rode past.

The pueblo, he thought, was like a cemetery. Death would only deliver these people from one degree of dirt to another—a return to the element with which they associated every day.

And yet, there was great beauty too. Beside the esperanza, bougainvillea waved wands of pink, purple, and white blossoms. Clumps of scarlet geraniums released their pungent fragrance when his horse brushed against them. His artist's eye caught the dappled shadows of a dusty lane and he followed it. It led to a crumbling adobe church, a fitting sanctuary for the drab village. The parish priest, Father Clemente, was a young man, but he wore his habit in as slovenly a manner as his communicants did their baggy pants. And he wasn't much cleaner, Santiago noticed.

"What is the name of your village, Father?" he asked.

"We call it 'Esperanza'—although we've lost all hope."

"Improvements are certainly needed," Santiago said, "but there is also much to recommend the place. Here you have peace, solitude."

19

"And time to get bored with both," the priest interrupted bitterly.

"I would like to live in your village of hope," Santiago suddenly decided.

"You would be very welcome, but I doubt that you'd be happy here."

"Why?"

"You appear to be a man of wealth. What could you find in this sleepy Indian village to amuse you?"

"What makes you think I want to be amused?"

"Everyone must have some form of entertainment, something to occupy his time. I have my church, the people their fiestas, but here there are no theaters, no music halls; why, we don't even have a school!"

"Good! This is the place I'm looking for. I'll busy myself educating the village children."

The priest smiled and shook his head. "When I first came here I had dreams of doing that. I was afire with enthusiasm. This was at one time the center of a mining camp, but the vein ran out, leaving the people without employment. They became what you see now. It's impossible to do anything with them—they have no ambition. You see, they are Indian."

"So am I," Santiago said. The embarrassed priest was profuse in his apologies.

"No offense was intended," he said.

"And none was taken," Santiago cut him off briefly. "Now, if you will show me some land . . ."

"I don't know that any is available."

"Who owns this area, the government?"

"No, it belongs to Señor Sebastian Salazar."

Santiago looked at him in amazement. "He was my father!" he exclaimed. He looked about him. "This village is a disgrace! How long since the mines have been worked?"

"Five or six years. Oh, once we were prosperous enough—at least the men had work and their families had food. That is when the men didn't drink or gamble their money away. Pardon my saying it, but Indians are like children. They need direction and, except for me, they have been without it for a long time. And no one cares."

"I do! I'll not have any part of my estate or the people on it looking like this! I'll live here. Will you come and help me select a suitable place for my home?"

Santiago wandered over the Valley and came to an area where springs bubbled out of the ground and a lake mirrored the wild growth around it.

"This is it. I'll build my house here, and a garden will enclose the lake."

He told Elodia of his decision, and she agreed to go with him. When the house in the Valley was ready, she had the furniture carefully packed and moved to the new location.

For a time Santiago was content. With the priest lending support he instituted a clean-up campaign. The fountain was cleared of the accumulation of debris; then its tiles were scrubbed and polished to newness. The plaza was planted with shrubs and flowers, and the benches around it were repainted. But the people could not be aroused to extend the renovating into their own homes. Santiago concluded that much of their inertia was due to poor diet, so he provided the proper food. He soon realized his mistake. The villagers accepted what he offered and asked for more. Then the news of his generosity spread to other areas, and instead of the twenty families he started with, Santiago counted fifty. In utter disgust he discontinued the program and set off on new wanderings.

A letter and his report card from Miguel reminded him of the boy's interest in the Mexican ruins, and he decided to see them again.

As though it were yesterday he could see again the majestic El Castillo in the moonlight. He had returned the next day to explore the area more fully, and he asked himself in almost agonized frustration, "When was this pyramid erected? Who did it? Where did its builders originate?" The questions were repeated at Palenque, and echoed among the ruins of El Tejin. Santiago had to agree with Dr. Prine—there must be a book!

He searched diligently in museums and libraries but without success. Finally he concluded that again Dr. Prine was right—the record was hidden somewhere, revered, perhaps worshiped in secret. From then on his quest had been among the people. There were times when he became discouraged but a return to one of the archaeological sites fanned his interest and renewed his determination to find the record.

Romero turned over and opened his eyes as the sun rose above the mountain peaks. He shivered in the early morning chill, then burrowed deeper into his poncho. He suddenly sensed that his grandfather was no longer beside him, and he raised his head to look around.

"What's the matter, Grandpa—you sick?"

"No, I feel fine. Are you ready for breakfast?"

"I'm always ready to eat." He arose, yawning, and followed Santiago to a sheltered spot on a small stream. They stepped out of their clothes and into the water.

"Wow!" Romero shouted. "This is cold!"

"It has no equal as a quick wake-up."

"I'd appreciate it a lot more a little later in the day," Romero replied, splashing water over his firm, young body. Santiago finished his bath, and, standing on the riverbank, let the sun and wind perform the duties of a towel, then dressed.

He filled the coffeepot upstream and returned to camp. When Romero joined him he found the pot boiling and the tortillas toasting over the bright coals. Santiago handed him a cup of coffee and some tortillas.

"Aren't you going to eat anything, Grandpa?"

"I want only my coffee."

"If I weren't with you on these trips you wouldn't need a thing but that," Romero charged.

"I like having you with me. I don't mind the extra pannier. I miss you when you're in school and I have to make the trips alone."

"Don't you ever get tired of this wandering around?"

"I thought you enjoyed it." Santiago evaded the question.

"Oh, it's better than staying in the Valley . . . anything beats that. It isn't bad when we're in the cities, but most of the time we hit only pueblos."

"You speak as if we're tramps. There is a purpose in what you call my wandering."

"I know that your visits mean a lot to the villagers, especially the old ones, but it's still a waste of time."

"Time spent in giving pleasure to others is never wasted, Romero. Besides that, someday I hope that in one of these isolated pueblos I'll hear of the book. I may not find it, but if I fail I want you to continue the search."

Romero looked up quickly. "Not me . . . I'm not going to spend my life chasing a feather! You don't know for certain that there is such a record."

"There *is* a book!" Santiago insisted.

"Then let someone else find it. I want no part of it!"

They sat without speaking until the labored sound of an approaching automobile roused them. They left the fire and hurried to the highway. A large car was advancing by fits and starts. When the driver saw them he stopped.

"Having trouble I see," was Santiago's greeting.

"Trouble! I've had nothing but trouble all night! I'm lost . . . have been for hours. I got off the highway sometime before daylight, I'm out of water, and I'm . . ."

Santiago halted the man's cataloguing of his woes. "There's water close by," he said. "My grandson will fill your radiator if you have a container he can put the water in."

"I have two five-gallon cans. I started out with them full, but the supply didn't last long enough." He took one can and handed the other to Romero. As he passed the camp, Santiago saw that his eyes rested on the coffeepot, so on the return trip he stopped him.

"How about a cup of coffee?"

"I was hoping you'd ask me," the stranger said as he accepted the cup. "I've driven all night, most of it in the wrong direction."

"Well, then, some breakfast is in order. Just a moment while I heat the tortillas," and Santiago duplicated Romero's meal.

"I certainly didn't expect anything like this, Mr. . . . ."

"Salazar—Santiago Salazar, and this is my grandson, Romero."

"I'm Ed Baker." He shook hands with both, then continued his breakfast. "I don't know what I'd have done if I hadn't met you, and I'm very glad that you speak English so well. I've had trouble in making myself understood since I've been traveling in this area."

"I had my schooling in the United States," Santiago told him.

"Grandpa went to Yale," Romero said proudly.

"A Yale man and you're here like. . . like. . ." Santiago chuckled at his guest's embarrassment.

"Yes, I'm happier here. This is where I belong. I am

24

Indian, Mr. Baker, and even though I lived for many years in your country, my roots are here."

"I see." The man was extremely uncomfortable and looked for some way to atone for his unintentional rudeness. "Your people must have a wonderful history," he said lamely.

"And a baffling one. With all the study and excavating that's been done, the scientists are just about as puzzled over it as a peasant farmer would be if he thought about it. I am sure, though, that somewhere there's a book which can unravel all the mystery surrounding our origin and perhaps give the reason for our decline."

"That reminds me of something I once heard about a golden book!" the visitor exclaimed.

"A golden book?" Santiago leaned forward eagerly. "Where did you hear of it?"

"You'll have to give me a moment to think. I'm a mining engineer, and I once worked in Mexico. But it's been all of ten years and I've been around the world since then. As I remember, though, we went west after leaving Zimapan. I picked up a guide at the hotel, for the people in that part of the country spoke a dialect I didn't understand. One night after we made camp we were joined by a half dozen men. They seemed to spring up out of the cactus. They began swapping yarns with my men and as I was unable to follow the conversation I asked for a translation. One of our guests said that at one time a relative had worked for an archaeologist digging around some ruins. . . ."

"Which ruins?" Santiago asked.

"I don't know. He said they were in a place far away."

"Who was the archaeologist?"

"I don't remember that he mentioned any name. It seemed that the men were digging in an area where extreme caution was necessary. They were resentful of their employer's watchfulness and as soon as his back was turned they grabbed their tools and went at it. They struck some massive object and thought it was the wall they had been looking for. As they dug around it, however, one of the stones moved, revealing a large concrete box. In this box lay the book."

"What did they do with it?"

"A very peculiar thing occurred, according to the storyteller. As one of the men reached out to take the book he fell back dead, and the others were knocked unconscious as by a giant fist. When they came to themselves the appearance of the place had changed. It bore no resemblance to the spot where they had been working."

"But didn't anyone follow this up and try to find the book?"

"Well, you know how superstitious these people are. When the story got around, no Indian would touch a spade to the ground. The archaeologist threatened to kill them all if they didn't produce the book. He accused them of taking it and hiding it."

Santiago buried his face in his hands and rocked back and forth in his disappointment. "Thank you, Mr. Baker, for your story, although it's discouraging to think how near we may have been to solving the mystery. There is some consolation in knowing that the book does exist."

Seeing how Santiago was affected by his recital, Ed Baker was sorry he'd mentioned the tale, and as if to soften future frustration said, "I wouldn't count too much on the truthfulness of the story. It may have been someone's imagination. But if it is true, I doubt that the book's still around. Someone would have come across it." He arose and said, "I must be going. I wish I could return your hospitality. Now . . . is there any way I can get on the main road without turning back?"

"Ten kilometers straight ahead will lead you onto it."

They waved him off, then broke camp and saddled their horses. Santiago led off up the narrow trail.

"Do you know where you're going, Grandpa?"

"I usually do, don't I? We're going home . . . but indirectly. I just thought of an old man who lives up this way who once worked with a National Geographic group. I want to ask him some questions."

For a time they rode in silence. The sun bore down, and there was no shelter from the heat. The mesquite bushes were sunburned, and their brittle limbs raked the sides of the horses as they passed. Lizards scurried through the dried leaves making small, rustling sounds. A cloud of dust, raised by a horse and his rider traveling ahead of them, outlined their course up the mountain.

While they were still a distance from the pueblo their approach was announced by the village dogs. Vegetation grew more scarce, and huge ant beds left large areas of the ground entirely bare. Soon they were in the village; the people paused to watch them. Santiago dismounted and, after the usual exchange of greetings, explained his purpose for being there.

"I would like to see Señor Guillermo."

"My José will show you," one woman volunteered. "José, take the señor to Uncle Felix."

Santiago followed the boy to where an old man sat with his chair leaned against the trunk of a tree. He was a colorful figure in faded pink trousers and blue shirt, his bare feet hooked around the legs of his chair. Romero trailed behind, then slid off his horse and lounged nearby. He was not unaware of the admiring feminine glances that followed him.

The old man, eyes filmed by time, stared straight ahead as Santiago questioned him. He smoked on for a time, then spoke slowly and with care.

"There should be a record, but I've never seen nor heard

of it. Unless someone writes the story of our people it will soon be forgotten."

"I know. That's why I want to find the book."

The aged one shook his head. "All I know is what my father told me, and his father told him, on back through many generations."

"And what did your father tell you?"

The old man bent over and traced on the ground the crude figure of a man, and below that, four similar figures. "Many years ago," he explained, "a man set out with his four sons from a land far away. They came across the sea in a boat, perhaps more than one . . . I do not know. But they came to this country and became a mighty nation. They built many pueblos—they and their sons and their sons' sons. I have seen them; the buildings were of stone." With a sweep of his hand he erased the drawing and leaned back. "Then, many years later, another man came. He was white, and his hair and beard were the color of corn silk . . . and he carried a cross."

"A cross?" Santiago repeated. "Why?"

"I don't know. He taught the people many things, and he healed the sick."

"Yes?" Santiago prompted impatiently. "What else did your father tell you?"

"That's all I remember. I've told you all I know!"

Santiago thanked him for his information, and the Salazars mounted their horses and left.

"Nothing new," Santiago said regretfully. "I've heard those stories dozens of times. Everyone seems to know of the four brothers and the white stranger, but no one can go beyond that."

"As stupid as I think our painting those memorial pictures is, Grandpa, it makes more sense then chasing after this book."

28

"Have you no desire to learn about your ancestors?"

"None. What I know of our present conditions sickens me. Those natives back there—slovenly, superstitious, illiterate . . ."

"We were not always like this, Romero. Our forefathers had a culture that flourished long before Greece or Rome became great," Santiago said.

"It's a pity we didn't inherit some of it. If, as you claim, the Indians were at one time a great nation—what happened?"

"I wish I knew! I assume their downfall had the same cause as all great governments of the past—moral decay. That's why I want to find the record. It will explain all."

"Well, if there is one, the chances are that neither you nor I will be around to see it. Let's get away from here, Grandpa! Let's get out of Mexico!"

Santiago rode on with bowed head. "No, Romero, this is home. I have a task here, and so have you."

"You've done your part. Aunt Elodia says you've made the Valley! Isn't that enough?"

"No, it's just the beginning. There is no time or place to stop until every person in Mexico who wants an education of any sort gets it."

"You've set yourself a pretty big job. Do you actually think you can do it?"

"Not alone. My task is to start from where I am with what I have. Doesn't your heart ache for those people back there? I doubt that much can be done for the old ones, but the children must have an education!"

"Grandpa, you know as well as I do that 90 percent of the people would rather have their children in the cornfield than in a schoolroom. Remember how hard it was for you and Aunt Elodia to get the Rodriguez kids in school?"

"Yes, but we did it, and now the children are teaching their parents!" Santiago exulted.

Romero realized he had chosen the wrong example. "Well," he insisted, "that's just one family. I still say that 90 percent will fight it."

"Aren't the 10 percent worth going after?"

"I think you're wasting a lot of time and money," Romero persisted, but seeing that he was losing the argument he asked, "Can't we stop somewhere until evening? This sun is boring a hole right through my hat."

"I was thinking the same thing. I noticed some women with their laundry baskets when we passed here earlier, so there's water somewhere near." A little later he took a trail that led to a small mountain stream. The horses were unsaddled and watered, then tied to a tree. Santiago went farther up the bank and found a shady spot for their siesta. Romero brought the saddle blankets, and they stretched out on them with their feet dangling in the water.

"Mr. Baker certainly had a good-looking car," Romero said.

"Yes, and it took a terrific beating coming up that mountain. I'm surprised he made it."

Santiago looked on with interest while Romero squirmed about, then sat up and removed a sharp stone from under his blanket. He settled back and continued. "He was surprised that you spoke English so well. Grandpa, tell me how it was when you were young. Aunt Elodia talks about it sometimes, but it's mostly party talk, dances, and balls."

"Elodia has many pleasant memories of her girlhood, for she was both beautiful and popular. What more can a señorita want?"

"Was that before the rich men had all their land taken from them?"

"Romero, you have an idea that the land reform was an

evil thing. Of course there was many an injustice—that always happens following a political upheaval. There have been many patriots who have tried to equalize the distribution of Mexico's wealth. There was a time when just a few families owned practically all of Mexico. That wasn't right, and my grandfather knew it. He divided a good part of his land long before the revolution. The new laws didn't touch us, for the family holdings had been so reduced that the government didn't bother to take what was left. My father was a good businessman, and when he came into the estate he invested in some profitable ventures in the United States and Europe."

"What became of them?"

"I disposed of the ones in Europe. We still operate some in the States. But let's forget about the family finances."

"Well, am I going to college in the States?"

"I don't know. I'd rather you stayed in Mexico. We have good schools here now."

"I'd like to go to one in New York. Didn't you like New York?"

"I suppose I did."

"What was it like? Tell me what you did."

"I wasted time, mostly. I opened my studio and spent part of my days dawdling. My mind wasn't on my art. I wasn't willing to pay the price success demands, so I failed. And all the time I knew what I was doing and resented the inner drive that forced my sporadic trying. But I finally managed to finish enough pictures for a very successful exhibit." Santiago paused briefly. "And that night I killed my wife."

"Grandpa . . . you never told me!"

"No, I won't discuss it, but I have nightmares. That's why I was up so early." Again Santiago paused.

"Go on."

"I told you I had a successful showing of my pictures.

Afterward I insisted on driving my car when I was so drunk I didn't know the steering wheel from the door. It was a foggy night, and I couldn't stop in time. Josephina was killed instantly."

There was silence while Romero thought this over, then asked, "Is that why you won't have a car? But why have you stayed here all this time?"

"Because it's where I belong. Even though I spent most of my life in the States, I wasn't, by temperament, fitted for the pace there. Neither was your father, nor—I am convinced—are you."

"That's why you want to keep me in the Valley," Romero concluded.

"I went out and killed my wife. Your father went out and killed himself. I doubt that I can survive another such tragedy."

"I'll never be satisfied here. I know I can do something really worthwhile if I can just get into the United States. There's where the money is."

"Are you interested in painting or making money?"

"Both. Don't you think it's possible to make money painting?"

"Not if money is your goal. There are far more hungry artists than well-fed ones."

"I know I can succeed if only I can get away from here. I wish we had the money we once had."

"We have our needs and reasonable wants. That's all any man is entitled to," Santiago told him firmly. Silenced, Romero lay looking up through the trees. His grandfather tilted his hat over his eyes and Romero followed his example. Soon both were fast asleep.

I t was darkening in the Valley, but the mountaintops caught and held the last bit of light. Romero rode ahead; when he reached the ledge, he slid from his horse and waited for his grandfather. Santiago joined him a moment later and dismounted to stand beside him. They turned to watch the setting sun.

"I'll send Panocha and Picante on to sort of warn Aunt Elodia that we're coming home starved." Romero gave the horses a sharp slap that sent them hurrying down the hill. "I'm so hungry I could eat a tortilla as big as the moon."

Santiago chuckled. "That would be a sizable one. I'm not particularly hungry, but I am tired."

"You've pushed yourself too hard, Grandpa. We should have stopped at Diegos overnight."

"I know, but there are so many things to see to about the place. Blanco is a good man, but not much of an overseer."

"Why don't you replace him?"

"I wouldn't hurt his pride that way. Someday he'll catch on. I've always hoped that you'd become interested. . . ."

"I hate the place! I hate the pueblo and the entire Valley!"

Santiago looked at him wistfully, but Romero refused to see the appeal in his grandfather's eyes.

"I'll die if I have to stay here another year! I want to go to school in New York as my father did. I want to go where there's some inspiration; there's nothing here worth painting."

"A good artist, Romero, doesn't have to leave his home to find subjects for his canvas. If you'd only open your eyes you'd find inspiration all around you. And speaking of subjects, have you ever seen anything to equal that?" His sweeping hand included the surrounding hills and horizon. Directly overhead the sky was an intense blue, shading to green, muted tones of yellow, then pink which deepened into crimson. The mountains were blue velvet in the twilight, and in a valley half hidden between two peaks, a single cactus was silhouetted against the sky.

"That picture," Santiago said tremulously, "can never be duplicated. It was painted by the hand of God."

Even the impatient Romero was humbled by the beauty of sunset. "I wish I could blend those colors," he yearned. They stood silent until the lights in the sky faded and those in the pueblo began to appear.

"Come," said Santiago, "let's go down. Our women will be worried, and the food will be cold." The trail led down the rugged slope but their familiarity with its rough surface made the descent easy.

Santiago moved slowly toward his home at the head of the Valley. It was set apart and overshadowed the smaller buildings in the area. Large urns filled with flowering vines spilled color over the high rock wall that enclosed it. Santiago unlocked the heavy gate and preceded Romero inside. He could see through the open door and across the hall into the patio beyond, where a fountain sprayed a fine mist over the plants bordering its marble rim. As he paused in the doorway his sister came forward to greet him.

"Santiago, it's good to have you home again."

"It's good to be home, Elodia. Santa Maria, but I'm tired!"

"I've told you repeatedly, Santos, that you shouldn't take those long trips on horseback. When you have to go, take a bus."

"Father, I was beginning to worry about you." Marquita came to stand beside him.

"I'm all right except for being tired."

"Where's the boy?" Elodia asked.

"He'll be along in a minute. He stopped to talk to the dog. I'm afraid we can't keep him here much longer. He's just as determined to leave as Tony was."

"You'll let him go?" Elodia questioned.

"I'll take him when the time comes. But here he is. Say nothing about it now. . . . I must think."

Romero ran in, his dog at his heels. "Hey, Auntie, what's for supper? I'm so hungry I could eat Camote—raw."

"Spare the dog, there's plenty of food. It will be ready by the time you get your bath."

Later Romero followed his elders to the table. He was so accustomed to the room and its furnishings that he didn't even see them, but Santiago, with his artist's eye, missed nothing. He looked around with deep satisfaction. The tile brazier filled one end and extended into the room. Across the top were a half dozen openings below which lay a bed of burning coals. On this stove, under Anastasia's watchful eyes, the family's meals were prepared.

"It's always good to come back to familiar things," Santiago said.

Romero looked up quickly and followed his glance. "Why don't the girls cook on the stove as women in the city do? And why do we eat back here when we have a comfortable dining room?"

"Aunt Elodia and I always eat here when we're alone. The dining area is much too large for the two of us. We didn't expect you tonight and didn't have time to change the table setting. The answer to your first question is that the girls won't cook on the electric stove," Marquita explained.

"Why not?"

"They say it has no soul."

"Stupid Indians! You see what I mean, Grandpa? And we're as bad! As long as we stay here we're no better than the peasants!"

"Leaving Mexico wouldn't change us," Marquita told him.

"Yes, it would! Things would be different in the States or in Europe. Aunt Elodia would be considered somebody if she were in France! As long as you stay here you'll teach grubby little kids their letters while Grandpa roams over the mountains painting pictures for their superstitious parents."

Marquita started to reply, but her father shook his head. But Elodia had something to say, and she said it.

"Romero Salazar, you listen to me! I refuse to sit here quietly while you abuse your grandfather and your aunt. They lived out of Mexico for years and came back here for a good reason. Now stop acting like the spoiled child that you are and eat your supper."

"And a good supper it is, too." Santiago hastened to avoid further controversy. "Anastasia is certainly giving the girls good training."

"It's a beautiful morning," Marquita said as she rearranged the flowerpots around the base of the fountain.

"It's Monday, and Monday mornings are never beautiful," Romero contradicted.

"Aren't you afraid you'll miss your bus?" Elodia asked.

"I have twenty minutes, and if I'm not there Gus'll wait for me." Romero arose, took his books under his arm, and sauntered through the door.

36

"I don't know what we'll ever do with that boy!" Elodia declared. "What's given him such a turn about going to the States?"

"Oh, he meets a lot of people from across the border. There are students from nearly every point of the continent registered at the university. You know how proud they are of their country. Naturally, they extol its virtues and are blind to its vices," Marquita replied.

"And he's not mature enough to see it."

Marquita picked up a small sprinkling can, filled it at the fountain, and carefully watered a bed of seedlings. Elodia sat watching her as she made repeated trips to the fountain.

"Do I hear cackling?" she asked.

"Yes," Marquita dropped her can. "Someone left a gate open! Bruno . . . Blanco . . . Juan . . . come quickly! Get these chickens out of here before they ruin my garden."

"Señorita, they just want the fat grasshoppers," Juan told her.

"Let them hunt them somewhere else!"

As they drove the chickens out, a flock of turkeys came through the gate, looking from side to side, uttering low gobbles of content. While the men were encircling them, a pig waddled in and began rooting in the damp flower beds.

Camote, returning from seeing Romero off to school, heard him and came on the run, barking furiously. They finally cleared the garden, and Marquita came to sit beside Elodia and catch her breath.

"I'll have to finish watering my flowers tonight. The bees are thick all over the carnations and jasmine. It sounds as though we have a hive set up in there."

"We should get some good honey this winter," Elodia said.

Marquita watched as her aunt manipulated her spindle.

Insects hummed for a while, then gradually grew still. "What do you think of Romero's going to New York?" she said.

"Who says he's going to New York?" Elodia asked.

"It's his Mecca, and sooner or later he'll get there."

"No good will come of his leaving Mexico," the older woman said firmly. She pushed her crown of white hair in place and reset the combs that held it. For a time her hands lay idle in her lap. "I just don't understand the disrespect Romero shows for his grandfather—and you and me, too, for that matter. Do you know that even after I was married I looked to my mother-in-law for guidance? I was ignorant of the customs of French nobility, and I had to have her advice. Romero doesn't think we know enough to pat our tortillas. I'm amazed at his rebellion. If he would only be content in Mexico!"

"He has his heart set on New York and he'll never rest until he gets there," Marquita said.

The day came to an end, and with the setting sun the farmers returned from the fields, driving their cattle before them. Candlelight shone through the windows, and smoke from supper fires hovered over the low rooftops.

Santiago sipped his chocolate slowly and thoughtfully. He smiled as Romero heaped his plate as though he hadn't eaten for a week.

"What's this I hear about your having a fight in the village, Romero?" he asked.

"It wasn't a fight." Mamie poured him a second cup of chocolate and pushed the cookies within easy reach.

"You don't call knocking two boys down a fight?"

Romero looked at his grandfather over the rim of his cup. "Not unless they hit back."

"I see. Well, what happened? There's a regular beehive of talk about it around the plaza."

"I hate a bully!" Romero declared. "Some people are

never satisfied unless they're tormenting someone smaller!" He was not inclined to discuss it, so Santiago turned to Mamie.

"You look as if you might know something about it, Mamie. Do you?"

"*Sí*, it was Flavio's granddaughter. She's new here, and they all make fun of her clothes."

"They were tearing her dress off her!" Romero added quickly. "That gang of girls and boys had her backed up against the wall, and they were all tormenting her. Not one tried to help her!"

"They tore her dress off?" Elodia exclaimed.

"Yes, she dresses sort of ... funny, you know ... not like the other girls. They just ripped it off her. She fought like a tiger, but she's so little she didn't have a chance. She was left standing there in her underwear. I couldn't get to her in time to stop them. But those peasants stood there laughing at her like the pack of idiots that they are. And she was all alone, crying! Some of the boys dared each other to take her pants off, too! So I laid them out, that's all!"

"What did the poor child do?" Marquita asked.

"Oh, she tried to cover herself with what was left of her dress!"

"Romero, he put her dress around her and carried her water pitcher home." Mamie was determined to get a word in.

"I am gratified, Romero, that you were kind to her. It makes me very proud of you," Elodia said.

"It wasn't anything. I was glad of a chance to take a poke at those characters. They've had it coming for a long time." He paused, then asked, "Did you get the strings for my guitar?"

"Yes, they're on the table in your den."

Romero went upstairs to get ready for his evening on the plaza.

"I wonder why they're so unkind to the child," Santiago mused.

"Children are sadistic little imps," was Elodia's explanation.

"No, there must be another reason for it. Do you have any idea, Marquita?"

"I'm not sure, Father. As Romero says, she dresses very poorly. I went by Flavio's shop the other day and asked him if I might buy her some school dresses. He was very surly and said if she had to have new clothes she could stay at home."

"The other children say she's too smart. She knows all the answers," Mamie put in.

"Yes, Velia says she's the brightest child she has ever taught. She recites with the fifth and sixth classes."

"How in the world . . ." Elodia began.

"She may be older than we think, and she has evidently gone to a mission school, although she won't talk about it."

"How old do you think she is?"

"I don't know, Father. In size, she's about six or seven, but mentally she's twelve or thirteen. I've been unable to approach her. She's very aloof and makes no friends."

"Yes, I've heard that. She's the first child to repulse me."

"Perhaps life with her grandfather is such as to make her wary of all men. From the neighbor's talk, Flavio doesn't want her and tells her so. At the least mishap he threatens to make her leave."

"Well, I'll have a talk with him tomorrow. I don't expect to accomplish much, though, for he's as stubborn as a donkey."

I am really not in the mood," Marquita said, yawning, "but I must write some letters. Tell the girls that if anyone calls I'm busy and can't be disturbed."

"What makes you think anyone is going to call?" Elodia asked.

"It's about time for Emeliano to propose again. I saw him when I was in the village this morning, and he had that look he always gets before he declares himself."

"When are you going to marry one of these men and put the rest out of their misery?"

"There's no hurry!" Santiago interposed hurriedly. "She has plenty of time to think of marriage."

"She should have married a year ago. That young man from Washington would have been a good match, and he was certainly willing."

"Don't think you're going to get rid of me so soon, Auntie. I have no intention of ever marrying. You know I can't leave Father. What would he do without me?"

"Just what other fathers do when their daughters establish homes of their own. You're not indispensable; no one is. I'm not saying you ought to marry Emeliano . . . in fact, I'd advise against it, but the next appropriate bachelor who seems interested . . ."

"Quit worrying about me and my unmarried state—I like things the way they are. Besides, I haven't met the man I'd want to settle down with, even if it were possible for me to marry."

Marquita left the room to get at her self-imposed task. But just inside the door she found one of the urns had been tipped over and its flowers scattered on the floor. As she started to summon a maid, she heard her father say, "You're entirely wrong, Elodia."

"About what?"

"Telling Marquita she wasn't indispensable. She is. Without her I wouldn't want to live. I hope she never marries."

"Why, Santiago, how can you say that? You married. I married. Tony married. Would you deny her the right to that happiness?"

"Is it a means to happiness? Yes, we three married, and every marriage ended in tragedy. I don't want her to go through the same experience."

"That, Santiago, is the poorest excuse for selfishness I've ever heard."

"Perhaps I am selfish, but can you imagine the garden without her . . . or the Valley . . . or the country?"

Elodia paused before replying. "No, but even so I wouldn't condemn her to a life of loneliness."

There was more said, but Marquita didn't stop to hear it. She wished that she had not waited to hear so much.

After a period of silence Santiago arose and went to the patio. Elodia, who felt the evening breeze, draped her rebozo over her shoulders and followed.

"Isn't this the night the council meets?" Santiago asked.

"Yes, but you're so tired, why don't you skip it this time?"

"Too many men are doing that now. I wish they would

realize how important it is for them to take part in their local government." So a little later Santiago set out, leaving Elodia alone until Romero came out with his guitar.

"Why don't you go to the council meeting with your grandfather? It's time you took an interest in the discussions," she said.

"And listen to a lot of old men arguing over the affairs of a backward Indian village!" he scoffed.

"You're just getting too smart for us, aren't you?" Elodia charged. "Don't forget that you're Indian, too."

"I can't forget it as long as I stay here." He touched the strings of his guitar and sang softly to himself. After a few moments he stopped and lounged idly in the doorway. Birds twittered in the jacaranda tree, and night insects hummed in the bougainvillaea that vined over the trellis. In a different mood he would have enjoyed the enveloping peace, but now he felt rebellious and the calm irritated him. Suddenly he slapped the strings of his guitar and stilled their echoes.

"Aunt Elodia, I'm going to leave Mexico. I have to get away. I hate to leave without Grandpa's consent, but if he won't give it I'll go anyway. I can't make him see my side of it. Won't you talk to him and explain?"

"What makes you think I understand?"

"Well, I think you do. . . . "

"No, I'm afraid I don't. I love my country and always have. I can't understand your eagerness to leave."

"But you've been everywhere!"

"Yes, I've traveled, but I remember when I left Mexico I'd be sick with longing for a glimpse of my home. I have no sympathy with your wanting to get away."

Romero sat with bowed head for a moment, then arose and went to his apartment.

The succeeding days were trying ones for the whole household. Romero neglected all tasks assigned him and spent his time staring at the mountains as if trying to see beyond them. Occasionally he took paper and pencil and drew designs no one was permitted to see. Santiago thought hopefully that at last he had found some worthwhile subject and asked him about it.

"There's nothing here to paint so I'm trying to draw some of the churches we've seen in the cities. We never stay in one place long enough for me to finish a painting, so the only way I can do it is from memory."

"Well, suppose we have a look at those in Toluca. The men are leaving for market in the morning . . . let's join them. I have some business to attend to, and you'll have two or three weeks to yourself."

As usual on market days Toluca buzzed with activity. The plaza was packed. Peddlers had trays of candy, balloons billowing over their heads, or long stalks of sugarcane over their shoulders. In the market area vendors spread their wares under thatch or canvas shelter, and when this space was exhausted they let their merchandise overflow onto the sidewalks. Delicately embroidered blouses and skirts were displayed next to heavy boots and sandals. Piles of handbags and baskets were neighbors to exquisite silver jewelry. Serapes, rebozos, ponchos, hats, straw mats, bags of transparent fish, heaps of onions, and baskets of beans were spread beneath palm leaf shelters. Over a portable grill a woman cooked pork cracklings and sold them as fast as she could lift them from the smoking pot. A little farther on the odor of coffee filled the air. These smells, combined with that of unwashed bodies, made Romero exclaim, "Whew, how do they stand that all day?"

"Let's go to the flower market," Santiago suggested.

"What are your plans for the day, Grandpa?"

"I'm going to take a bus for Cuernavaca. I was to have met a friend here, but he had business there and had to leave.

I'll be away for a couple of weeks or more, so you'll have time to paint or amuse yourself in your own way."

Romero, pleased with the idea of being on his own, was not reluctant to see his grandfather board the bus that afternoon.

When Santiago returned two weeks later he found Romero absorbed in his painting, so he sought out old friends and sat talking with them—as usual, about the book.

"Why don't you come and see my son, Moclovia?" one man asked. "He's a tour guide and sees all kinds of people. He'll be home tonight, so come with me. Maybe he can tell you something."

Moclovia was sitting in the doorway playing a mouth organ when they arrived. Overhead in a cage hung against the wall, a parrot fluttered its wings and cried, "Here comes Zapata!"

"That parrot . . . sometimes I think I'll wring its neck! My grandfather taught him to say that; now every time he sees a stranger he thinks it's Zapata," the host said. He introduced Santiago and explained his visit.

Moclovia was thoughtful for a moment before replying. "No, I've never heard of such a book, but a funny thing happened about two years ago. I had a tour at Cholula. I was telling my people how the pyramid came to be built. . . . You know the story?"

"Tell me," Santiago urged.

"Well, this man suddenly appeared in the village one day. He was a white man with brown hair and beard and he wore a loose robe that seemed to float around him as he walked. He settled down in the pueblo and lived as the natives did. He went to work in the fields and sat in their council meetings. Now these people were idol worshipers, but this man wouldn't go to their altars with them. Instead he talked of God—much like our priests do today. And he could heal all

45

sorts of sickness with just the touch of his hand. Because of his kindness the villagers loved him, and to please him they destroyed their idols and worshiped him as their god. It was then that they built the pyramid to honor him." Moclovia shifted his position, took the parrot from its cage, and rested it on his arm.

"Is that all the story?" Santiago asked.

"No, that is only the beginning. The Fair God, as the people called him, lived in the village for a long time, and news of his power and his beautiful temple spread throughout the country. One day another stranger came to see the temple and to meet the God. When he was told that he was out in the fields helping the men with their harvest, the stranger laughed and said, 'He's no god! Would a god work in the fields like a common farmer? He has you fooled. He says you should share your food with others. Why? You worked for it . . . let others do the same.' He talked until he had the people convinced that they had been deceived. So when the Fair God came in with the men that evening, they made him leave. He was sad, but he went down to Yucatan and taught as he had at Cholula. The people there loved him, too, and followed his teachings. One day they looked out to sea and saw a beautiful ship with sails so thin they seemed to be made of spider web. As it came closer to the shore the Fair God walked across the water, got into the boat, and sailed away. But before he left he told the people that he would return someday." Moclovia set the bird on his shoulder and paused to light a cigarette.

"Did he tell anyone where he came from?" Santiago asked.

"No, but when I finished telling my story one of my tourists said, 'Moclovia, the Fair God was Jesus Christ. He came to this continent after his resurrection in Jerusalem.' "

"What utter nonsense!" Santiago cried.

"One moment, Señor Salazar. Down in Yucatan there is a tribe of Indians that have very peculiar religious ceremonies, and when they take the Holy Communion they speak some words in the language that Jesus knew. Now what was it called?" Moclovia snapped his fingers trying to remember.

"Aramaic?" Santiago prompted.

"Oh, yes. They say these words in Aramaic."

"And what are those words?" Santiago wanted to know.

Moclovia raised his eyes to meet those of his guest as he repeated solemnly, " 'Father, forgive them. They know not what they do.' "

"Oh, well, the priests taught them that."

"Pardon, Señor, they were saying those words when the priests got here."

"Do you believe the story?" Santiago asked.

Moclovia's cigarette left a comet of sparks as he tossed it away in the darkness. "Me," he said, "I am a good Catholic," and he crossed himself reverently. There was a little murmur of agreement, and Santiago looked around to see that they had acquired an audience.

"That's the first time I've heard that story, Moclovia," one of the guests said. "I am a guide, too," he explained, turning to Santiago. "Tourists are always asking me questions about the Indian. I am glad to have another story to tell them. I wish someone would put these stories in a book."

"Somewhere there is already a book . . . if we could only find it," Santiago told him.

"A book, you say, Señor?" another guest asked. "There are many books. Haven't you heard?"

"No, where are they?"

"Let me call my son. His teacher told him about them. . . . Trinidad, come tell the señor what your teacher said about the gold books." He pushed the boy to the front.

"Well," the child began, "my teacher said this man was

flying his plane over the jungle near Salvador when it broke and he had to land. He climbed to the top of a hill to see if there was a pueblo near. He saw a big hole in the ground and as he walked around it he fell into a cave. He was scared when he saw a big man standing in front of him and he jumped back. But then he saw that it was a stone man guarding some gold books that were spread out on a stone table."

"Did he bring them out?" Santiago asked eagerly.

"He couldn't. They were chained to the table."

"But didn't he tell the authorities or do anything about it?"

"He tried to. He went back to the United States because he was in the army and had to stay until his time was up. Then he came back with some men to get the books, but he could never find the cave again. My teacher says the mountains are full of such things. Someday I'm going to find the books, and then I'll be rich."

"I hope you do, Trinidad. If you do, not only you but all of Mexico will be the richer."

he following week the Salazars returned to the Valley.

"It always reminds me of a jewel," Santiago said as they paused on Lookout Point.

"What does?"

"The village—an iridescent jewel set in emeralds. Look how the forested hills hold it in the cupped hands."

"You're a dreamer, Grandpa. I don't see anything jewel-like here," Romero replied.

As they entered the Valley, Santiago said, "We're going to need more schoolroom space soon. Just look at all those children!"

"Yes, the Indians are a prolific breed. And what will become of them when they grow up? There's certainly no opportunity for them here."

"Opportunities can be made, Romero. Take yourself, for example. You think you must leave Mexico to paint, forgetting how many artists from all over the world come here to paint. Cuernavaca is filled with them; so is Pueblo and Mexico City. You don't need to leave the Valley to find interesting material. Where would you find anything more picturesque than Bernal over there?" Romero followed his pointing finger.

"Bernal? On a donkey?"

"Yes, an old Indian on a donkey riding down a dust-clouded lane under a canopy of mimosa trees. Or when we came out of the mountains and looked down on mist-enshrouded Santa Tomaz. It seemed to be suspended in space. The houses were just dark smudges . . . the spire of the church the only distinct object as it rose above the haze in the valley."

They were hailed from the doorways as they passed through the village. Dogs, aroused from their sleep, barked until they recognized them, then settled back to scratch their fleas and doze again. Children crowded past their parents and ran after Santiago crying, *"Papacito! Papacito!* It's my turn to ride with you!"

He reined in his horse and waited until they had caught up with him. Then he reached down and helped them up one by one until his mount was literally covered with children and his arms were full. One little boy panted up too late to join Santiago's cargo, so he turned with upraised arms to Romero.

"My horse is too tired," he said, and the child's eyes filled with tears as he turned away.

"Romero, I'm ashamed of you!" Santiago reprimanded.

"Oh, all right, come here," he called to the child who in turn shook his head.

"No, you don't want me," he said.

"Well, I want you, Nicolas," Santiago assured him. "We'll make room for you somewhere. Here, you can ride on my shoulders. Put your arms around my neck and off we go."

He circled the plaza, then said, "I'm going to take them back now, Romero. Wait for me here." And he rode down the street, letting each child off at his home.

"How do you stand it?" Romero asked on his return.

"Stand what?"

"Having those dirty kids swarm over you every time you

ride through the village. And the garden is filled with them. They even crowd into your apartment!"

"I wouldn't have it any other way. I love them." At Romero's challenging look, he continued, "I sincerely love all these children. You would, too, if you'd let yourself. You're so full of resentment, you keep your better nature bottled up as though you were afraid people might learn that you had it."

"I don't love anybody, and I don't want to."

"Romero, the person who doesn't love doesn't live."

"Then I'm dead, and I intend to stay that way! If you love people you're tied to them, and I'm never going to be attached to anything or anybody! I'm going to be absolutely free!"

"As long as you have that attitude, Romero, you're a slave to your own selfishness. Where did you get this thinking? What conditions in the home fostered this feeling?"

"Nothing in particular. I just don't see that love gets you anywhere. Everyone knows how you feel about the people in the Valley. You say you love them, and I suppose you do, but what do you get out of it?"

"Romero, there is no price on love!"

"The way I see it there is, and that price is a lot of grief!"

"Where did you get that idea?"

"Well, since you ask me, you loved my grandmother and she died. My father loved my mother, and she died. Auntie loved her husband, and he died."

"People die whether or not they are loved. Death is the common lot of man. But isn't it better to know that during the time you live you make a place in the hearts of your associates and that your passing will be noted at least by a few? Clemente says that one of the most pathetic passages in the Bible was written concerning an early king. It says that he died without being desired. It's sad when a man dies without leaving anyone to mourn his passing. You're limiting love to the romantic quality, and that has its place. But the emotion we started out to discuss covers a broader scope, and unless you have a concern for people—unless you become involved in something outside yourself—you're limiting your capacity for living."

"I don't want any part of it!" Romero said. "I'm never going to become involved with other people. I don't want anyone having a claim on me."

"Then you're going to live an entirely self-centered life?"

"You might say that. Someday I'm going to the States and paint a picture that will make me famous. Then I'll travel all over the world doing only exactly what I want to do. And after I paint that picture I doubt that I'll ever pick up another brush."

They rode the rest of the way without speaking.

After supper Romero took his guitar and walked over to the plaza. Santiago asked for another cup of chocolate and sat at the table sipping it thoughtfully. He finished it without speaking and handed the cup to Mamie, who washed it and put it away.

"You may go now, Mamie. We're through for the night," Marquita told her.

"Well, Santiago," Elodia said as soon as the maid left the room, "what have you decided?"

"I visited with Glen for a week. He's the same old friend I knew in college. My cotton trousers and sandals didn't disturb him the least."

"But what about the boy?"

"Glen isn't teaching now, but his son Allan is. He's agreed to accept Romero as a pupil. I'm taking the boy to Monterrey on the twenty-eighth. We'll meet the Parkers there. They'll go to New York after the first of the year."

The three sat in silence until bedtime.

If he noticed the subdued atmosphere the next morning Romero didn't mention it. After the family was seated at the breakfast table Santiago said, "Romero, I've arranged for you to study art in Monterrey. We leave in two weeks."

"Will I live in Monterrey?"

"For the present. Later on you'll live in New York."

In his excitement Romero tipped his chair over backwards. "Why didn't you tell me yesterday?"

"Because I wasn't sure of it myself. I've given it a lot of thought since our conversation yesterday, and I have finally decided to consent to your going."

"I don't know what to say!"

"Then keep quiet," Elodia advised. She knew what the decision had cost Santiago.

But Romero couldn't keep quiet. "I'm getting away at last!" he exulted. "Where will I live in Monterrey?"

"In the Parker home. But eat your breakfast. I'll tell you about it later."

Romero hurried through the meal and left the table. Thereafter he worked diligently and without complaint. When the time came for him to leave an elaborate meal was prepared, and at its conclusion Santiago suggested a walk to the point.

When they reached the lookout, Santiago said, "I have some things to say to you, so we may as well sit down." He leaned back against the face of the cliff and bent forward, his hands clasped around his knees. "I haven't had the opportunity or perhaps I didn't take advantage of it, to discuss this change in your life. And you've been so eager to get away that you haven't been interested enough to ask."

"I know that whatever you do will be all right."

"I doubt that you sincerely believe that. I'm worried about you, Romero. I have the feeling that you're not so much interested in learning to paint as you are in getting

53

away from home. You will not be free of restraint, even though you're away from us. As I told you, you will be living in the Parker home in Monterrey and New York. I have made Allan Parker your guardian. If at any time he feels that you're beyond his control he will bring you back to the Valley. You will continue your schooling wherever Allan lives, but I hope that you'll return to Mexico for your college years. You will account to Allan how you spend your allowance. I'm deeply concerned over this whole venture, and I'm not at all sure that I've been wise in this decision."

"Why?"

"In spite of all the traveling we've done you're still unaware of dangers and disappointments and hurts. You have a lofty disdain for the old and the proven. You'll learn that not everything modern is good, and that there is much of worth in preserving the old. You have been in all of Mexico's most prosperous cities and have been impressed by what you saw. You lack the discernment to see that they contain gilt as well as gold, and it takes wisdom to distinguish between the two."

"I'll get along all right."

"I hope so. I expect to hear good reports of your schoolwork and your art. Don't do as your father did. Tony had great talent and it was acknowledged. For a time he rode on the crest of public favor, but he was content and stopped there. Remember, Romero, the moment you become satisfied with yourself and your work you begin losing ground."

"Tell me more about my father." Romero didn't relish the advice and wanted to change the subject.

"I think we've told you the important things. I made the mistake of giving Tony more money than he had the wisdom to handle. There was never any need for him to work except for art's sake, and it didn't mean that much to him. Then he married a wealthy woman much older than he was, and she indulged him more than I had. We didn't see him after his honeymoon trip home until you were born and your mother died. A little later your father joined the United States Air Force, and Elodia and I went to New York and brought you home."

"Did Father ever come to see me?"

"Frequently. He was home just a week before the crash that killed him." Santiago got to his feet slowly.

"Come, the light's fading." Romero arose, and they turned to the mountain cleft and watched as darkness crept into the Valley.

Father Clemente sat beneath the jacaranda tree that shaded his doorway, his rosary clasped loosely as he fingered its shining cross. He looked up as Santiago came through the gate.

"Welcome, Santiago. Come, sit down. How do you feel now that you've thrown your grandson to the wolves?"

"I had to let him go, Clemente. I have no right to force my will on my family."

"I'm going to worry about Romero. As long as he was here I had hope. Now that he's away I'm afraid the church will lose him."

Santiago thought this over before replying. "The church never had him," he said at last. "It can't lose what it's never had."

"True, true . . . and may I remind you that it's your fault your children were never baptized?"

"I don't think church membership should be compulsory. You take a baby that is unconscious of what's going on, sprinkle some water in its face, and declare it one of your group. What right have you to impose your will on a child incapable of making a decision?"

"Its inability to think for itself is the reason the parents and the church decide. We know what's best for it."

"Who says so?"

"I don't know why you're so stubborn, Santiago. You've always been a rebel! You can read, but think of the thousands that can't."

"That's why I'm always campaigning for more and better schools and teachers. When people learn to read they won't have to depend on you for an interpretation of the Bible."

"Learning to read won't qualify them for that!" the priest said with finality.

"I don't see why it wouldn't, and I don't know why you men think you have a corner on understanding the Bible! It urges people to search and study and says something to the effect that no one need remain ignorant of its teachings."

"As I said before, Santiago, you're a rebel; you read too much and put your own interpretation on the scriptures."

"I'm just taking a page out of your book, my friend."

They sat in companionable silence for a time, then Father Clemente said, "Well, now that we've had our usual verbal battle, let's hear the purpose of your visit. You're not here to discuss the education of our children. You came through that gate like a man with something on his mind. I surmise you've heard some new tale about the book."

"Yes, I have," and Santiago repeated the story of the pilot and the golden books, then waited for the priest's reaction.

"Well, Santiago, it's possible that the tale is true. I don't doubt that there are numerous hidden records. But even if the book is ever found and translated—and we haven't been able to decipher the hieroglyphics on the pyramids, remember—of what benefit would it be? I think you put an exaggerated value on it."

"I always forget, Clemente, that you are not Indian, and that you can't be as interested in the history of my people as I am. I heard another story while I was away—not about the book, but when it's found this account may be in it." When

Santiago retold the guide's story of the building of Cholula's pyramid Clemente lifted his hands in horror.

"Not another word, Santiago—this is blasphemy!"

"Why, do you think it's impossible? Don't you think He had the power?"

"Nothing is impossible with Him, but what reason was there for his coming to this continent—or anywhere else? He came to the Holy City, founded his church, and gave the keys of authority to Peter. Do you think He revealed himself to all the people of the world?"

"Yes," Santiago replied after a moment, "when I stop to consider it, I believe he was just that sort of person, and the attributes ascribed to this fair stranger could belong only to the Son of God. You claim that unless one is baptized he will go to hell. If this is true—and mind you, I don't believe a word of it—wouldn't a just Lord extend the same opportunity to all men? Would he favor only those in Jerusalem?"

"Santiago, if Christ had visited any place other than the one we know as the Holy Land, it would have been recorded in the Bible."

"Perhaps it is . . . in a veiled way. Many things are presented symbolically."

"No, believe me, there is absolutely nothing in the Bible to suggest such an event," Clemente insisted. "Why don't you forget this fruitless search and concentrate on your land, stores, groves, factories, and a dozen other enterprises? And, my friend, although you have forbidden me to mention it, why do you go around dressed like a peasant farmer, painting those memorial pictures, when you could be using your talent to produce worthwhile canvases?"

"Because it's humbling, Clemente! It's a good antidote for my pride—and pride is a sin, isn't it?"

"What's happening in the village?" Marquita asked. The usually quiet pueblo had suddenly come to life, with all the people running in the same direction.

"I might as well go see. If it's a fight I'll be called on to arbitrate." Santiago started out when Clemente, the skirts of his robe flapping about his feet, halted him.

"Where are you headed in such a hurry, Clemente?"

"Here . . . I came to get you. I just left the weaver's! He dropped dead a moment ago!"

"Flavio? Where is the child?"

"I don't know. I suppose she's there. I didn't ask for her. It happened so suddenly that I didn't get there in time to administer the last rites." The priest was disturbed over this omission. Santiago donned his hat and accompanied Father Clemente to the small house where a crowd had gathered.

"Marquita, you'd better go see about the girl," Elodia suggested.

"I suppose you're right, Auntie; I'll bring her home with me."

But Chavelita was not to be found. Santiago sent some of the neighbors to look for her but they returned, unsuccessful.

That evening the old weaver's body was placed in a coffin in front of his home, a circle of burning candles around it. Mourning women prostrated themselves around the bier, while inside the house the village men gathered to extol the merits of their friend. In the midst of the confusion, Santiago, who had been sitting with the men, heard a child's cry.

"Grandpa, wake up!" He hurried out to find Chavelita shaking the old man's body, screaming her command. When Santiago tried to take her in his arms, she screamed louder and bolted into the darkness.

Flavio was buried the next morning. Chavelita went with the group to the cemetery and stood by during the service.

But when the coffin was lowered into the grave she turned and ran back to the village. Some of the women started to follow, but Santiago waved them back.

He heard her frantic cries long before he reached the weaver's house.

"Come back, Grandpa! Come back!"

Santiago paused at the open door. Chavelita was standing with her face pressed against the loom. When she sensed his presence she looked up quickly and backed into a corner, her tear-filled eyes wild with fright. For a moment she stood irresolute, then Santiago opened his arms and she ran into them. He held her close until she had sobbed her fear away. When at last her body had ceased its convulsive throbbing he took his handkerchief and dried her tears.

"Now that's better," he told her. "How would you like to come home with me and be my little girl?"

She studied his face for a moment before asking, "You will be my *Papacito*?"

"I surely will." She struggled to get to the floor, and without a backward glance at the home she was leaving, put her hand in his and walked out.

The household had returned from the cemetery when Santiago arrived with his charge.

"Elodia! Marquita!" he called.

"We're out here, Father."

He led the child to them. "Chavelita has come to live with us," he said.

"I think that's splendid. This garden needs a little girl to run through it, make doll houses, and sail boats on the lake." Elodia drew her near and kissed her.

Marquita knelt beside her. "I'm glad you've come to live with us. You'll be my little sister."

"Why don't you take her upstairs and let her select her own room," Santiago suggested. "I don't suppose you have a dress that will fit her any better than the one she has on."

"No, but I'll see what Mr. Cantu has that will do until we can get into Mexico City to outfit her. Come, Chavelita."

"Marquita, if you like, while you see that she has a shampoo and bath, I'll walk up to the store and select something for her," Elodia said.

"Oh, will you? I'll appreciate it."

Chavelita submitted to the cleaning process meekly, but when it came to a choice of her apartment she was firm.

"Where does *Papacito* sleep?" she asked.

"You mean my father?"

"No, my *Papacito!* Where does he sleep?"

"This is his bedroom, next to mine."

"I'll sleep here," Chavelita decided promptly.

"Oh, you can't do that, dear! Little girls don't sleep in gentlemen's apartments."

"I do," she said, and Marquita had no argument that would move her. Santiago came up during the discussion.

"Oh, have her bed brought in here for tonight! Her world has been torn apart and she's completely bewildered by the day's events. Your aunt got some very pretty little dresses. Do you want to see them, Chavelita?"

The child immediately transferred herself to Santiago's care and went skipping down the hall.

Chavelita had set her doll house under an orange tree at one end of the fountain patio. As Santiago watched, three of the village girls joined her.

"Let's play doctor and nurse," Chavelita suggested. The medical team assigned to the Valley had visited the school the week before, and Chavelita had been fascinated by the doctor's kit.

"No . . . you have to have a boy to be a doctor, and boys are no good," Matilde objected.

61

"Why does a boy have to be the doctor?" Chavelita demanded.

"Did you ever hear of a lady doctor?"

"No, but a lady could be if she wanted to."

"I don't think so, Chavelita. Ladies don't have enough sense."

"Don't say that. . . . I have as much sense as any boy! I'll be the doctor, Elena; you be the nurse—and Katie, you be the mama."

"No papa?" Katie asked.

"No, he's at the cantina or the cockfights," Elena said knowingly.

Santiago had been lying in the hammock listening to the chatter. As he heard Chavelita's prescription for the ailing doll—so much herb tea, so many pills, and an injection given with a rose thorn—an idea formed in his mind. When the visitors had gone and Chavelita had put her toys away, she climbed in the hammock beside Santiago.

"Chavelita, would you like to be a nurse when you grow up?"

"I'd rather be a doctor."

"I doubt that a woman doctor would get very far here, but a nurse . . ."

"Do you want me to be a nurse?"

"If you'd like to be. But there's time to decide."

It seemed to Santiago that after that no game was ever played but doctor and nurse. Chavelita often took the nurse's part at first, but she soon would take over the doctor's role. One day Santiago took her into Mexico to visit a hospital. She looked on with awe as the nurses went about their duties, and by the time they left the building Chavelita had made her decision.

Marquita, would you and your aunt like to go into Mexico with me?"

"Why are you going?" his daughter asked.

"If that isn't like a woman! Ask her a question and she answers with another. I have some business to attend to. Now will you answer my question?"

"Yes, Father. I need some clothes, and this will be a good time to get them."

"I don't suppose we can take Chavelita with us . . ." Santiago suggested.

"No, we can't keep her out of school that long. I sometimes wonder . . ." Marquita paused, and her father prompted her.

"You wonder what?"

"About how long we can keep her interested in school here. She's advanced far beyond the children of her age group, but she's too young to be sent away from home."

"Let's discuss that later. Make her Consuela's particular charge while we're away. Now, how soon can you and your aunt be ready?"

"Ready for what?" Elodia had come in in time to hear the question. Marquita explained.

"It won't take me long, and I'll be glad to get away. Even

with Chavelita's noise the place is too quiet, now that the boy is gone."

"Very well, get ready as soon as you can."

Santiago entered the hotel dining room a week later with Elodia on one arm and Marquita on the other.

"I'll wager no other man in Mexico can boast two such beautiful women," he said.

Elodia was dressed in sheer black which enhanced the loveliness of her silvery white hair. And as Santiago looked down at Marquita he said, "You're so like your mother. She, too, was very beautiful. And the first time I saw her she was dressed much as you are tonight."

The bodice of Marquita's pink dress fit snugly, and the full skirt swirled below her knees.

Two men seated near the foot of the stairway looked up as they entered. Both arose involuntarily, and as Marquita looked down into the black eyes of the younger man she caught her breath sharply and grasped her father's arm.

"What's the matter, Dulce?"

"I almost turned my ankle," she fibbed.

There were many present who recognized Santiago, and he returned their greetings gravely. Neither Elodia nor Marquita looked up until they were seated at their table.

"I never saw a more striking resemblance!" the older of the two men exclaimed.

"Who do you think they are, Dad?"

"I'm sure that's Santiago Salazar. I used to visit my uncle in Mexico, and his ranch adjoined the Salazars'. I once fancied myself in love with his sister. She went to Europe and married a French count but was widowed soon after. Santiago went to the United States and studied art. I met him when your mother and I were buying pictures for Woodwind."

"But the girl, Dad, the girl!"

"She must be Santiago's daughter, although I never heard that he had any children. I would like to speak to him, but it might remind him of an occasion he'd rather forget."

"Why?"

"Your mother and I entertained for him the night his wife was killed."

"Well, I don't understand why that should make any difference now. I want to meet that girl! Did you ever see anyone so beautiful?" He took out his card and motioned to a waiter.

"Phillip, you can't do that! I'll see if Santiago will receive me," and he crossed the room to the Salazar table.

"Santiago, have you forgotten me?"

Santiago looked up, paused for a moment, then arose with arms extended.

"Carlos, my friend!" They embraced, then stood with clasped hands. "Your having added a few pounds since I saw you last explains my delay in recognizing you."

"After all these years ... we meet again!" Carlos marveled.

Santiago borrowed a chair from the next table and pushed his friend into it. "You remember my sister, Elodia Tobar, and this is my daughter, Marquita."

Carlos was on his feet again acknowledging the introductions when his son took his arm.

"Dad, have you forgotten why you came over here?"

"No, Phillip, but you haven't given me time to explain. Santiago, my son is eager to meet your family."

Santiago arose and shook hands.

"Mrs. Tobar, my son, Phillip." Elodia bowed.

"Miss Salazar, Dr. Phillip Parmarez." Marquita smiled.

"You're a doctor of medicine?" Santiago asked.

"Yes, Mr. Salazar."

"Are you practicing in Mexico?"

"No, my work is in Chicago. I'm here temporarily." His eyes never left Marquita's face.

"Since Phillip is so sparing of his information, Santiago, I'll fill in for you. He's here to do some lecturing before nurses and student doctors in one of your hospitals. He's committed for a year, but I hope he finds some attraction to keep him in this part of the country permanently since there seems to be none at home."

"Where is your home, Carlos?" Elodia asked.

"In Guatemala . . . but we're delaying your dinner, and I'd forgotten ours. Has it been served, Phillip?"

"No, I canceled the order. Perhaps Mr. Salazar won't object to our joining him here."

"I was about to suggest it. Sit here beside me, Doctor."

The seating was rearranged. Carlos took a chair beside Elodia, and the doctor crowded his in between Marquita and her father.

"This is delightful!" Carlos said. "I never dreamed of seeing you again, Countess."

"Drop the title, please. I never use it—it's too pretentious. Call me Elodia as you used to."

"Thank you. Do you know that you and Santiago haven't changed much except for your hair? But your niece—she could pass for Josephina." He looked across the table to Marquita.

"I was just telling your aunt that you're the image of your mother. Are you married?"

"No, I'm not married."

"I worry about these children of ours, Santiago. We married young and had our families early in life. How are we ever to have any grandchildren to spoil? I've paraded the most beautiful women in Guatemala before Phillip, but he's not impressed. He was down last year for a short time, and I

66

invited all my friends with marriageable daughters in to meet him. My neighbor's youngest is a beauty, and when she came in that night I thought sure we'd found the future mistress of Woodwind. She wore a low-cut gown, and all the men there—except my son—gravitated toward her. When I asked him for his opinion he said, 'She forgot her fig leaf.' He's the first man I ever knew who objected to a woman displaying her charms."

"Nudity is no treat to me," Phillip said. "I see enough of it at the hospital."

"Ah, a hospital!" Santiago sighed. "That's what I want for our Valley. I have a project I'd like to discuss with you, Doctor."

"All right, sir." And Phillip turned his attention to Santiago.

Elodia and Carlos were soon recalling the past and remembering old friends. The doctor was, to all appearances, deeply engrossed in Santiago's conversation. But Marquita soon felt his hand enveloping hers as it lay in her lap. She tried to free it, but he held it firmly. As Santiago's attention was diverted for a moment, he whispered, "I'm only trying to count your pulse, Miss Salazar. Your face is flushed as if you had a fever."

"That's my war paint you see," she replied. "And there's nothing wrong with me. I've never felt better."

He opened her hand and folded it in his. "Keep still, or you'll run the count up with your struggling."

"Dr. Parmarez, may I remind you that I'm not your patient, that I have not consulted you? Besides, that is not the way you take a pulse count."

"It's my way. I can see that you're very nervous. You must try to control yourself. If you don't, you're going to tip the table's contents on your aunt and my father. Now I don't

67

know about your aunt, but a lap full of silver and a baptism of ice water wouldn't please my father at all."

"Then why don't you release my hand?"

"Because," he said, spacing his words, "I . . . want . . . to . . . hold . . . it." And he held it until dinner was served. He continued to be attentive to Marquita but dutifully divided the time with his elders. Santiago was greatly impressed with his interest in the Valley's needs.

"From correspondence I had before agreeing to this assignment, I understood that the government requires all your new doctors to spend some time in isolated areas," Phillip said.

"It does, but we don't graduate enough of these men to go around . . . or perhaps we have an oversupply of needy districts," Santiago replied. "We had a young doctor once, but he couldn't win the people's confidence. He was abrupt, had no patience with their superstitions, and wouldn't give them time to describe their ailments. When he tried to rush them through the account of their illnesses they became confused and agreed to any symptom he might suggest. Then he lost a patient—a baby—and the few who had been showing up for treatment quit coming."

"What about that team that goes out periodically—a doctor and nurse?"

"Yes, they come occasionally, but they get around so seldom that they've aroused little interest, and even less confidence. The school children are about the only ones who really benefit. However, I'm not too concerned about getting a doctor, for we'll soon have one of our own—full time."

"How can you be so fortunate when there is so much demand for even a part-time medic?"

"We recognized our needs years ago and prepared for it. We are educating a young man for the post. He's studying in the States and will soon be ready to take over."

"Does he understand that? Has he agreed to settling in your valley?" The doctor was skeptical.

"Yes, he got the money for his schooling with that agreement. When he comes home I want a small hospital ready for him."

"Tell me about your valley, Mr. Salazar."

Out came pad and pen, and Santiago drew a map of Esperanza.

"We occupy a rift in the mountain chain," he began. "In our area the rift opens into a large, fertile plain. We're in what we call Lower Esperanza. At this point the valley narrows, almost closing the gap, then widens again into Upper Esperanza. . . . It's a larger, busier place—mostly industrial—while our end of the valley is pastoral. Our homes are made of adobe brick and lighted mostly by candles. You have no idea of the charm of candlelight until you've stood on the Point and looked down into the Valley. We cook our food over tile braziers, or, if the weather permits, over open fires in our dooryards. You'll find us very primitive, according to your standards, but it would be hard to find a place lovelier than our Valley of Hope."

"With such primitive conditions, how do you expect to operate a hospital?" Phillip asked.

"I've heard," Santiago said, smiling, "of instances where doctors have operated in worse surroundings and by the light of a torch."

"So have I, but that doesn't mean that they couldn't have worked with greater efficiency if they'd had electric lights and sterilizers."

"We do have some conveniences, Doctor, including electricity."

"You're sure your young medic is coming?"

"Oh, yes, I can count on Luis Mendoza."

"Don't you think you'd better wait on your hospital

until he gets here? He may have definite ideas about the place in which he is to work."

"No, I don't want him hampered in any way. That may be one reason Dr. Diaz was unhappy with us; we had no convenient work space. I don't want Luis to become discouraged before he launches his practice."

Elodia indicated that she was ready to retire, but before the Salazars left the dining room they had agreed to lunch with Carlos the next day.

"Now that," Santiago said as they went to their rooms, "is the doctor I'd like to have for the Valley."

"You *are* aspiring," his sister told him. "If you had him every woman in that part of the country would discover ailments she didn't know she had before. I might develop a few myself. There should be a law against a man being that handsome. Beauty belongs to women—strength and virility to men."

"Well, Auntie, I don't think he's lacking in those qualities, either," Marquita said, remembering the firm touch of his muscular hand.

"He's a likable man. I hope we see a lot of him while he's here," Santiago said.

His wishes were fulfilled, for each day the doctor called on the Salazars. It was his first trip to Mexico, and they offered to show him the museum, the Cathedral, Chapultepec Park, the Floating Gardens, and the pyramids at Teotihuacan. Elodia went along as chaperon until she declared herself exhausted.

One evening as Marquita prepared to go out, Elodia said, "Did your father tell you that we're going home soon?"

Marquita whirled around quickly. "No, he didn't. How soon?"

"Early next week, I think."

It was Sunday night when Santiago made an unexpected

announcement at dinner. "I've bought a car . . . a station wagon."

"Whatever for?" Elodia asked. "You haven't owned one in years."

"Are we going home in it, Father?"

"Yes, I expect to use it in the Valley."

"Well, if you're going to drive, Santiago, I'm not at all sure that Marquita and I should go back with you."

"Don't fret, Elodia, I have no intention of ever driving it. Dr. Parmarez has offered to go with us and do the driving. He's interested in our hospital plans. I've asked him to advise me about the location."

"Oh, I see! This is all for medical science," Elodia teased.

"Absolutely," he agreed, and gave her a knowing wink.

The Salazar car was at the hotel entrance early the next morning. The women came down followed by porters inundated with luggage.

"What have you two been doing? Stripping the city of its feminine finery?" Santiago asked, eyeing the mound of boxes and bags in the lobby. "I think we need a truck instead of a station wagon." He stepped out to oversee the placing of the load.

"And how are you this morning?" Marquita felt an arm around her waist and looked up to see Phillip smiling at her.

"Quite well, thank you."

"And you, Mrs. Tobar?"

"With you in the car, who cares about the state of her health?" Elodia quipped.

"Is he bothering you, Elodia?" Carlos had come up in time to hear her reply.

"Not so far. Why did you let him study medicine, Carlos? You should have known he'd never succeed as a doctor."

Phillip whirled around, a frown on his face. "Why do you say that?"

"Because you're too handsome. All your patients will be rich old ladies who want their hands held."

"Mrs. Tobar, aren't you ashamed of yourself! Wait until I prescribe for you . . . I'll hold your hands all right!" he threatened.

"Where are your bags, Dr. Parmarez? These women haven't left much room," Santiago said.

"I'll find some space, sir." As Phillip ran down the steps to the car, Santiago asked, "Carlos, are you sure you can't come with us for a few weeks?"

"Not now, Santiago. I came in only to meet Phillip and help him get settled. No doubt we'll be seeing each other frequently. I'll be flying in to check on this son of mine. And I want you three to plan on coming to Woodwind for a visit. I'll send the plane for you anytime."

"Thank you, Carlos, we'll give it some thought. . . . And now, girls, if you're ready we'll be on our way."

Phillip returned to embrace his father.

"I want you to lose some weight, Dad—twenty pounds, at least. And get some exercise. You've got to get rid of this," and he gave his father's stomach a gentle poke. "You stick with the diet I've put you on, and I'll be down to check on you as soon as I can get enough time off to justify the trip. Or, better yet, why don't you come here and share my apartment? After all, I'll be here for only a year."

Carlos took his arm and walked to the car with him. "If that girl can't keep you here permanently I'll be disappointed in you."

Phillip smiled. "I'm planning to take her back with me!"

Marquita had joined Elodia in the back seat, and Santiago's eyes twinkled when the doctor discovered it.

"Why are you sitting back here?" he demanded.

"You and Father want to discuss the hospital. That's why you're coming to the Valley . . . isn't it?"

He smiled as he leaned in to whisper. "It's your ball now, Miss Salazar, but don't forget, I'm coming up to bat." He got in beside Santiago and with a farewell salute to his father eased the car into traffic.

The ride home was pleasant and the time passed rapidly. They made one rest stop, and when they returned to the car Phillip maneuvered Marquita into the front seat.

"You are most persistent," she murmured as he took his seat.

"I know it. And I might give you this warning—I go after what I want and I usually get it."

"My father calls that being obstinate and he accuses me of having the same trait. We seem to have something in common."

"Good. Now if we have the same objective . . ."

"I hardly think that's possible."

"Then let's synchronize our aims, shall we?"

"Let's talk sense."

"All right. What shall we talk about?"

"How about bullfights?"

"Bullfights! That's hardly what I expected from you!"

"Watch your blood pressure, Dr. Parmarez," she cautioned. "That is usually the first thing a newcomer to Mexico asks about. My father has never let me see one, so I couldn't fill you in on the details. Now let's sign a treaty, smoke the peace pipe, and bury the tomahawk."

"You sound like an Indian."

"I am Indian."

"You are? Good, so am I. We do have something in common after all. Now that peace has been restored between Mexico and Guatemala, perhaps you'll explain all those orderly rows of cactus. The entire mountain is covered with

73

it. If all that is used in making tequila, Mexico is destined to have one thundering big binge."

"She will have. But the maguey plant is also used in other ways. Twine and rope and wicker furniture are made from the fibers," Santiago explained. "Our people couldn't get along without it. Some species are used as food. The leaves make an edible salad, and the fruit can be crystallized and eaten as candy. It also makes a very good jelly."

"There's our highway store," Marquita pointed out a little later.

"You'd better begin slowing down, Doctor. About five hundred yards ahead we turn to the right. We have to go through Upper Valley." Following directions the doctor turned onto a country lane where the car was almost hidden by its own dust. It reeled over rocks and ruts and Phillip had all he could do to keep it on the road.

"Why did you settle in such an isolated place, Mr. Salazar?"

"Because it is isolated, I suppose. But when you see the Valley from the Point you'll be able to answer your own question. Marquita, you must take the doctor up there some evening at sunset."

"Well, it will certainly need a lot to justify its inaccessibility," Phillip said.

"I think it has it. Now turn right again. Our streets in the other end of the Valley are too narrow to admit a car, so we'll leave this at the garage straight ahead and walk to the house. Let me round up some youngsters to carry this plunder home."

Phillip got out and stretched. "I'll enjoy the walk. Mrs. Tobar, will you take my arm? The path looks pretty rough."

"Thank you, no, Doctor. I want to oversee the transfer of this plunder, as my brother calls it. He'll have another name for it when he gets Marquita's bills. You two need not wait in this heat." So Marquita and Phillip started on.

"This way is a shortcut through the garden," she said, leading him past flower beds and fountains around the house to its broad entrance. Phillip had only a glimpse of barred windows and heavy bronze doors.

"Come in, please," Marquita invited. He obeyed and looked about with interest.

"I've been cheated," he said. "Where is the candlelight and the outdoor ovens your father promised me?"

They had entered a high-ceilinged, circular room. The floor was marble, and the woodwork was finished in ivory and gold. Porcelain vases were placed on tables set against the walls. Two broad, winding stairways led to the second floor. A console organ occupied the space at the foot of one of these.

"Father didn't say we indulged, only that there were homes where such was used."

Elodia and Santiago came in followed by the boys carrying luggage.

"Our bedrooms are on the second floor, Doctor, and it's siesta time. How about a nap?" Santiago suggested.

"No, thank you, Mr. Salazar. I haven't been in Mexico long enough to acquire the habit. But don't let me interfere with your rest."

"Come on up and get rid of your coat. It's too hot to wear one." Phillip climbed the stairs after him. "Here is your room. Your balcony overlooks the garden if you care to sit outside. Your bedroom is there and beyond is your bath. Towels will be sent up in a moment. If we've forgotten anything tell the girls when they bring your bags." Santiago left, closing the door behind him.

Phillip stepped out on the balcony and inhaled deeply of the perfumed air. Directly below a tiled patio stretched for a hundred feet or more. Around this, at intervals, lampposts of wrought iron were spaced, and swinging from these were baskets filled with flowers and vines. In the center of the patio a marble fountain sent up a fine mist that rained down into a large basin in which he could see tropical fish darting about in alternate sun and shade. Flowering shrubs and trees had been set in the flooring, and among their branches bamboo cages housed brilliantly colored birds. Looking down the length of the house he could see other patios similarly equipped.

The garden was an unpaved extension of the courtyard. Numerous walks crossed each other at different levels and meandered off among the trees. Some led over narrow footbridges to a lake. A rap at the door called him back into the room.

"I am Consuelo, Señor. I have come with your bags. Adele has the towels for your bath." The maid set the luggage down and waited with downcast eyes while Adele scuttled across the room to the bath. Phillip thanked them, and they left giggling.

After a shower he decided to explore the grounds. He paused for a moment outside his door to admire the circular corridor into which it opened. As he started down he saw Marquita leave her room and descend the opposite stair. They met at the door.

"Would you like to walk in the garden, Doctor?"

"I'd like it very much. I've been admiring it from my balcony. It's a veritable Garden of Eden—except that I saw several Adams trimming trees, and there wasn't a single Eve in sight."

"The Eves are busy in the house. At least we try to keep them there. We've had a number of romances bud and blossom here."

"The atmosphere is certainly conducive to romance. Didn't I see a lake somewhere?"

"Yes, we take this trail to it." Trees bordered the walk closely and often the branches of mimosa, jacaranda, and oleander grew so closely they were forced to walk single file.

"What is that heady fragrance? I smelled it from my balcony."

"That's gardenia, my favorite flower." She bent over a bush covered with creamy buds, broke off one for him and one for herself. "You'll find at least one of these in every yard in the Valley."

"And what is the yellow flower that grows so riotously?"

"That's esperanza. The Valley is named for it. It means 'hope.' "

"The Valley of Hope," he said. "Rather poetic, isn't it?"

"And prophetic, we like to think. You wanted to see the lake. It's right around this grove of orange trees."

Following a bend in the path they saw its smooth expanse of water. The sky and mountains were mirrored on its surface, and blossoming trees and shrubs bordering it met their own reflections. Butterflies flitted among the lilies, and two swans skimmed over the lake as lightly as clouds.

The two roamed idly through the garden until Santiago came in search of them and called them to supper.

Phillip was aroused the next morning by a slight stir in the patio. He dressed quickly and stepped onto the balcony. Elodia and Santiago sat at the table with their coffee, and Marquita stood a little distance from them, a parakeet on an extended finger. As she reached up to return him to his cage she saw the doctor.

"Come on down," she called. "I've waited for my coffee until you could join us."

He ran down the steps, and after greeting the others said, "Why didn't you throw stones at my window?"

"Oh, I've survived the delay. I'm sure you're tired after yesterday's long drive." She poured his coffee and then hers.

"If you're ready I thought we'd start looking for the hospital site today, Doctor," Santiago said.

"Any time, Mr. Salazar."

"Elodia, we'd like an early breakfast so we can be back by lunchtime."

"We're going to eat out here, and I see the girls coming with the trays now."

As soon as the meal was eaten Santiago arose.

"We'll go before it gets too hot," he explained. "You'll need a sombrero; we'll stop at Olivia's for one. And your shoes will never do. Nemecio makes good huaraches; we'll patronize him." At Phillip's look of surprise he said, "We'll make a native of you in no time."

After they were gone, Elodia said, "I wonder what Santiago has in mind."

"Why, nothing, Auntie. Dr. Parmarez offered to help, and Father is giving him the opportunity."

"Now, Marquita, you know, and I know, and your father knows that Dr. Parmarez did not come here to look at real estate!"

Marquita blushed. "You're entirely too suspicious. Father isn't getting the doctor away because of me. He has never asked any other of my friends to share his walks."

"Of course not!" Elodia agreed readily. "None of them were eligible. Your father knows that you could become interested in Phillip, and he's jealous! The doctor isn't used to this heat and will likely come back so blistered he'll never want to see Esperanza again."

But Phillip survived that and a good many similar tours before a site was selected.

78

Are you busy, Father?" Marquita paused at the library door; then seeing that Phillip was present excused herself. "I didn't know Dr. Parmarez was here."

"I'll get out, Miss Salazar. We aren't solving any world problems."

"There's no need for you to leave, if you don't mind being bored with ours. Where's Chavelita? I haven't seen her since I got back from the City."

"I'm having to punish her. She's in her room studying. At least I told her she was to select a book from Romero's library, read it this week, and give me a written report on it this evening," said Marquita.

"Why is she being punished?"

"She was impertinent to Jesse. She's bored having to stay in that class. She told Jesse she wouldn't answer her stupid questions. She disrupted the entire class with her outburst, then left the room without permission and came home."

"When did this happen?"

"Right after you left."

"Has she been out of school all this time?"

"No, I sent her to Father Clemente."

"Perhaps I'd better talk with her. And Doctor, I'd like for you to sit in on this conference. We may need your help."

Marquita rang and had Chavelita come down. The minute she saw Santiago she squealed with delight and ran into his arms.

"Papacito!" she said, pressing her face against his.

"What's this I hear about you and Jesse?"

"She says I've been bad," she whispered.

"Do you think you have?" When she nodded her agreement Santiago asked, "What made you act that way?"

"I don't know." She concentrated her gaze on his chin. He studied her thoughtfully for a moment, then asked Marquita, "Do you think she's had enough discipline for the day?"

"It depends, Father. Chavelita, did you finish the work I gave you?"

"Yes."

"Very well, bring me the book and what you've written about it. Then you may go play."

She was back in a moment with the book and a sheaf of papers. Marquita looked at the title.

"Anatomy!" she exclaimed. "Why did you choose this when you couldn't understand it?"

"I like it a lot better than I do Romero's books. They're all about boys who are handsome and intelligent—and that's seldom true."

"All right, you may go." Marquita shook her head in bewilderment as the child left. She looked over the papers then gave them to Phillip.

"This is more in your line than mine, Doctor. What do you think of her efforts?"

He glanced through the report. At some of her observations he frowned; at others he chuckled. "She's an extremely bright little girl. Some of her thinking is rather advanced."

"How does your aunt feel about this, Marquita?"

"We discussed it with Jesse. We think the only thing to

do is to put her in school in the City. We spent a day in Mexico checking on private schools there, and we believe we've found the ideal place."

"Well, I'll think it over, and we'll talk about it later."

Marquita was substituting at school. One of the teachers had pleaded illness and asked to be relieved while she went into Mexico to see her doctor. Phillip had spent the afternoon in the garden, and after his nap Santiago joined him there.

"Mr. Salazar, I haven't been able to get that child off my mind," Phillip said after their greeting.

"You mean the Ochoa girl?"

"Yes, the one with the crooked spine. There's a possibility that she can be helped."

"I tried to persuade her parents to let me take her into Mexico to a specialist, but they refused. They said it was the will of God that she have this deformity, and they won't interfere with Providence."

Phillip shook his head. "It's cruel to let a child grow old in that condition when it might be remedied. I've been wondering if the sick would come to me if we reopened that little dispensary. I'm here nearly every weekend, and while it isn't like having a full-time medic, it would be better than nothing."

"Why, Doctor, that's a wonderfully generous offer! Elodia, did you hear that? Dr. Parmarez has suggested that we open the doctor's office again!"

"Tsk! Tsk! Tsk! Such a dedicated young man!" She winked at the doctor, and he winked back.

"Well," Phillip said, rising, "with that settled I'll go meet Miss Salazar. It's about time to dismiss classes."

He was early so he sat in the shade of a tree until the children came marching out. When Marquita appeared they swarmed around her. Phillip was surprised to see her guiding a man through the door and pause with him just outside.

"All right, Augustine, you may take Gregorio home. See that he gets there safely." At that there was an instant clamor and waving of hands. Every child wanted the task. "Quiet!" Marquita called. "We will do this alphabetically. Each of you will have a day. Now, *adios!*" She looked over and saw Phillip. "I didn't know you were here. Have you waited long?"

"A bare ten minutes. Why are the children so eager to see the man home? I can tell that he is blind, but I thought you were going to have a riot on your hands. And what is a blind man doing in your classroom?"

"Gregorio moved to the Valley recently because he heard we had a school. It never occurred to him that he couldn't learn here unless he had his sight. I don't know why children are so cruel. From the time he began coming here they seemed to take delight in tormenting him. He doesn't know his way around the village yet, and these little demons turned him around to further confuse him. Last night he didn't get home until long after dark. I suppose he would still be wandering around if his wife hadn't come to look for him."

"How did you change their attitude?"

"I blindfolded every one of them and turned them loose in the schoolyard. They soon learned what blindness is. Even though there were some who treated the experiment as a big joke, Gregorio will never again lack a champion."

"What caused his blindness?"

"I don't know, and I doubt that he does. He says he saw his first child but lost his sight soon after."

"It may be cataracts. If it is, it will be an easy matter to

82

correct. Can you arrange for me to talk with him tomorrow?"

"Will you be here?"

"Yes, I'm free until the middle of the week. Suppose I come back tomorrow at this time."

The next afternoon Marquita led Gregorio to where Phillip waited. The doctor clasped his hand firmly and held it while he tried to explain the possibility of his having his sight restored. When Gregorio learned that a stay in the hospital would be necessary, he refused. It took all the argument that Marquita and Phillip could muster before he would agree to it, and then only if his wife would consent.

"You've never seen your baby daughter, Gregorio, nor Ricardo nor Pedro. Think how wonderful it would be to see your children," Marquita coaxed.

"And I can come to school?"

"Of course. We'll go home with you now and discuss it with your wife."

Celestina was deeply impressed by the visit of the teacher and the doctor. It would give her quite a standing in the neighborhood. She spread *petates* on the floor for them to sit on. Marquita won her confidence when she took the fretful baby and stilled its crying.

After much discussion it was decided that Gregorio would go to Mexico with Phillip on Wednesday.

Marquita and Phillip made a triumphant entry into the library where Elodia and Santiago were sitting.

"You'll never guess what we've done!" Marquita challenged.

"Then tell us," her aunt said.

Marquita related all that had happened.

"It's an opening wedge!" Santiago exulted. "I'll go in with you, Doctor, so Gregorio won't feel so alone."

Gregorio was waiting with his small supply of clothes when Marquita, her father, and Phillip met him at the garage on Wednesday evening. Marquita saw them off, then went slowly back to the house.

Santiago read the letter again and his smile broadened.

"You have laid a good foundation," Glen Parker had written. "There is no doubt of the lad's having talent. He's rebellious and has a certain amount of impatience over the plodding details that make a good artist. But he's young; he'll learn. Allan is showing the work of some of his students and Romero has submitted two paintings. Why don't you come and look them over? I'm sure the boy will be glad to see you."

So a week later Santiago stood in the lobby ready to mount the steps to the studio. Evidently the affair had been well publicized, for the stairway was crowded, and he was shoved back repeatedly by someone more stalwart. At last he was near the top and looked up to see Romero facing him on the landing. He tried to attract his attention but failed. He struggled to get nearer and finally called his name. Romero didn't respond, but his companion touched his arm and said, "Is that old gentleman trying to catch your eye? He seems to know you."

Romero looked around over his shoulder. "Must be someone else he's looking for. I don't know him," and he turned back to look into his grandfather's beaming face without a sign of recognition.

At that moment something in Santiago died. He stumbled down the steps and onto the sidewalk. He roamed the streets until he had control of himself; then went to his hotel and sat staring with unseeing eyes until morning.

"What could have happened to your father while he was in Monterrey?"

"I wish I knew, Auntie"

"Did he mention his visit with Romero?"

"Only that he saw him and that he was looking well. He wouldn't discuss his paintings, so I'm sure he's disappointed in his progress."

"Well, I'm worried about him. Do you know where he is now?"

"I surmise he's at the hospital site. He said something about putting the few adobes they have made under shelter. Poor dear, he was so eager to have the building ready by the time Luis got here. It's a good thing Dr. Parmarez persuaded him to write Luis before completing it."

"I wonder why Luis objects to having a fully equipped hospital ready for him to walk into. Most young doctors would welcome such an opportunity."

"Dr. Parmarez thinks he has his own ideas about the arrangement."

"Have you heard from the doctor since he was here last?"

"Yes, he wanted to drive down this weekend. I wrote him that he was always welcome but that I was expecting a guest from Puebla."

"Well, we won't look for him, then. I'd hoped he'd be here to help arouse Santiago out of his depression. He always brightens up when the doctor is here."

When Friday came, so did the doctor. He picked Santiago up in front of the highway store.

"How did you get here, Mr. Salazar? Not through that dusty lane."

"No, we have a shortcut that brings us to the rear of the store."

"Now tell me about Gregorio."

"Dr. Almendarez has removed a cataract from one eye."

"Will he need to remove the other also?"

"Not for a while. The second operation depends on how well he gets along following this one. I've been thinking that it might be better to keep him where he is until both eyes are healed. If he finds he can see with one eye he may refuse further surgery."

"You have a point. When did they operate?"

"Yesterday. We aren't sure of the results yet, but Dr. Almendarez feels confident that sight will be restored." Phillip eased his car into the space allotted him.

"I appreciate the ride, Doctor. Occasionally I forget how hot the sun gets at this time of day."

They found Elodia with her needlework and Marquita just coming out, followed by a maid with her arms full of books.

"Your books came today, Father, and I opened the package, hopeful that I'd find something I wanted to read. Won't you ever get enough of these things on archaeology?"

"Not as long as a new one is published." Santiago examined the titles. "They've been so long in coming that I'd almost forgotten I'd ordered them. Dr. Parmarez, have you ever heard of a book on the origin of the Indian?"

"Well, frankly, I've never given it any thought. There must be dozens of books about Indians."

"There are hundreds of them—all written about the Indian but none by him. There must be a record some-where—kept by someone who cared enough about his culture to leave a history of it. You saw the ruins at Teotihuacan, didn't you?"

"Is that where we went?"

"My good doctor, don't you know where you've been?" Elodia demanded.

"At the time I was in a daze. I knew only that I was in Mexico."

"And to think of the time I wasted explaining the Temple of Quetzalcoatl!" she lamented.

"Sometime before you leave the country, Doctor, we'll visit ruins in other areas," Santiago promised.

"Why don't you forget them?" Elodia said.

"I can't. From the first time I remember hearing them discussed they've been a lure and a challenge. How I wish someone would find the key to their mystery. I get so impatient waiting, I've about concluded that only an act of God can produce the answer."

"Father, I have a letter from Dr. Parmarez. He writes that Gregorio's bandages will be removed on Saturday. And he says he is coming out Friday and wants all the Herrerra family ready to go back with him that afternoon." Marquita glanced over the papers in her hand and slipped them into the envelope again.

"You'd better send word to Celestina at once so she can get their clothes ready." Elodia said. "On second thought, I doubt that they have anything suitable to wear into Mexico. Have her take the children to the store and outfit them. And if there's something she can wear, get that, too. Tell Horatio to charge it to my account. Marquita, why don't you go with her?"

The news spread rapidly through the village, and when the doctor's car appeared a self-appointed lookout announced his arrival. By the time Phillip stopped at the garage a large crowd had gathered.

"Let me say hello to the Salazars and we'll be off," he said. "Where's Mrs. Herrerra? Isn't she ready?"

"She changes the baby. She will be here soon."

When Phillip returned Mrs. Herrerra stood a distance from the car and refused to let the children get near it. The villagers were loud in their efforts to encourage her, but they were without success. Santiago added his word of assurance, but Celestina only shook her head and drew back still further. Marquita tried persuasion, and Elodia scolded, but they, too, were unsuccessful.

"Marquita, do you suppose she would go if you did?" Phillip asked hopefully. The suggestion met with instant approval.

"But I'm not ready!"

"Well, get ready, my dear. One of the girls can pack a bag while you change clothes."

A half hour later she returned. Phillip seated her in front while the Herrerras packed into the rear. Marquita watched as they huddled together—as much from fear as necessity.

"Let's take two of the children up here," Marquita suggested. "They're too crowded back there."

Santiago made the change and closed the door after them. The villagers cheered as they drove off.

"Why are they so frightened?" Phillip asked. "Have they never been in a car before? She's back there with her eyes closed, counting her rosary beads."

If they were frightened of the car ride they were terrified when they were taken into the hotel elevator and whisked up to the apartment Phillip had reserved for them. He called for them early the next morning, and they entered the alien territory of the hospital. Another elevator ride, a walk down the long corridor, and they opened the door to Gregorio's room. He was sitting up in bed, his eyes bandaged. The children whimpered and backed away, but Marquita called them back.

A nurse came in and adjusted the window shade. Dr. Almendarez entered, followed by an assistant. Marquita gripped Phillip's arm nervously as the bandages were removed.

"All right," Dr. Almendarez said, "open your eyes, Gregorio."

His eyelids fluttered as though loathe to admit the light denied them so long. After a moment's hesitation, he blinked a few times, then cried, "It's light! I can see the light!" He leaned forward.

"Take it easy." Dr. Almendarez put out a restraining hand.

"Where is my wife . . . my children? You said I could see them."

"Celestina, bring the children where he can see them." Marquita, calm now that the success of the operation was assured, urged them forward. They crowded around him, and Gregorio examined each face intently.

"My children," he kept repeating, "now I can see my children."

Celestina wept silently as she caressed his hand. At the sight of her tears the children began crying too. They were hurried out of the room and to the elevator.

Now that his sight was restored Gregorio scrutinized everything around him. What he had previously known only by touch became a wonder. Before he left the hospital he was fitted with glasses.

"Wear them as you do your shoes . . ." The doctor hesitated, remembering the heavy calluses on his patient's feet when he arrived. "Wear them like you do your pants," he amended. "Put them on when you get up and don't take them off until you go to bed at night. Dr. Parmarez, I'll turn him over to you. Let me see him in a month."

Santiago was waiting for them at the garden gate and shepherded them to the patio where Elodia served ice cream and cake. It was a day worthy of celebration.

Excitement ran high throughout the Valley, and the villagers crowded around Gregorio to hear the wonderful story of how he received his sight. All credit was given to Dr. Parmarez, and the next morning patients began coming before breakfast. Phillip ate hurriedly and opened the dispensary to the first arrivals.

"We'll have to keep a record of these cases," he told Santiago. "I can't remember names nor treatments prescribed." So Elodia was pressed into service and set up a file. Santiago acted as interpreter, and Marquita was Phillip's assistant.

It was growing dark when Phillip closed the door behind his last patient. Marquita leaned heavily against the table and sighed.

"Exhausted?" Phillip asked.

"Tired," she admitted. "But wasn't it a rewarding day?"

"Marquita, why don't you take Dr. Parmarez up to the Point to watch the sunset?" Santiago asked the next evening.

"Are you too tired to do some climbing, Doctor?" she asked.

"No, I'd like to see this sunset, and I'm sure I'll enjoy the walk."

"It will be a perpendicular one. Won't you come with us, Father?"

"No, I'll stay here with your aunt."

91

"Then come, Doctor. We'll just about have time to reach the point before sundown."

As they approached the incline Phillip looked up, gauging its height. "How do you get to the top of this?"

"There's a trail we use when we're in a hurry to get to the highway."

"I would think it would take dire emergency to induce you to climb this."

"Oh, it isn't bad. And the view from the top is worth the struggle." They were silent as they labored to reach the ledge.

"Here we are," Marquita panted a little later. "We have a minute, so let's sit down and rest."

"I'm more winded than you are," he said.

"I do more walking than you do. Now when we go to the highway, there's a trail that branches off from this a little farther down. It isn't as steep as this; perhaps it's been worn down by constant use. Not many people come to the Point. Now, look at the sky. See how it's beginning to change color?"

He arose and walked to the rim where he had an unobstructed view. One moment the sun was a golden ball, then it was gone, leaving colors that shouted their magnificence. Marquita came to stand beside him, and they watched until twilight deepened into dusk. They looked down into the Valley at the candlelit windows, at the smoke rising from supper fires, at animals being driven in from the fields. They listened to all the homely sounds of the village, the lowing of cattle, the barking of dogs, and the far-off braying of donkeys. Fireflies swarmed up like sparks from a Roman candle.

"You have to get to the top of the mountain to properly appreciate it, don't you?" Phillip asked. "Has your father ever put this on canvas?"

"Not to my knowledge. Now we'd better go while we can

still see our way down." No more was said until they reached level ground, then Phillip philosophized, "Your father was lamenting the fact that the old people of the village get so little out of life. I wonder if the answer to that isn't in the village itself."

"What do you mean?"

"Let me think about it a little while before I put my thoughts into words."

Phillip was already in the patio when the family came down to breakfast the next morning.

"You're up early, Doctor," was Santiago's greeting.

"Yes, after watching the sunset last night I hoped to get a glimpse of its rising."

"You have to climb a mountain to get that, too. What did you think of the view?"

"I've traveled widely, Mr. Salazar, but I've never seen its equal anywhere. In fact, all I've seen of the country is one big picture postcard, and I love it! I've said a lot about the ruggedness of Mexico, but there is a beauty in your mountains I'll never forget. While we were up on the ledge last night I got an idea. Why aren't artists swarming over the Valley as they are in other parts of the country?"

"I really don't know."

"They tell me at the hotel that there is a steady increase in tourists every year."

"Yes, I've seen crowds of them in the cities."

"It's been my experience, Mr. Salazar, that large cities are much the same the world over, but how many Esperanzas are there? I met some people at a dinner party last week who were boasting of a small pueblo they had found as if they had discovered another Paracutin. There is no reason the Valley should not be an even greater find . . . and that brings up another possibility. You once spoke of the futile existence of the oldsters, saying that the high point in their lives once had been to attend a market. Why not create a market for them right here? They wouldn't be doing much getting around, but they'd see people and no doubt do some trading."

"Upper Esperanza has a fairly large market every Wednesday," Marquita said.

"I know, I've seen it. But much of what is offered has been imported."

"Well, that seems to be what the villagers want."

"But we aren't catering to villagers. We're aiming at tourist trade, and those people aren't going to be interested in an ashtray or key ring they can buy at the drugstore back home. They'll want native handcraft. This should give your old people gainful employment."

Santiago's eyes were beaming even before Phillip had finished speaking. "I think you have something!" he said. "There are men and women here with skills they haven't used in years. It will be a resurrection for them."

"How will you get tourists in here?" Elodia asked.

"We'll do what manufacturers do when they put a new product on the market, we'll advertise. I know a man who supplies material for one of those pictorial magazines. I'll write him, and if I can get him to see this as I do, he'll be down on the next plane. This valley would be a source of pure delight for camera fans, and I've seen enough since I've been here to make an artist ecstatic." Phillip paused for breath.

"What shall we do to prepare the Valley for this bonanza?"

"Absolutely nothing. It's ready now. The simplicity of the village life has great charm. Let the people go about their business as usual, bring their work into the dooryard, and cook their food over open fires."

"It sounds wonderful, Doctor."

"Then I'll write my friend."

"The sooner the better."

"Good morning, Clemente. I hope I'm not disturbing you." Santiago joined the priest under his grape arbor.

"No, I'm just finishing breakfast. May I offer you something?"

"Thank you, no, I had mine hours ago."

"What brings you out so early?"

"It isn't early for me. You're a procrastinator."

"Is that what you came to tell me?"

"No, I came to tell you of Dr. Parmarez' plan for helping the Valley." And he outlined the doctor's program. "This will give purpose to their lives and a little ready money."

"My dear friend, what makes you think tourists will come here? We're the counterpart of hundreds of villages."

"Clemente, you splash something besides holy water in a man's face. Now listen to this and I defy you to find fault with it."

"I'll have to agree, Santiago, that it sounds feasible," Clemente said, when the plan was laid before him. "It will be good to see these old men doing something besides sitting aimlessly around the plaza. Now there's another chap I'd like to see get busy at his craft again."

"Who?"

"You. It's a sin, Santiago, for a man to neglect such talent as you have."

"Sometimes I'm tempted, but I'm afraid I've lost the touch."

"No you haven't. There are some memorial pictures you've painted that should be in an art gallery instead of on the walls of a country church."

Santiago thought this over before replying, "No, Clemente, that's all behind me now."

"Foolish! Foolish!" the priest murmured. "How soon will you start preparing the village for your project?"

"It's ready now. Dr. Parmarez thinks the success of the venture lies in the people being themselves and leaving things as they are. He says the cobbled streets, adobe houses, and dooryards filled with flowers will be major attractions. The women will prepare tortillas over an open fire, and the men will bring their work out and sit beside the women."

"Santiago, you're a man of contradictions. Last week you were going to modernize the village. This week you want to go back to plowing with a forked stick and grinding corn between two stones."

"Clemente, you're being difficult. We've had a gristmill for years, and most of the women patronize it, but you know as well as I do that some of the older ones refuse. They say they can't make good tortillas unless they use masa of their own making. Where modern machinery is practical, we use it; but there are areas where we can't even get the equipment, much less operate it. As for having the people revert to the old ways, I'm not. But for those who reject modernization, there'll be no change in their living habits. We'll just commercialize what the world considers their quaintness . . . and I'll admit that it has many attractions. Our generation will remember the old ways, but when we're gone our children will forget the things we've known and cherished. Perhaps it's just as well, for some day the Indian will take his place in society and make his contribution to world culture."

"You seem so certain, Santiago."

"I'm positive."

"And you think the book will point the way."

"I'm not sure, Clemente, what to expect of the book. I

think that when we have the real story of the Indian we'll know why he fell to his present level. Perhaps we can use that knowledge for his reclamation."

"I never could understand your obsession about the book nor your assurance of its existence."

"Clemente, every legend is based on fact. You've heard of the book from various sources. Somewhere a record was kept, and I am convinced that it was hidden at some crucial period in the history of the Indian. The stories we have heard tell of books being seen in caves or buried in stone boxes. We've heard of the four brothers who came across the waters in boats and were the founders of a civilization. Perhaps they didn't do all the things ascribed to them, but they existed! I am also convinced that the legend of the bearded white man has a foundation of truth. Some of our scientists advance the thought that the stranger may have been one of the apostles. Personally, I don't believe that the activities and attributes given this personage could belong to anyone but the Christ."

"That, Santiago, is . . ." but the priest was stopped before he could voice his objections.

"I know you think it's blasphemy. I see no sacrilege in it. It's very comforting to me to think that He cared enough about the people in this part of His world to bring them a message of hope."

"I never expected to see you become religious, Santiago."

"I've never been irreligious. I just can't accept the tenets of the Catholic Church. But we've never quarreled over it, and we won't start now."

"No, there's no need to discuss it. By the way, tell me, what do you hear from Romero?"

"Very little. The boy is as poor a correspondent as I was at his age. Mr. Parker writes that he's happy about being in New York and likes the school he's attending. Allan thinks he has exceptional talent."

"I'm sure you're proud of him."

"The news is gratifying," Santiago admitted modestly.

"I suppose the doctor is still being kept busy?"

"Yes, the Valley people seem to appreciate what the doctor is trying to do for them, but up in the hills . . ." Santiago shook his head hopelessly. "We can't get those people down at all. And Dr. Parmarez says conditions are ripe for epidemics there."

"I wish we could keep him."

"No possibility of that. Anyway, we'll soon have Luis, and when he comes I don't anticipate any trouble in getting the sick to him. He's one of them. They'll trust him."

r. Salazar, I heard from my photographer friend. He'll be in Mexico next week and I'll bring him out when I come on Friday. I suppose you can put him up for a few days?"

"We'll be happy to have him as long as he wants to stay."

When Phillip came out the following weekend he brought Greg Larson and an assistant. Santiago met them at the garden gate. Marquita had seen the doctor's car, and she and Elodia were waiting on the patio. They heard the visitors exclaiming over the beauty of the place before they appeared.

"How much of this will I be permitted to photograph?" Greg asked.

"Anything you consider worthwhile. I hope you find your main interest in the village—we want to make that the chief attraction," Santiago answered.

"I hope I've brought enough film." Then turning to his assistant, Greg asked, "Mac, is your vocabulary extensive enough to describe this?" Without waiting for a reply he continued, "Who designed all this, Mr. Salazar?"

"Professionals originally plotted the garden, but my daughter has made so many changes that I think it can be considered her plan. Doctor, will you take the lead here? I'm sure we'll find the ladies on the patio."

Two weeks later, as Gregory Larson left the Valley, he said, "I'm coming back. I want to get this working as soon as possible, or I wouldn't be leaving now."

"I hope your magazine can use the feature soon. I'm eager to get our project started."

"It takes time, Mr. Salazar. Don't be impatient."

When the article appeared Phillip triumphantly waved a copy of the magazine as he came up the walk. He had dozens more in the car. "I bought all I could find," he said. "I knew everyone in the village would want a copy. I wanted to call and tell you the news. Can't you get a telephone in the Valley?"

"I've never tried," Santiago said. "I hate to spoil the peace and quiet. Besides, they're hard to get."

"I have an idea your doctor is going to insist on having one."

"I'm sure you're right. I'll check into the matter soon."

"And have you discussed business with the people at the tourist bureau, or whoever is in authority?" Phillip asked.

"I attended to that last week. They were agreeable and willing to try it."

"Well, that's all we need now."

"Where are the ladies?"

"Marquita had to take a class today. Velia is ill. Elodia is calling on a family new to the Valley. She heard that one of the children was ill and thought something might be needed. Here she comes now."

"How is your patient, Mrs. Tobar?" Phillip asked.

"Very ill. The baby is teething, and his mother has been feeding him beans and tortillas! We spend twenty years teaching them how to save their children, and they still kill them with the same old weapons! Frankly, I'm disgusted."

"Now, Elodia . . . perhaps the baby isn't as sick as you think he is," Santiago tried to reassure her.

100

"He's having convulsions!" she said grimly. "I came home to see what remedies we have in the dispensary. Now that you're here, Doctor, perhaps you can suggest something."

"Do you think she'll let me see the baby?"

"If you're willing to look at the poor little thing you certainly shall."

"Then let me get my bag, and I'll go with you."

Phillip had to stoop to enter the small house. It was windowless and dark, and filled with a fetid odor.

"The first thing to do is to knock out a wall and get some air in here. The place is stifling."

A fire burned in an open brazier. Its light and that from a flickering candle threw eerie shadows across the floor and climbed the opposite wall. The baby lay close by, gasping for breath.

"Small wonder the child is ill," Phillip growled. He picked him up and carried him to the door, the mother shrilling her protests. Elodia spoke to her sharply and quieted her.

"We need some place to take cases like this—a place where the diet and care can be supervised. If we leave this baby here, he'll die. He may, anyway. Is there a woman in the village we can trust to follow instructions who would be willing to take care of the baby for a few days?"

"Let's take him home with us!"

So the baby was placed in a cool room of the big house. The mother crouched in a corner fearful and sullen. Alice, one of the maids, under Elodia's direction, bathed the restless child. Phillip came in with a hypodermic needle and gave an injection. He stayed with the baby all afternoon, and Marquita joined him for the night watch. By morning the child was better, but Phillip refused to let the mother take him home.

"No, Anna," Elodia said when Phillip appealed to her,

101

"Jorge is going to stay here until he's entirely well. You go home and take care of the other children. We'll take care of Jorge."

"If she'd taken him home," Elodia said as the mother left, "she'd be feeding him beans and chili for breakfast. With your help, I'm going to keep this child alive . . . if I have to breathe for him."

The first of the patients arrived while the family was at breakfast the next morning, and there was a constant stream of them after that. Elodia was busy checking the files.

"Doctor, shall I destroy this record on Antonio Lopez now that you've dismissed him?"

"No, indeed. We want a complete, up-to-date file on every patient for Dr. Mendoza. If Antonio ever comes back, the doctor needs to know our diagnosis and treatment."

Teresa dropped Phillip's instruments into the sterilizer and watched the water bubble up around them. Alice was gathering soiled towels and gowns and putting them in the hamper. Marquita and Phillip were storing bandage, adhesive, and unused medicine in the cabinets.

"I believe this has been our busiest day so far," Phillip observed. "I think we'd better give some thought to training Teresa. She seems to like the work."

"I do, Doctor, I do!" Teresa exclaimed.

"Good. I'll bring some books out next weekend, and you can begin studying. Now, are we through for the day?"

"Yes, Antonio was our last patient," Marquita said. "I'll get something cool to drink and meet you in the patio. Aunt Elodia, you're joining us, aren't you?"

"No, thank you. I'm going to my room and have my nap."

Marquita was strolling among the flowers when Phillip

came down. At his low whistle she turned and walked back to meet him.

"I would think you'd be glad to rest after being on your feet so much."

"I find it restful to walk out here and listen to the birds. But come, let's sit down over here." He eased himself into the swing beside her and leaned back with a sigh.

"Was that an indication of exhaustion or boredom?" she asked.

"Neither, just pure joy. But speaking of boredom, do you ever feel any? The village is so quiet, and judging from the people I've met here there is little mental stimulation to be found in their company."

"I get bored with myself frequently. And when I do I go into Mexico or to Monterrey or one of the other cities. I shop, visit, see the latest shows—and then can't wait to get back to the Valley. I have a lot to do here that prevents my becoming bored. I teach whenever I'm needed. We have an extensive library. I play the piano indifferently, the organ worse—but I'm an artist on the record player."

Phillip didn't relish the lightness of her reply but didn't quite know how to get the conversation on a serious level. The silence was growing awkward, and Marquita tried to relieve it. "I'm sure you find it very dull here. Perhaps we shouldn't have let you sacrifice your weekends to tend our sick. We do appreciate it, even though we may have been slow in expressing it."

"You owe me no thanks. I have received far more than I've given. I have made no secret of why I've been coming out here. No," he said as Marquita started to get up, "it's time we settled things." She arose and walked away. He followed close behind.

"Why are you running away? Are you afraid of me?" He stopped her at the arbor. "I love you, Marquita. And you know the main reason I've been coming out here is to ask you to marry me. You'll have to admit that there hasn't been much opportunity for me to declare myself. When I'm not treating patients your father has me up in the hills corralling more sick people. And if he's too tired to do any mountain climbing, you seem to have the garden full of other suitors. My father cautioned me to use patience in my courtship, and I've tried hard to conform to the amenities of Mexican society, even though I'm not in complete accord with them. But it hasn't gotten me anywhere, so I'm going to risk a refusal by asking permission." The doctor lifted her chin and left a long kiss on her lips. She struggled to free herself, but he only held her closer.

"Aren't you ashamed of yourself?"

"Not a bit! You know my year in Mexico is nearly over and I'm going back to Chicago. I want to take you with me. How soon can we be married?"

"I'm not going to marry you. Marriage for me is impossible."

"Nonsense!" he exclaimed.

"May I ask the reason for this outburst?" They turned quickly at the question.

"Mrs. Tobar, am I to consider you an enemy or an ally?" Phillip asked.

"Ally to what?"

"Don't pretend ignorance. Every one of you know I've been trying to court Marquita ever since I met her. Now I want to know if I can rely on you in the event of a skirmish."

"From where I stand you seem to be doing all right without any help." An embarrassed Marquita slipped from his arms. "And I doubt that I'd have any influence one way or the other. Santiago is your opposition."

"There's no use talking about it. I can't leave Father."

"What's the talk about leaving?" They had been so busy

discussing Phillip's proposal that they failed to see Santiago when he walked up.

"Oh, there you are, Mr. Salazar! You're just the person I want to see."

"Yes?"

"I have just asked Marquita to marry me, and she's giving me a bad time."

Santiago ignored the remark and turned to Marquita. "Can you put your hand on the Aguilar and Sons contract? I want to see what we signed."

"I can tell you, Father," she began, but he waved her off.

"I have to submit it to their lawyer. Get it for me, please." As she left, he turned to Phillip. "You proposed to my child, and she refused you. What do you want me to do about it, Doctor?"

"Well, I know you're concerned with the man she marries, and about what her future will be. Aside from my inheritance my personal investments are sound, and I am well established in my profession. As to my character . . ."

"Wait, Doctor, there's no need to go into that. I have no objection to you as a son-in-law, but I can't suggest that she marry you if she doesn't care enough. And I don't think she loves you, or she wouldn't have refused you."

"Mr. Salazar, my love for the girl would arouse a similar feeling in, in . . ." he looked around for a suitable comparison, "in that marble figure over the fountain."

Santiago smiled at the analogy. "She'll have to decide for herself. Her answer is mine."

Marquita came out with the document her father wanted. She had stopped to order the afternoon coffee, and now one of the maids followed her with the tray. The coffee was drunk in silence, then Elodia excused herself, and Santiago withdrew to consider the Aguilar account. They mounted the stairs together.

105

"We Salazars have many weaknesses," Elodia began, "but never until now did I think stupidity one of them! Here the most eligible man she's ever met wants to marry her, and she turns him down without your saying a word in protest!"

"I'm not sure he's the man for her, Elodia. I couldn't stand it if she wasn't happy."

"Do you think she's going to be happy when we're gone and she's alone in this mauseleum?" And Elodia slammed the door after her.

Dinner that night was a cheerless affair. At its conclusion Elodia went to her apartment and Santiago to the library.

Marquita and Phillip sat in the slowly moving swing. The garden was full of shadows. A sudden breeze set them dancing and swept the fragrance of roses and gardenias before it.

"This is my first experience at proposing marriage, and I'm sure I'm being very awkward about it," he began. "I talked with your father . . ."

"Dr. Parmarez . . . Phillip, there's no need . . ."

"Please let me finish what I have to say. Your father accepts your decision, whatever it is; it's entirely up to you. As I see it, the only reason for your refusal is that you don't love me. If you can tell me that, I have nothing more to say."

"How I feel has nothing to do with it."

"It has everything. To me, love is all that counts."

"It isn't that I don't love you, for I do, but I can't think only of myself. There are people who depend on me, and I can't desert them."

"Marquita, I don't know why you feel that you're bound to Esperanza. Surely someone can be found to take over your tasks."

"I am not thinking only of the village needs. I am also

considering what it would mean to my father. His philanthropic work is more widespread than you know. It is a business with him, and I believe I have a better understanding of the program's purposes than many of those who are paid to manage them."

"I don't think this is an insurmountable problem," Phillip insisted.

"The most important reason of all is my father. This is personal, and I hadn't intended mentioning it. When I tell you this, you'll understand. My father's life has been filled with tragedy and disappointment. At one time, so Aunt Elodia told me, he was considered a very gifted artist. My mother was killed the night of his greatest acclaim. He has always blamed himself for the accident and has never painted seriously since then. His only son was killed in an airplane crash, leaving a baby boy for Father to rear. He idolized Romero. Since leaving home to go to school Romero has cut himself completely off from the family. I'm all that he has left . . . besides his plan for his people. He wants a doctor and a hospital for the Valley. Luis will soon be home to fulfill the first, and he will have the hospital, too. I'm not going to have him hurt again."

Phillip arose and walked from the shadow of the trees and continued as if she hadn't spoken. "It isn't as though I'm asking you to go across the world. Chicago is just a few hours away by air. You can come home as often as you like, and your father and aunt will be welcome any time. My home is in Chicago—my office, my business interests, and my friends are all there. I've spent years learning my profession and more years building my practice. You can't ask me to throw all that away."

"I'm not suggesting that you do. You have your work; I have mine. It just happens that we have different interests and in widely spaced areas. This isn't easy for me either, Phillip. I'm in love, too."

"You don't know the meaning of the word. If you really cared you'd want to be my wife, mother of my children . . ."

"Stop, Phillip! I can't hear anymore." She was beside him now, grasping his arm. "Please go! If you want a family, there are many women . . ."

He stopped her and turned her face to the moonlight while his own was in shadow. "Marquita, do you really want me to marry?"

"I wouldn't feel so responsible for your aloneness, so guilty, if I knew you were happily married." She refused to raise her eyes to his, and for a moment he regarded her silently.

"Well, right now, with your rejection of me so very present, another woman is the last thing I want to think of. But every normal man wants a wife. He wants children of his own—at least that's what the books say. I think I'm normal, so I suppose that some day I'll marry. It won't be easy for me to find a companion, for I'm afraid I'll be searching for another Marquita. Perhaps after a while I'll forget how you look tonight and how I feel at this moment. Time has a way of blunting the sharp corners of our disappointments. . . . Now, since I can't change your mind, I won't be coming out again. It's been the hope of winning you that has kept me driving out here week after week."

"Perhaps it's better that way, Phillip. But even though we don't see each other, I hope we can still be friends."

"I don't want to be your friend, Marquita. I want to be your husband. I'd rather say good-bye now." He held out his hand.

"Must it be this way, Phillip?"

"Yes. When you've finished reading a story, you close the book and put it aside. I'm sorry ours couldn't have had a happier ending. Now run in and go to bed. It's beginning to mist. I'll walk you to the door."

"Aren't you coming in?"

"Not now."

She went directly to her bedroom and locked the door. For a time she lay across the bed sobbing, then she arose and knelt at a window overlooking the garden. Phillip had wandered away from the house, and she saw him dimly through the mist as he moved slowly down the winding walk. At times he would be hidden by trees and shrubs, then would reappear, like a shadow, farther on. He finally retraced his steps and entered the house. She remained at her post until she heard him close the door behind him.

When the family arose the next morning Phillip was gone. A maid brought his note to Marquita as she dressed. She opened it eagerly and read,

> My Dear,
>
> There's no point in my seeing you again, so I'm leaving. By going now I'll get into the City quite early and have time to check some material for this week's lectures.
>
> Many thanks to you and your family for the happy hours I've spent in your home. I'll write your father and aunt later.
>
> I hope that our conversation didn't keep you awake last night and that you can soon forget the unhappy occasion,

She took the note and went to his apartment. In the past he had often left a shirt, a jacket, or a tie hanging in the wardrobe—a tube of toothpaste or shaving cream in the bathroom. But now there was nothing to indicate that he had ever, even briefly, occupied the apartment. It seemed that he had indeed closed the book.

When Phillip left that morning the sun was just coming up over the mountain. When he took the shortcut through the garden he walked through pools of fragrance, each a different aroma. He started once to look back, then thought better of it and went on resolutely through the gate to the garage. A few of the villagers in Upper Valley were astir and waved when they recognized his car. He drove slowly until he reached the highway, then stepped up his speed. The sooner away the better, he reasoned. He wouldn't be coming this route again. It was too bad that he wouldn't be there to treat the sick the next weekend, but Mendoza should soon be on hand.

He stopped at a roadside cafe for his morning coffee. The place was empty except for a native. While he was waiting to be served this man approached him and held out his hand and began talking rapidly. Phillip clasped the hand but couldn't understand a word being spoken. He appealed to the waiter.

"He thinks you're the doctor from Esperanza."

"Yes, I am Dr. Parmarez."

"He says you saved his little boy. He didn't have any money, but he's working now and wants to pay you. Is a peso enough?"

Phillip was on the point of refusing until he saw the man's look of pride.

110

"Oh, yes, that's quite enough," he hastened to say. When he got into his car later the man was standing beside his laden donkey, waiting with a comradely smile to wave him off.

Marquita went about her tasks with unsmiling lips. Santiago avoided the house except at mealtime. The servants felt the tension and quarreled among themselves. Elodia tried patiently to maintain peace and lift morale.

Marquita could hardly convince herself that Phillip wouldn't come on Friday as usual, and sat at her window overlooking the land. Santiago, perhaps hoping he would return, had not advertised the Doctor's absence, and by early morning the sick were arriving.

"What shall we do, Father? We worked so hard to get them to come it seems a shame to send them away."

"There's nothing else we can do. We don't know enough to prescribe aspirin."

"Well, I can sterilize wounds and put on bandages. And there's an ointment that the doctor used for cuts and sores." So the patients were screened, and those that Marquita could care for were called in. The others were sent home.

The third week passed before Marquita heard from Phillip. It was a short note. He said he'd been hard at work with end-of-the-year business. The doctor who was to replace him had arrived, and he'd been briefing him on the routine. He would be going to Chicago in a day or two to see about resuming his practice there. Then he would spend a few weeks with his father in Guatemala before going to work.

Marquita went to her room crying. Elodia followed and sat beside the bed where she had thrown herself.

"Marquita, are you sure you love Phillip?"

"Oh, yes, Auntie. I loved him the moment I saw him."

"Then why did you send him away?"

"You'll never know how I've had to fight myself to keep from writing him to come back for me. Then I would see

Father's face and know I couldn't be happy if I left him. But when I think of Phillip and how much I love him, I'd be torn to shreds. Father needs me here," she sat up and reached for a Kleenex, "but I like to think Phillip needs me, too."

"Marquita, you must be practical. You'll be here a long time after your father and I are gone. Have you ever thought of what it's like, being alone? I speak from experience when I tell you that the weeks and months and years grow increasingly lonely, sometimes almost past endurance."

"I guess I never thought of that. I'm sorry I've been so blind and selfish. You won't see me moping around anymore."

"Good. Now before you do anything else, sit down and write to Phillip. Perhaps you can reach him before he leaves Mexico."

Phillip drove across the International Bridge at Nuevo Laredo, passed through customs, and on into Texas. "Well, that's the last of Mexico for me," he mused as he drove down the highway. "It will be good to get back to work in my own environment."

The first person he met when he reached Chicago was Ian Dent, a former associate.

"Are you back to stay?" Ian asked after their initial greeting.

"My year in Mexico is over," Phillip replied evasively. "Tell me what's been going on here."

"That's a large order, but come, I'll fill you in on the main events while we have lunch." The next hour was spent in shoptalk, but Phillip found that he wasn't very interested. He had lost touch while he was away.

"Are you ready to go to work?" Ian asked when he sensed that Phillip's attention was wandering.

"Not immediately. I'm not sure what I want to do."

"Great Caesar, man, practice medicine, of course! What else is there for you to do? We need more space at the clinic but we hesitated to make any change until we were sure of what you were going to do. John said he was going to write you, but I doubt that he did. He's having in-law trouble, as usual. Every time I see his tax exemption I'm less resentful of having to pay Uncle Sam. I've got to get back to the office now. Why don't you come up with me?"

"Not now, Ian. I haven't even been out to my place yet, but I'll be in soon. And Ian, I'll appreciate it if you don't say anything about seeing me."

"I won't mention it," he promised.

But Phillip's presence didn't remain a secret very long. His phone continued ringing as one and then another heard of his return. After a year of peace and quiet the constant demands irritated him and he was more determined to get out of town. He had tried to locate his father but found that Carlos had left the Florida house two weeks before. The caretaker said he never reached the Guatemala place. Phillip became alarmed and was ready to fly down when his father called him.

"Hear you've been trying to get me," he said tersely.

"Where have you been? You had me worried."

"I went deep-sea fishing with some people. If you'd come home occasionally I wouldn't have to depend on acquaintances for companionship."

"Dad, I've got to talk with you. Do you want to come up here . . . no, I'll fly down to Woodwind. I want to get out of Chicago. I'll see what plane connections I can make, and I'll call back."

"No need—I'll send Redfield up. He'll call you as soon as he lands."

113

Although he had spent his early childhood at Woodwind and had returned year after year, Phillip never felt at home in its grandeur. It was a show place, and when Carlos was not there it was opened to a limited public. People paid to go through its palatial rooms and wander among the flowers of its formal gardens. The money from these tours was used to buy lunches for needy school children.

Carlos was waiting at the airport when the plane landed, and the two embraced affectionately.

"How was the flight?"

"Smooth, as usual."

"Redfield's the best pilot we ever had. Have you finished your stint in Mexico?"

"Yes, I've been back in Chicago several weeks."

Carlos forebore asking any more questions until after dinner that evening. "Let's go to the library," he suggested. "How about a drink to loosen your tongue, or are you still an abstainer?"

"You know I never touch it."

"I can't understand a son of mine being a teetotaler."

"Dr. Abbott put the fear of the Lord in a good many of his students," was Phillip's reply.

"A little liquor and a good cigar never hurt anyone," Carlos argued, pouring himself a drink.

"Never did anyone any good either." Phillip was equally argumentative.

"You look about as cheerful as the guardian angel on a cemetery gatepost. I take it Marquita refused to go to Chicago with you."

"That's why I'm here. No woman ever affected me this way before. As I left the Valley I could hardly keep from turning the car around and going back."

"Why didn't you?"

Phillip looked up quickly. His father was intent on

trimming the end of his cigar. "A good many reasons. First, she sent me away. That's reason enough. Perhaps the difference in our ages . . ."

"Age has nothing to do with love, Phillip. Your mother was my senior by eleven years. It didn't make any difference to either of us, and our love has endured even though she's been gone for nearly a quarter of a century. What are Marquita's reasons for refusing you?"

"She thinks she can't leave Esperanza because of the family's work with the poor of that area."

"What was your argument? I suppose you had one."

"The reason any man has. I have established myself in the United States. My home is there. My business interests are there. A woman should go where her husband's work calls him."

Carlos spun the stem of his glass between his fingers, watching the encircling wine thoughtfully.

"In other words, you expected her to give up her work and follow you."

"Marquita's work is not her means of making a living."

"Neither is yours." Then at Phillip's look of surprise, "What I mean is, you aren't depending on your professional income for your living. Her work is as important to her as yours is to you—and to me it's quite as worthwhile."

"I know . . . I've known it all along. But think of all the years I spent learning to be a good doctor, and if I stay in the Valley I'll have no use for my skills. Santiago has a young medic coming in. I've also considered your disappointment in my letting anything come between me and my practice. But Dad, it boils down to this—it's Marquita or medicine. I have no choice."

"Well, now, I don't see why you have to sacrifice either. Marquita won't leave the Valley, and you can't practice medicine there. Is there anything to prevent your opening an

115

office in Mexico City? You've been driving back and forth courting her; I see no reason why you couldn't do the same if you were married. Arrange your schedule so you won't need to open your office more than two or three days a week."

"You won't be disappointed at my leaving the States?"

"Phillip, I'd be heartsick if you gave up your work completely—if you wasted all your years of study and forgot your skill. I'm proud of what you've done and that you were unwilling, as so many sons of rich men are, to treat life as one long holiday. But pride makes a poor diet. You can't live on it. As you well know, I've wanted you to marry, for more reasons than one. A man alone is only half a man. And I want grandchildren. I want heirs to succeed you in the operation of this modest empire I've founded. This is the first time I've known you to show the least interest in any woman, and I've exposed you to a good many. Nothing would please me more than to see you married to Marquita.

"I proposed to your mother seven times before she agreed to marry me, so don't accept Marquita's first refusal. Go on back to Mexico and marry the girl. I repeat, I want grandchildren! Now get going before she marries someone else."

Marquita was putting on her gardening gloves.

"You surely aren't going to work out in all this heat!" her aunt exclaimed.

"I have nothing else to do. If I feel it too much I'll come in," Marquita promised.

"Have you heard from Phillip?"

"No, I suppose my letter was too late," and Marquita passed through the hall to the garden.

"What have I done to merit such a family?" Elodia demanded. A crash in the kitchen called for her attention, so she didn't see Santiago's stricken face when he came in. He was sitting with bowed head when she returned.

"Are you ill, Santiago?"

"Read this." He handed her a letter.

"From Luis? How soon will he be here?"

"Read the letter," he repeated. She opened the single sheet and read:

Dear Mr. Salazar,

Since neither my wife nor I feel that our children should be reared in the primitive surroundings of Esperanza, I have decided against returning to the Valley.

I hope you will soon find someone better suited to the work there than I am.

My wife joins me in sending best wishes.

Elodia looked up. "Did you know he was married?"

"No, he never mentioned it. He's been getting more money from the fund each year. I believed him when he said he was studying other branches of medicine and needed it for tuition. I surmise that what he really needed it for was his family."

"Do you suppose his parents know?"

"Yes, I've just come from there. Luis has been married and practicing medicine in Los Angeles for three years. He has two children."

"And there's nothing you can do."

"Nothing. I have never asked anything but a verbal agreement from any of the young people. Luis promised me he would come home and stay here for at least a year. I had confidence that a dedicated young doctor, with his living assured, would want to respond to need when he saw it."

"Evidently he's known for some time that he wasn't going to come back."

"Yes, that's why he didn't want me to go ahead with the hospital. I've been very stupid."

"Not stupid, Santos, just too trusting."

Another month passed without a word from Phillip, then one afternoon he came striding into the garden. He kissed Elodia and embraced Santiago as he dropped his bag to the floor.

"Where is she?" he asked, looking around.

"Inside with a patient."

"A patient?"

"Yes, Ismael Torres had an infected finger, and she's dressing it," Santiago explained.

"I'll see if she needs any help."

Marquita's back was turned to the open door, and the old

man was intent on her ministrations. Neither of them knew that Phillip was in the room until he reached out and took over. He made quick work of the bandaging, hurried the patient through the door and locked it after him. Then he turned with outstretched arms, and Marquita ran into them. For a long time they embraced in silence, then Phillip held her away from him.

"Let me look at you . . . just let me look at you!"

She attempted a smile, then hid her face against his chest. "You said the book was closed."

"That was a lousy ending. We're going to rewrite that last chapter."

"When you didn't answer my letter I thought you weren't coming back."

"I didn't get it. What was in it?"

"I asked you to come back for me."

"You're willing to leave the Valley?"

"I'm going with you, regardless of where you go." She was amply repaid for her declaration. "I'm so happy that you're here, Phillip, but when I think of leaving Father and Aunt Elodia I feel guilty."

"We're not leaving Esperanza. Perhaps this separation was good for me. . . . I learned that I was asking a sacrifice of you that I was unwilling to make. So I disposed of my Chicago practice, and I'm here to stay. Now I think I'd better finish that conversation I began with your father several weeks ago. I'm going up to my apartment for a moment. Then I'll soon be down."

"Well, *niña,*" Elodia said as Marquita came starry-eyed through the door, "you had a nice surprise, didn't you? Where is he?"

"He went to his room. He'll be down in a moment.

119

Phillip says he never got my letter. Did you have anything to do with his coming back?"

"If I didn't, I wasted a lot of time on my knees. Another week of looking at those tears would have driven me to joining the church so I could beg intercession of the saints."

"Well, I'm going to freshen up. I know I look frightful."

She and Phillip came down together a little later.

"Has Marquita told you, *Papacito?*" Phillip asked.

"No, what's the news?"

"I've given up my Chicago practice. I'm here to stay."

For a moment Santiago was silent, then he said, "No, Doctor. You can't do that. Marquita must not let you make the sacrifice."

"It isn't a sacrifice. I love Marquita."

"Have you considered all that you're giving up—your practice, your prestige, your position in medical circles? And your father, how will this affect him? He was so proud of your record."

"Yes, I've considered the cost of my decision, and I'd repeat it. I'll admit that I did a lot of thinking about it. I argued it from every angle and always came to the same conclusion. Dad only confirmed my resolution."

"You've discussed this with your father?"

"Yes, when I realized that I had to come back, I wanted Dad to understand why. He has always taken such an interest in my career, I didn't want to hurt him if I could avoid it. Dad and I have been very close. I've never made any important decision without his knowledge. He couldn't get me to Esperanza fast enough. He suggested that since Marquita doesn't want to leave the Valley I could open an office in Mexico two or three days each week. That way I'll keep in practice and satisfy both of us. And I know I can find enough work in the hills to keep me busy at other times. I'll stay out of Mendoza's territory."

120

"Luis isn't coming back, Doctor," Santiago said after a pause.

"Not coming back? The doctor you depended on?"

"No, he's been practicing in Los Angeles for some time."

"Then the Valley is mine?"

"You don't want it, Doctor. You've been kind and considerate in treating all those who came to you, but you've known that you'd have only a few hours of such service and could wash your hands and forget them for another week. But if you gave it your full time, there would be no break. Frankly, I don't think you could take it day after day. I appreciate your offer, but with your education and background I'm afraid it wouldn't work out. I know I'm stating it poorly, but I hope you understand."

"Do you remember once telling Dad that it was immoral not to share with those in need whatever you had, whether it was time, talent, love, or money? And you said that there were times when love and understanding were of more value than money. Well, I have a certain amount of medical skill I'd like to share, and I don't know of a more needy place than the Valley. These people get to you. I couldn't forget them. Their silent, patient faces were constantly before me when I was away. . . . Something happened on my way to Mexico when I left here. I had stopped for a cup of coffee and while I was waiting for it an Indian farmer approached me and wanted to pay me for attending his baby. He handed me a peso. I can't tell you how it affected me. Every time I put my hand in my pocket I touched the peso and remembered, not only him and his baby but all the others I had treated. So he and his baby became another strand in the cord that was pulling me back to Esperanza. I'm here to stay."

Santiago was deeply moved and held out his hand in wordless acceptance.

"And now with that out of the way, let's get to the most

important question. When can we have the wedding? How about Sunday?"

"Sunday!" Marquita said. "Are you serious, Phillip?"

"I've never been more serious. We've wasted too much time already."

"A girl should have at least a year's engagement. She needs time to plan her trousseau and prepare for her marriage. It's the happiest time of her life."

"Are you insinuating, Aunt Elodia, that Marquita will enjoy the anticipation more than the reality of being married to me?"

"I wasn't thinking that way, but with your trigger temper, perhaps she would," Elodia agreed in mock seriousness.

"Sunday is out of the question, Phillip. You must know that. I have clothes to buy . . ."

"Let me say a few words here," Santiago interrupted. "Marquita is my only child, Doctor . . . Philip, and I want her to have the kind of wedding her mother would have arranged for her. I won't insist on a long engagement, but I do want things done properly."

"I'll agree to that, but we need a date—and not one twelve months away. I won't be able to function effectively as a doctor until my future is assured."

"Well," Santiago turned to Elodia, "can you name a day so this man will give me some peace?"

"We'll discuss it privately, Santiago. Right now Mamie is trying to announce supper," and she walked with Santiago into the dining room.

"Since arranging for this wedding is going to be my responsibility I'd better begin on a guest list immediately. If anyone has any suggestions let me have them now," Elodia said after the meal had been served.

"I'll be glad to help, if you'll tell me what to do," Marquita said.

"You won't be capable of doing anything as long as Phillip is in sight."

"Are you suggesting that I head back to Mexico tonight?" he asked.

"Would it do any good if I did?"

"Not the slightest. I've been away too long and nothing short of a tornado will get me out of Esperanza before morning."

It was the evening before the wedding. After dinner Phillip and his father had taken a walk, and now the doctor was continuing that walk through his apartment.

"I haven't seen Marquita in three days," he mused aloud.

"You don't look any worse for it."

"I can't see what 'Auntie' hoped to accomplish by this separation. I don't know if it's a Mexican custom or just something she thought up."

"It's the custom, I suppose. If you're determined to walk let's get out where it will take us somewhere. You're getting on my nerves."

"I'm getting on my own nerves," he confessed, as he followed his father from the room.

"What time do you expect your attendants?"

"The plane is due at eleven. I've ordered lunch to be served at twelve, and we'll leave at one. That will give everyone a chance to get acquainted, time for the rehearsal, and the ceremony at seven."

They met the plane the next morning and in two hours were on their way.

Santiago was waiting at the gate to greet them. He turned to Carlos after meeting Phillip's friends.

"Carlos, it's always good to see you."

Phillip took the lead. "This is going to be a fairyland tonight," he said when he discovered the half-hidden floodlights that at dusk would be focused on some of the more beautiful spots.

"What is that fragrance?" Dr. Dent asked.

"That comes from the gardenias which were emptied into the lake a short time ago. Would you like to see it?"

"Say, where are the swans, Santiago?"

"They were moved several days ago so this area could be cleaned. Here we are." They stopped at the lake and watched as the gardeners worked with long cane poles to separate the flowers so that each blossom floated free on the surface of the water.

"This looks more like the stage setting for an extravagant movie than a private garden," Dr. Wise said.

"It's the setting for our daily lives, for we practically live in some part of it. This has been my daughter's greatest pleasure."

As they started on Elodia and Marquita appeared around a turn in the path. Phillip left the group and hurried to meet her.

"Are you all right, Marquita?" he asked, bending to kiss her.

"Phillip!" Elodia spoke sternly, "aren't you forgetting something?"

"Don't be so impatient, Auntie ... I'll kiss you in a minute."

"Why, you ..."

"And stop sputtering. It's most unbecoming in a lady of your grace and charm," and he silenced her with a kiss. "Now, wasn't that worth waiting for?"

"Have you no regard for the rules of polite society?" she demanded.

"None in the world, but which one have I smashed now?"

"Do you realize that your father and those four strange men are watching?"

"And every one of them is envious."

"I don't know how I'm going to stand living under the same roof with you, Phillip."

"Oh, you'll love it," he assured her.

The prolonged chord from the organ at the foot of the stairs stilled the whispering of the guests. The soloist finished his song and with the first notes of the wedding march the bridal attendants proceeded in order. Then Marquita walked in on her father's arm, a long satin and lace train rustling behind her. Taking her place beside Phillip, she listened to the words of the marriage service:

" . . . to love and to cherish . . . for richer or poorer . . . in sickness and in health . . . till death . . ."

The phrase startled her. It should not be a part of the service. What had death to do with marriage? Why should sorrow be linked with joy?

Her breath came tremulously. She felt weak and helpless until Phillip's encircling arm and kiss gave her assurance.

They stood at the entrance of the great reception hall to receive the good wishes of their friends, then climbed to the balcony to watch the fireworks being exploded in their honor.

It was past midnight when they mounted the stairs and Marquita paused to toss her bouquet into a sea of waving hands. Hastily they changed into traveling clothes and returned to the reception room and their guests. But as they went through the garden to Phillip's car only Elodia and the fathers were with them. Marquita started out between Phillip and her father, then Phillip dropped back, leaving them alone.

"I think you have married a fine man, dear, and I'm sure you're going to be very happy."

"I know, Father, and if I didn't love him so much I would never leave you and go with him. Now while I'm away ..."

"While you're away you're to think of no one but yourself and Phillip. Do as I'm going to do for the next few weeks, forget the Valley. We may be surprised at how well the villagers get along without us."

"What do you mean by that, Father?"

"We had intended keeping it a secret until you came down to Woodwind, but Phillip thought you should be told now. At his and his father's insistence we're going to fly down to Guatemala with Carlos."

"Why, I think that's wonderful! Now I won't worry about your being lonely without me."

"Elodia and I are looking forward to the visit and to a cruise. Carlos has had the boat readied and it's waiting for us. But here we are at the gate, so I'll return you to your husband. . . . And Phillip, I'm afraid that you've trimmed your time pretty close. Unless you drive faster than you should you won't get to the airport at the time agreed on."

"As far as I know there's no reason why we must leave Mexico tonight. If we can't make it with safe driving, I'll call Redfield and cancel the flight." And with final farewells they were off.

A month later Marquita ran from the plane into her father's arms.

"How have you been, Father? You and Aunt Elodia look rested and younger than ever."

127

"I don't know when I've felt so well. There's such a thing as being too close to your problems. Phillip, how are you?"

"Fine, Father." He embraced Santiago after paying his respects to Elodia. Marquita put an arm around her aunt and left the men to follow them to the car.

"There's no need to ask you how you are. Your radiant face speaks for you," Elodia said.

"I'm very happy but we're both eager to get back to work."

"I think we are, too. We've been royally entertained, and we've had a marvelous time, but frankly, Marquita, all this magnificence becomes wearing after a while. It's hard for me to realize that this is all I knew during my early life. I don't know how I endured it. Perhaps our village girls are slow, but I think I prefer battling them to living with this staff of perfection."

Marquita understood her aunt's feeling when she saw the expanse of richness of Woodwind.

"After spending your childhood here, Phillip, I'm surprised that you were satisfied away from it."

"It weighs me down. Dad finds it so and never stays long at a stretch. He opened the place because he wanted you to see it, and to entertain your aunt and your father. Now, if you're ready, we'll go down. I'd like you to see the garden and greenhouse."

But when they joined the fathers and Elodia, Carlos took Marquita to himself. "I want to become better acquainted with my daughter," he said.

"Well, what do you think of Woodwind?" Phillip asked as Carlos led Marquita from the room.

"It's magnificent," Elodia said.

"Quite a layout," he agreed, "but scarcely a home. Had my mother lived it would have been different, I'm sure. It's a

128

great place for parties. Do you know when Dad is planning to entertain for Marquita?"

"Tomorrow night, I believe."

"Good! I'll be glad to get all these superfluities out of the way so we can go home and get busy."

Santiago's face glowed with satisfaction. "The boy is a son after my own heart," he exulted.

"Well, I'm not accustomed to so much idle time, and there's so much to be done in the Valley. I hope they have enough adobes ready to get that hospital off paper and onto the ground."

A little later Marquita and Carlos returned.

"Phillip, I asked Marquita about your taking the yacht out for a month or so as a sort of honeymoon finale. She says you're leaving next week for Mexico."

"Yes, we need to get back. Remember, I have to establish myself in an entirely new environment."

"You were in the States too long. You've adopted the North American's hustling habits," Carlos accused.

"Well, you didn't acquire all this sitting under a tree with a sombrero pulled over your face," he countered.

"I hurried so you wouldn't have to."

"I appreciate it, but I'm not the sombrero type, either."

"Well, Elodia, you and Santiago will stay on?" Carlos asked hopefully.

"They will not!" Phillip said emphatically. "We have a hospital to put in operation, and we'll need all the help we can get. If you aren't careful I'll draft you and put you to work up there, too."

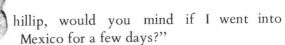hillip, would you mind if I went into Mexico for a few days?"

"Of course not. I can't get off to take you, but Aurelia can go in with you. What's happening in Mexico?" Phillip was intent on a specimen he had under the microscope.

"One of my friends is getting married and she has asked me to be her matron of honor. I may be gone a week or ten days," she added with some hesitation.

Phillip looked up. "Well, I suppose I can manage for that long. If I can't, I'll come after you. I want José to drive you in, so let him know when you want the car."

Two days later Phillip walked her to the garage and saw her off.

"Phillip, is that you?" Elodia asked one morning a week later.

"It is . . . and what are you doing up so early? It's only six-thirty."

"I've had a headache for the past hour, and I thought some strong coffee . . ."

"I'll wager you were up until all hours reading, weren't you?"

"That has nothing to do with my headache. Besides, what am I supposed to do when I can't sleep? And where have you

130

been? You look as if you'd spent the night at Sampson's bar."

Phillip ignored her remark. "The next time I go into Mexico I'm going to take you with me. We'll have your eyes examined, and I have an idea you'll come back wearing glasses."

"I'll do nothing of the kind. I don't need glasses. How would I look, going around all goggle-eyed?"

"Such vanity I didn't expect in you. Almost everyone, sooner or later, has to wear glasses."

"You didn't tell me where you'd been, and if you don't quit needling me about glasses I'll tell Marquita you've been out every night since she left."

"You do and I'll have Pete Perez put you in the thickest lenses on the market. . . . Lord, but I'm tired! After you give me a cup of that poison you're brewing I'm going to bed for a week."

"Who was so ill?"

"No one, that's what rankles. Leola Morales had her baby an hour ago. For centuries these women have been giving birth with only a midwife or a witch doctor. The minute I come on the scene they aren't satisfied unless I'm in constant attendance. I could have slept some but every time I got out of her sight she had hysterics."

"Well, sit down and I'll have Mamie get your breakfast."

"No, I'd rather not eat now. I'll have something when I get up... Good-morning, Father. You okay?"

"Fine, Phillip. Did you know you had a call from Mexico? Alfred's looking for you." Phillip hurried out.

"Elodia, can you spare me a cup?"

Santiago had just settled down with his coffee when Phillip returned.

"I've got to go into Mexico City immediately," he said.

"That call was from the hospital. Marquita's been there all week."

"All week?" Elodia looked puzzled.

"I'm leaving at once."

"I'm going with you," Santiago said.

"So am I," Elodia decided.

Phillip left instructions regarding his patients then followed Santiago and Elodia who were hurrying through the garden.

"Who called you?" Santiago asked as Phillip backed the car out of the garage.

"Dr. Gomez."

"Did he tell you what the trouble was?"

"He said there was nothing seriously wrong but he felt I should come in this morning."

Marquita was in bed with her face to the window when Phillip entered.

"What's the matter with my girl?" he asked, placing his hand on her forehead.

She turned quickly, her arms out. "I was wishing you were here!"

"What hurts?"

"Nothing. Phillip, we're going to have a baby! I had begun to think I wasn't normal, and I couldn't stand it . . . not having children."

"Are you sure?" He could feel her nod of confirmation against his shoulder.

"All the tests are positive. Aren't you pleased, Phillip?"

"I'm more than pleased . . . I'm delighted."

"I can hardly wait to tell Aunt Elodia and the fathers."

"You won't have to wait to tell two of them. Your aunt and father came in with me." He stepped to the door and opened it.

132

"Well, Grandpa, you and Granny can come in now."

Marquita started to get up, and Phillip cautioned, "No, stay there until I talk with Frank."

"Isn't it wonderful—that we're going to have a baby?" she asked.

"Yes, it is wonderful, but we thought from the doctor's phone call and Phillip's anxiety that you were seriously ill."

"I nearly scared them out of their white pants, last night. I had a nightmare. I thought I was having the baby and I couldn't find Phillip."

The door opened and Phillip entered, followed by Dr. Gomez.

"Where's your robe, Marquita? Dr. Gomez is dismissing you." A nurse brought the wrap and helped her into it.

"Thanks for taking care of her, Frank. We'll be back in about seven months to let you finish the job."

arquita, have your bags packed so we can go into Mexico tomorrow. The time is growing short. We can expect the baby any day now."

"Why can't I have him at our own hospital like the other village women?"

"Because you aren't just another woman. You're my wife."

"Well, I'm not going to Mexico! I'm not going to have some strange doctor taking care of me. It was embarrassing enough when I had the examination."

"We've been over that before, Marquita. Now do as I say."

"If you were a natural father you'd want to deliver your own baby."

"No doctor takes care of his own wife's delivery. There's too much emotional involvement. Now we won't discuss this any further. Have Aurora get your things together."

Marquita was furious. No one had ever dared talk to her like that, and she had no intention of taking it from her husband. She picked up a book and aimed it at the doctor's head, then looked around for a weightier missile when he successfully dodged the first.

Phillip stared at her as though he was seeing her for the first time. His black eyes flashed, and without another word he turned and stalked from the room and down the front stairs. With equal fury, she lumbered down the back way into the garden.

The doctor went to the stables, had his horse saddled, and rode off toward the mountains.

Marquita took the path to the lake. Her eyes were filled with tears of rage and she mentally composed a speech she intended to deliver when she saw Phillip again. Then, she caught the toe of her shoe on a rock and pitched face down onto the hard ground. Her head struck the walk and she lost consciousness. Some time later she was roused by sharp pains and knew that she was in labor. As she tried to get to her feet her one thought was of Phillip. She called his name repeatedly. Her cries finally reached one of the gardeners who came running. Her face was covered with blood from the gash, and at the sight he bent quickly to raise her.

"Señora, what happened?"

"Help me, Pepe. I'm going to have my baby."

He staggered with her toward the house. Elodia met them at the door and helped them inside.

"Get the doctor, quick, Pepe. He's at the hospital," Elodia ordered.

He left on the run but soon returned with the report that Phillip hadn't been at the hospital since early morning.

"Then find him. If he left the village someone must have seen him leave. Learn which way he went and follow him! Aurora, see if Mr. Salazar is in his room and tell him to come here at once. And send someone to the hospital and tell Alicia that we need her here."

Alicia came, bathed Marquita, and got her into a gown.

"What do we do now?" Elodia asked.

"Wait."

"But can't something be done for the pain?"

Alicia shrugged her shoulders. "Maybe Mrs. Garcia has something."

"Nonsense! I'm not going to call in a witch doctor! Haven't you watched Dr. Parmarez? What does he do?"

"Sometimes he gives a shot."

"Oh, Lord, Aurora, where is my brother?"

"He isn't in the house. I've sent Dora and Rita to look for him."

"Little one, what are you trying to do?" Elodia bent over Marquita and caressed her face.

"I'm going to find Phillip! You must come with me!" She struggled to her feet, wavered for a moment, then fell back.

"Señora Elodia, let me get Mrs. Garcia. She has delivered many babies," Aurora pled.

"No," Marquita protested, "I want Phillip."

"We can't find Phillip and something must be done," Elodia declared when she heard an angry but welcome voice coming from the hall.

"What's the matter with this confounded pueblo? Where is everybody?" Carlos demanded.

Elodia met him at the door, concern showing in her face.

"Is Marquita all right?" he asked.

"Oh, Carlos, she's been in labor for hours and Phillip isn't here."

"Well, where is the blithering idiot? What does he mean leaving home at such a time? Have you tried to get a doctor out of Mexico?"

"No, I didn't even think of it."

"Here, you," to Alicia, "get the hospital in Mexico on the phone," Carlos ordered and stalked into Marquita's bedroom.

"I want to know why Phillip isn't here where he belongs!" he thundered. "Do you think you can make the trip into Mexico? No? Well, we'll have a doctor here as soon as I can get Mexico on the phone. Why didn't Santiago call?

136

Must I come all the way from Guatemala to see that my grandson is ushered into the world safely?"

"Someone please get Phillip!" Marquita wailed.

A door slammed downstairs, there was a scurry of footsteps in the hall, and Phillip dashed into the room.

"I'm here, darling. Dad, clear the room, please, except for Alicia and Aurora. Aunt Elodia, you'd better stand by, too. Let me wash up and I'll be right with you."

Now that Phillip was in command Marquita relaxed. "I'm not going to die, am I?"

"Of course not! You're going to have that baby before you know it." And an hour later Phillip delivered his son. As soon as he was sure the baby was all right, he put him in Elodia's arms and turned back to Marquita.

"Is he all right?" was her first question.

"Perfect. But you're exhausted, and as soon as we get you more comfortable. I'm going to put you to sleep for a while. I'll be right here beside you, so don't worry."

Day was breaking when Marquita aroused and called Phillip.

"I'm right here, dear." He arose from the reclining chair where he'd spent the night. "Are you ready to see that boy? I think he wants his mother. He's been fussing for the past hour."

Phillip brought the baby in and stood looking down at the small, restless bundle. Marquita raised on an elbow to watch him.

"Phillip," she called in alarm, "what's the matter with him? Why are you looking at him like that?"

"Can't a father admire his son without there being something wrong? For your first attempt, Mrs. Parmarez, I think you've done extremely well," he teased as he put the baby in her arms.

"Oh, isn't he beautiful?" she asked in an awestruck voice. "I didn't know he'd be so wonderful!"

"He'll do," Phillip agreed. "Are you sure you want to nurse him?"

"Of course."

"Well, he thinks he's hungry, so we'd better see what success you have feeding him."

"Have his grandfathers seen him yet?"

"Have they seen him! They hung over his crib all night. Your father was in to see you a little while ago but you were asleep."

"I want to see them as soon as they're awake."

It was near noon when Phillip opened the door to them. Carlos darted in while Santiago followed more slowly. He bent over and kissed Marquita and stood by caressing her face. The baby was nursing again and he touched its cheek gently. But Carlos couldn't control his exuberance. "I knew you would do it, Marquita! I knew you'd give me a grandson! I hope this is just the beginning. I hope you aren't going to stop with this one child."

"No, Dad. Phillip and I want a large family. Just let me get over having this one before I start on another."

"You know," Carlos said thoughtfully, watching the baby, "I've been reading a lot about the care of babies, and according to one authority it isn't good for a mother to nurse hers."

"Well, I'm going to nurse mine, and no doctor is going to tell me I can't!"

"Oh, I don't mean to interfere. I only want what is best for my grandson," Carlos hastened to say.

"He's getting it, Dad," Phillip assured him. "There may be instances where it's best to bottle-feed a baby, but I'm of

138

the opinion that the Almighty knew what he was doing when he made this provision for a mother to feed her young. From the way this one is nursing I'm not sure if I sired a boy or a little pig."

here is Conchita Mendoza going in such a hurry, and why is she crying?" Elodia asked.

"Well, since she's in our garden I assume she's coming to see us and I can't think why she's crying."

"I'll go speak to her. She always seems to be embarrassed when she sees any of us. She may think we hold her responsible for Luis' behavior." Elodia arose and went down the path. When the two women met Conchita took her hand and held it to her breast. She was sobbing so violently that Elodia couldn't understand what she was saying.

"Control yourself, Conchita. Here, sit down. . . . Dora, bring Mrs. Mendoza a cup of strong coffee. She's had a severe shock. Then tell my brother that I want to see him here."

By the time Santiago joined them Conchita was calmer and produced a letter from her pocket.

"What's the trouble, Conchita?" he asked, taking the letter.

"For a long time, Señor, we don't hear from Luis. Then today this came."

Santiago opened the single sheet and read the abrupt note.

> I am writing you as a last resort, or rather another patient is writing for me. Six months ago I had polio. I am paralyzed.

When my wife learned that I'll be crippled for the rest of my life, she left me and is getting a divorce. She has taken what little money we had, and I am penniless as well as helpless. Do you think I can come home, and can you send me the money to travel? I've nowhere else to go.

Santiago returned the letter. "Do you have the money to send him, Conchita?"

"We have some. Joaquin has gone to see his boss. He thinks he can borrow the rest from him. Do you mind his coming home?"

"Of course not. Where else would he go? But I want to talk this over with the doctor before Luis leaves California."

"Phillip," Marquita called to her husband on the balcony, "Father has something to discuss with you."

"I'll come right down."

When he had joined the group, Santiago said, "Phillip, you've heard us speak of Dr. Mendoza. His mother has just received a letter from him. Luis has had polio."

"Oh, no!"

"Yes, he's completely paralyzed. Would there be any chance of his regaining even partial mobility with therapy?"

"Frankly, I don't know, but it's always worth trying."

"I think so, too."

"Conchita," Santiago said, turning to the distraught woman, "tell Joaquin to forget about borrowing money. We'll advance it from the hospital fund. We're going to see what can be done for Luis before we bring him back. Have Joaquin get ready—we'll take a plane for California tomorrow if we can get tickets."

With many expressions of gratitude Conchita left.

"Isn't that heaping coals of fire on the man's head?" Phillip asked.

Santiago's eyes twinkled. "Luis may practice medicine in Esperanza after all," was his only comment.

"And now, Marquita, can I leave you without having to worry about you and the baby that's coming?"

"Yes, Father. I'm going into Mexico next week to stay until time to go to the hospital."

"And Phillip, I hope you won't be away doing any mountain climbing."

"You can bet on it! We'll get along fine, so don't worry."

"Good. Elodia, will you give instructions about the packing of my bags? Allow for two weeks at least."

"I'll attend to it, Santos. Are you sure Hilario understands when you want the car?"

"I'll see him tonight."

"Now about Chavelita while she is on vacation. If you have to leave here before I return I want her to go in with you. Where is she now?"

"Visiting somewhere in the village, I suppose," Elodia said.

"No, she and Amanda took Carl to the lake to feed the swans," Marquita corrected. "Here they come now."

Chavelita and Amanda, with Carl between them, came slowly up the path. The baby's steps were sluggish as he was growing tired. He lifted his arms to Chavelita and she picked him up.

"He's the smartest, most beautiful baby in the whole world," she declared when she had joined the group. Carl reached for his mother, and Marquita took him.

"Chavelita, we may have to cut your visit short this time."

"Why?"

Santiago explained.

"Let me go with you, please, Papa. I want to see how they give the treatments. After all, I'm going to be a nurse, and I should know these things."

"Well, I'm not sure . . ."

142

"Please, Papa, please, please!"

"Elodia, what do you think?"

"I think it's a sound idea. She's never been out of Mexico, and the trip would be educational. She must have an older woman with her, of course."

"Why?"

"A young lady doesn't travel with a gentleman unless he's a relative."

"Well," Chavelita protested, "he's my father!"

Santiago smiled. "Call Mrs. Hernandez and tell her to prepare to go with us. She chaperons you in Mexico, so I'm sure she will be acceptable in the States. We leave here early in the morning, so get your clothes packed tonight."

The family was having early morning coffee in the patio when Conchita appeared, more agitated than she'd been the day before.

"Now what's wrong?" Elodia asked.

"Joaquin can't go to see Luis. He fell; he can't walk," she cried.

"Fell? From where?"

"He was climbing the fence and he fell off."

"Where is he now?" Phillip asked.

"At home."

"Dora, tell Armando to bring my bag. And don't wait breakfast for me. I'll have something later."

Marquita finished her coffee, fed the baby, and waited anxiously for Phillip.

"What will you do, Father, if Joaquin can't make the trip?"

"We'll go without him. I hadn't intended seeing Luis . . . thought it might embarrass him, but perhaps I'll have to."

Phillip returned an hour later.

143

"You'll go without Joaquin, Father. He has a multiple fracture of his right leg."

"How did it happen?"

"That bull he keeps was in a bad mood this morning and chased Joaquin over the fence when he went into the pen to feed him. The poor old man took a high dive from the top rail. He may never walk again. Old bones are brittle and slow to mend. Very often they don't."

"Can Conchita take care of him? She's almost as old as he is and not so strong."

"I put Joaquin in the hospital, Aunt Elodia. If you have time, I wish you'd look in on Conchita today. She's so distraught over this, piled on top of her son's misfortune, I told her to stay away from the hospital until tomorrow. If she's left alone she'll sit there imagining all sorts of horrors."

"And now I'll worry about you, Father," Marquita said. "You be careful while you're away."

"Oh, I'll be all right. I'm never ill. Chavelita, we'd better be on our way."

Chavelita said her good-byes and followed Santiago through the garden.

Two weeks later they were back again and joined the rest of the family at the apartment in Mexico.

"We didn't expect you so soon," Elodia said. "Tell us about Luis."

"There isn't a lot to tell. I talked with the doctors at the hospital where Luis had been a pathologist. They were heartsick over his misfortune . . . they consider him brilliant. Luckily, the disease didn't affect his mind, just crippled his body. But a doctor without hands or feet is certainly handicapped. Luis was terribly embarrassed when I walked into his room. We had a long talk about what had happened. He has no hope of improving and resisted therapy. He cried when I told him my plans for him."

"And what are those plans?" Elodia asked.

"Well," Santiago began almost apologetically under his sister's stern eye, "I thought Phillip might use him in a sort of advisory capacity."

"Phillip has about as much use for an adviser as I have for a hayfork!" she declared.

"Well, at least he can talk shop with Luis. I'm sure Phillip misses having someone to discuss medical problems with. And who knows, Luis may regain partial use of his body." Marquita quickly rallied to her father's defense.

"We're going to put in a fully equipped laboratory. I heard Phillip say he needed one. Luis can run that."

"How soon will he be home?"

"Not for some time. Possibly a year or longer."

Marquita came home a month later with her second son. She wanted to call him Santiago after her father, but at her father's request named him Frederick after a favorite brother. Carlos was as jubilant as when the first grandson was born. He joined Marquita one day in the garden. "That's my girl!" he smiled. "Two grandsons! The Parmarez name will live on. By the way, where's Carl?"

"Amanda has him somewhere in the garden, more than likely at the lake. . . . Did you see Chavelita while you were in the City?"

"Yes, we had lunch the day I got in. She's taking her college entrance examinations. She seems too young for college."

"We don't know. She may be older than we have always thought. She has a fine mind and has always received top grades in her schoolwork. But she has always worked too hard! She has the greatest determination to excel in whatever she attempts."

"Yes, I discovered that while talking with her. In one of her studies—I think she said it was physics—she's the only girl in a class of twenty, and she's leading. She has two rivals for her place at the top and one of them is very close. She says she has to widen the gap."

"She's very ambitious. I hope she doesn't wear herself out studying."

"She looks well. Ah, here comes my boy! Come to Grandpa, Carl."

The child looked up and when he recognized his grandfather gave a happy squeal and came running on sturdy, bare feet.

"Amanda, where are his shoes?"

"I have them, señora. He didn't want to wear them."

"Make him keep them on, anyway.

"Carl, you're a naughty little boy."

"Naughty boy," he repeated.

"Just look at your feet!"

He obediently turned one chubby foot over and regarded it gravely.

"Foot dirty," he said, and tried to wipe it on Carlos' coat sleeve.

"No, no, Carl! Don't let him do that, Dad."

"Oh, let him alone. The coat needs cleaning anyway."

"Amanda, take him in and clean him up. I don't know how I'll manage if Ricky is as mischievous as Carl is."

Carlos hugged him close before turning him over to his nurse.

"Hurry back with him," he told Amanda.

"I haven't seen Elodia or Santiago since I came. Are they in retreat?"

"No, they're in Mexico on business connected with the estate. I'm surprised that they've been gone so long."

"And I suppose Phillip is at that little adobe pile you call a hospital."

"Don't belittle it or underestimate its usefulness, Dad. A great many people have been helped during the short time it's been in operation. We're very proud of it."

"You know, Marquita, you amaze me. You've had a good education, you've traveled widely, and you're certainly one of the world's loveliest women, yet you seem content here in the valley. I believe you're happy."

Marquita's laugh rang out. "Of course I'm happy. I live in the most beautiful country in the world; my home is—to me—the best in all of Mexico; and I am married to the most wonderful man. . . ."

"Hey, where is everyone?" Phillip called.

"Out here, dear."

Phillip came out leading Carl. "Why, hello, Dad. I didn't know you were here. What do you think of our youngest?"

"He's fine, Phillip. Looks just like Carl."

"We see the resemblance, too. I'm getting quite a family in spite of my late start." Then as the baby began to whimper he picked him up and cuddled him in his arms. "I believe if we had a dozen the last would be as thrilling an experience as Carl was. Is it anywhere near his snack time? He's nuzzling around as if he's hungry."

"I'll feed him now. And you're right, each one is a miracle, I wonder what's keeping Father and Auntie so long."

"They're here. They came in as I did. They'll be over in a moment."

And a little later Elodia and Santiago strolled over to join them. Elodia sat down, sighing deeply.

"Tired, Auntie?" Marquita asked.

"Exhausted. I don't know how people live in the city year after year. The noise and confusion would drive me crazy."

"Did Chavelita say anything to you about college, Father? I know you saw her."

"Yes, she mentioned it."

"Well, what do you think?"

"It isn't what I think but what she's capable of. I talked with her teachers, and they think she can pass the tests. It remains to be seen."

"I wish she wasn't in such a hurry to get through school. There isn't any reason for it," Marquita said.

"She thinks there is. She's eager to get into nursing and out so she can restore health to the world. The child is as much of a dreamer as I ever was," Santiago said.

"Well, if her dreams come as near to fulfillment as yours have, we'll have reason to be very proud of her." Elodia was always loyal.

Father, Auntie and I have decided to have a dinner party for Chavelita when she comes home this summer. We'll invite some of the students from college."

"That's fine, Marquita. Is anything required of me?"

"No, we'll attend to everything."

"Are you sure you're up to all this, with the baby so soon?"

"Oh, yes. It's good for me . . . takes my mind off myself."

But the party never materialized, for Chavelita came home the next weekend.

"We didn't expect you until the fifteenth," Marquita told her. "What brings you home ahead of schedule?"

"Where's Papa?" Chavelita asked by way of answer.

"He's sitting in the swing waiting for his snack and deciding on the boys' future," Marquita jested as she led the way to the garden, only to find the swing empty.

"Now where did he go? Father?"

"I'm over here trying to keep Ricky from wrecking your flower beds. Back to your playpen, young man! No," Santiago protested as the baby began struggling, "I know you want your freedom, but your mother wants a few of her flowers left." He brought Ricky back to the patio with Carl trailing after, his toy duck held close. He dropped it and ran to Chavelita as soon as he saw her.

"Why, Chavelita, what brought you home so early?" Santiago asked. She embraced him fondly with one arm while she held Carl on the other. The maid came out with the tea cart, and the boy squirmed free and ran to the tray.

Amanda took charge of his feeding, and Marquita attended to Ricky.

"Now let's all relax while this child tells us the news. I know she has something on her mind," Santiago said.

"Here come Aunt Elodia and Dr. Phillip. I'm glad we're all together to discuss my plans. I've been doing a lot of thinking lately and since I'm going to be a nurse there's no point in my spending any more time learning things I'll never use. I want to go into training at once. I've had two years at college, and I can get my diploma by attending night classes. Is that all right with you, Papa?"

"I think every girl is entitled to a college education," he said after a thoughtful pause. "I'm afraid that once you leave you'll not want to go back."

"Yes, I will, I promise. I've talked to the directors at the school of nursing, and they'll accept me."

"You're so young and so lovely, Chavelita. Are you sure you want a nursing career?" Marquita asked.

"I'm positive! I've always been."

"I'm sure you'll be an exquisite one," Elodia said.

"What do you think, Phillip?" Marquita turned to her husband, a puzzled look on her face.

"This isn't our choice, dear. Chavelita must decide for herself. As a doctor, I look upon a good, conscientious nurse as God's gift to an understaffed profession."

"It seems to me, Chavelita, that in getting an education you have sacrificed many pleasures a girl should have,"

Marquita argued. "We had planned to have a party for you...."

"Good. Let's have it this weekend because I won't have time to get home again soon. I've agreed to help out at the hospital for a while."

Marquita struggled through the blackness of anesthesia to partial consciousness. She was tired, so terribly tired! She tried to turn her head, but the effort made her dizzy.

"Phillip," she called.

"I'm here, dear."

"Shouldn't the baby ..." She opened her eyes and focused them with difficulty. "Shouldn't he be here now?"

"Both of them ... safe and sound."

"Both? Then we did get twins. Are they boys?"

"No, two identical little girls."

"Let me see them now, please."

Phillip left the room and returned a moment later with the babies. A nurse followed and taking one small bundle placed it beside Marquita. Phillip lowered the one he held gently on the other side, and uncovered the little faces. "Aren't they beautiful?" he asked.

"Oh, yes, they are, they are. I was so sure we'd have another boy."

"It did look as if we were in a rut," he agreed. "Have you decided on names for girls or did you concentrate on labels for boys?"

"I thought of girls' names just in case. I considered Marcia and Macaria, but I wasn't sure which I liked the best."

"Well, now you won't have to decide. You can use both. And we'd better send these young ladies back to the nursery so you can rest."

I am glad to see that you've replaced that old wooden bench with this one of concrete, Clemente. I don't know how that poor old thing supported your bulk all these years. Why, it had reached the point where it creaked every time you even looked at it," Santiago teased.

"And on the other extreme, you could perch on a violet stem without bending it," Father Clemente returned.

"Yes, we look like before and after, don't we?" The two sat down together and the priest, from force of habit, began fingering the cross on his rosary.

"Go ahead and say your prayers if you think your sins demand supplication."

"You were the subject of my petitions," the priest replied good-naturedly. They fell comfortably silent, as good friends do. A babel of voices roused them and they looked up to see a group of tourists approaching the small church.

"Will your services be needed?" Santiago asked.

"No, Marcos can handle the crowds as well as I can, and his small body leaves more room for the sightseers, too. This tour business has been a lifesaver for the Valley, Santiago. The people were never so prosperous as they are now."

"Yes, the villagers are kept busy, and they are happier and more self-reliant."

There was silence again for a moment, then, "Santiago, do you ever hear from Romero?"

"No, I haven't had a letter since before he left Mexico."

"And that was ten years ago."

"Yes. I often wonder what sort of man developed from my young rebel."

"I'm sorry, Santiago. I know it's been your deepest grief."

"He was all I had left of Tony."

"Marquita's marriage was a blessing. The doctor filled a need not only in the Valley but in your family circle as well."

"Phillip has no equal. He's a devoted husband, a good father, an exceptionally fine doctor, and most important, he's kind and compassionate. He is all that I can ask for my daughter and her children."

"Yes, I know. He's loved and respected everywhere. And what he's accomplished with that hospital! I know he's been handicapped for lack of efficient help. Dr. Mendoza can't do a great deal. By the way, how is Chavelita doing?"

"Fine. When she finishes training we'll have a nurse who will stay with us." He looked at his watch. "I have some letters to write, so I'd better attend to them."

But he had to postpone his letter writing, for Chavelita had come in his absence and was waiting for him.

"I didn't see you come through the village," he told her after their greeting.

"No, I came through Upper Valley. I've bought a car and learned to drive it. Come sit over here, Papa, so I can talk with you."

Santiago took his chair by the window, and she sat on a hassock close by.

"Papa, will you be terribly disappointed if I don't complete my nursing education?"

Santiago's heart skipped a beat as he remembered his

153

boast to the priest less than an hour before. "Why, no, Chavelita, you chart your own course."

"I know, but you've been so generous all these years."

"There were no strings attached—there never have been. Did you bring him home with you so I can meet him?"

"Bring whom home, Papa?"

"Your young man. Aren't you trying to tell me you have fallen in love and want to be married?"

"Me? Married? Who in the world would I marry? No, Papa, I want to study medicine. I want to become a doctor."

"A doctor! A woman doctor?"

"Why not?" she demanded heatedly. "Do you, like a lot of others, think a woman lacks the brains to compete in what has been considered a man's field?"

"Smooth your feathers, my dear. You know that I have faith in your ability to accomplish anything you set your mind to do. I'm just surprised that you would select such a demanding profession. From Phillip's comments I assume it is a tough one."

"I know it is, Papa, but that's what I want. I thought at first that nursing would satisfy the need I felt, but it hasn't. I've had enough of it to know that it isn't what I want to do. I'll stay with it if you want me to, but I'll tell you now that someday there's going to be 'Doctor' in front of my name."

"Will you discuss this with Phillip before going any further with your plan? I'd like his opinion. I'm not opposed, you understand, and I'm proud of your ambition. I just want you to be sure of what you're doing."

When the matter was laid before Phillip that night he was silent for several minutes before voicing his opinion.

"Mentally," he began at length, "you're capable of it—perhaps temperamentally, too. But in appearance, you're just not the type. You're too small and dainty. I doubt that anyone will take you seriously."

"Well, they'd better! I'm not just talking! I'm going to be a doctor, and I'm going to concentrate on women and children's illnesses."

"It's a long, hard pull, Chavelita, but with your determination you won't be influenced by anything that I can say."

"You're right, Dr. Phillip, and I'd like to start right away, if Papa's willing."

"If it's what you want, I'm for you all the way," Santiago assured her.

lodia! Marquita! Come here, will you?"

Elodia dropped her book and ran in the direction of Santiago's voice. Marquita and Phillip, hearing the call, came in from their quarters. The three met in the downstairs library where Santiago sat with the Bible open before him.

"What is it, Santiago?" his sister asked, breathing heavily. "You frightened me."

"Sorry, I didn't mean to. And I didn't want to rush you, but I want you to listen to this. Sit down, all of you." They obeyed, and he turned to the Bible and read, " 'And the vision of all is become unto you as the words of a book that is sealed . . .' "

"Is that the beginning of the quotation, Santiago?" Elodia interrupted to ask. "So far it doesn't make sense," she added critically.

"No, that's the eleventh verse of the twenty-ninth chapter of Isaiah. It starts off, 'Woe to Ariel, to Ariel!' "

" 'Woe to Ariel!' " Marquita exclaimed. "That doesn't make sense either. Ariel is a mischievous fairy in one of Shakespeare's plays."

"Ariel is a star, or a comet, or some other heavenly body," Elodia corrected.

"And ariel is a small African antelope," Phillip informed them.

156

"You're all wrong as far as this text is concerned. If you'll let me continue without interruption, Isaiah explains. 'Woe to Ariel, to Ariel, the city where David dwelt!' That would be Jerusalem, wouldn't it?"

"I suppose so. Jerusalem was the seat of the government, such as it was, and I assume that David, as king, would live in the capital," Elodia agreed.

"That was my conclusion. Isaiah was predicting the calamities that were to come. Now I don't understand this next bit. 'And thou shalt be brought down, and shalt speak out of the ground, and thy speech shall be low out of the dust, and thy voice shall be as of one that hath a familiar spirit, out of the ground, and thy speech shall whisper out of the dust.' Now what do you make of that?"

"Santiago, since you've been poring over the Bible so much you come up with some of the most perplexing questions! I've always before found it such a comfortable book to read," his sister complained.

"I doubt that it was meant to make us comfortable. Perhaps its purpose is to stir us up into doing something."

"Let me read that passage, Santiago. I never could get anything out of another's reading," Phillip said. Santiago moved aside to make room for the three of them. They bent over the opened Bible with interest.

Phillip was the first to speak "Well, I think the first phrase refers to the destruction of the city and her people," he said cautiously. "But how do people speak out of the ground? In that one short verse he expresses the same thought four times."

"And the next phrase, 'Thy voice shall be as of one that hath a familiar spirit,' " Elodia read. "Whatever it is that speaks out of the ground is similar to something that is known."

"Perhaps Father Clemente could explain this," Marquita suggested.

"No, I've asked him. I've been puzzling over this all week. I can't seem to get past the twenty-ninth chapter. I keep returning to the possibility that the verse we just read is linked in some way to the eleventh and eighteenth."

"Read them," Marquita prompted.

Santiago turned back to the book. "In the ninth and tenth verses Isaiah says that the spirit of revelation has been taken from the prophets. Clemente and I agreed on that . . . after much argument I'll confess. Now this follows: 'And the vision of all is become unto you as the words of a book that is sealed.' Then in the eighteenth verse, 'And in that day the deaf shall hear the words of the book, and the eyes of the blind shall see out of obscurity, and out of darkness.' "

"What day is referred to?" Phillip asked.

"The preceding verse evidently dates that event. This is how it reads, 'Is it not yet a little while, and Lebanon shall be turned into a fruitful field, and the fruitful field be esteemed as a forest?' "

"What does that mean?" Marquita asked.

Santiago shook his head. "I don't know," he confessed. "From this you'd suppose Lebanon's lands would be barren for a period of time and then would be cultivated successfully again. I'm sure it has a deeper meaning."

"I don't know how many times I've read the Bible, but I don't remember ever seeing that passage before. It shows how very shallow my reading is," Elodia said thoughtfully.

Phillip drew the book across the table and, resting his head on one hand, studied the passage. "The book referred to couldn't be the Bible, could it?"

"No, I don't think so. If you read on you'll note that the book is to be shown to an educated man who will say he can't read it because it's sealed."

158

"How sealed?" Marquita wanted to know.

"You can ask some puzzlers yourself, Marquita. The only way I can think of a book being sealed is that it's written in a language I don't speak or understand. One printed in Arabic would certainly be sealed to me."

"Well, this is sealed to me, although I can read it," Phillip said. "If you accept the Bible as divine truth, a book is to be produced. You can't dispute that. It will be a joy to the meek and a blessing to the poor. In that way it resembles the Bible."

"Wouldn't it be amazing if this is the book I've been looking for so long?" Santiago asked in awed tones.

"Now, Santiago . . . what a fantastic idea! Isaiah was talking to the Israelites in Jerusalem."

"The warning was given to them, but I don't know that my idea is so fantastic after all. For years scientists have advanced the theory that we, the Indian people, are descendants of the Lost Tribes of Israel," Santiago argued.

"I don't hold with that. Both North and South America were peopled with Indians, not Jews, when the explorers got here."

"Agreed, but how and when did they come? Oh, if we just had the book, all these mysteries would be solved."

"For your sake, Santiago, I wish there was one, but . . ."

"I know what you're going to say, Elodia, and I maintain that there is no 'but' about it. There is a book!"

The atmosphere was growing tense, and to cool it Phillip broke in. "You know, I never realized that the Bible was so—so human, so sort of everyday. And these chaps knew what they were talking about. Here we're told that business pressure causes dreaming, and a man displays his ignorance by talking too much. And here's a poor devil suffering from indigestion."

"Phillip," Elodia reproved, "you should not speak lightly of the Bible."

"I'm not, Auntie. It's right here in Ecclesiastes. I just put the words in modern English. See if I'm not right." Phillip found his place in the book again. " 'For a dream cometh through a multitude of business; and a fool's voice is known by the multitude of his words.' Now isn't that exactly what I said?"

"Suppose you read the passage about the man with indigestion," Elodia suggested dryly.

"It may have been an ulcer," Phillip conceded. "We aren't given enough of the symptoms to make a positive diagnosis possible. I'll read what's written here. 'A man to whom God hath given riches, wealth, honor, that he wanteth for nothing for his soul hath all that he desireth, yet God giveth him not the power to eat thereof, but a stranger eateth it. This is vanity and an evil disease.' "

"Wouldn't you know a doctor would put that interpretation on it!" Elodia exclaimed.

ovita, as soon as my brother comes down we'll have breakfast in the patio." Elodia paused a moment to center a floral arrangement on the dining table, then walked outside. Jovita came out a little later with the coffee.

"*Papacito* sleeps late," she said.

"He was not feeling well last night. Perhaps you'd better tell Felipe to look in on him." Elodia sipped her coffee slowly. As she waited, Marquita and Phillip came out to their own patio.

"Good morning, Auntie. Where's Father?" Marquita called.

"He hasn't come down yet. I sent Felipe to see if he's awake. He was tired when he went to bed last night so I suppose he's resting. Come on over and have your coffee. The urn is full."

"We'll have Petra bring ours over as soon as it's ready." They joined Elodia, and a moment later their maid came across with their breakfast.

"Have one of the rolls, Auntie. Carlotta made them this morning."

"Thank you, but I'll wait for your father."

"Phillip can't wait, so we'll go ahead with our meal."

They had just begun when Felipe appeared.

"Yes, Felipe . . . did you arouse Senor Salazar?" Elodia asked.

"He is awake, but he can't get up," Felipe replied.

"He can't get up?" Phillip was halfway to the door in an instant. "I'd better see what the trouble is," he called back as he ran in. The women followed, but he met them at the top of the stairs.

"Get word to Rudy at the hospital that he and Gilbert are to bring the stretcher. Have Menchaca get the ambulance ready at once. We have to get Father to the hospital in Mexico immediately. He's had a stroke. Call the hospital and say I'm bringing in an emergency. And if you girls want to go in with me you'd better get ready at once."

The women rushed to their separate apartments and met nervously a little later in the downstairs hall.

"I wish Chavelita was here," Marquita voiced the wishes of both.

"We'll have to get word to her immediately. Do you have her address, now that she's finished her internship?"

"She's still available at the hospital." A commotion on the second floor attracted their attention, and they looked up to see the orderlies start down with Santiago. Phillip was directly behind them. Marquita bent over to kiss her father.

"You girls are not to worry," Phillip told them, seeing their faces. He put a reassuring arm around each of them. "I want you both to ride in with Escobeda. I'll be with Father in the ambulance."

"But, Phillip, I . . ."

"There isn't room for all of us, dear, and I must go in with him."

Marquita said no more but hurried after him to the garage where Menchaca had the ambulance out and the motor running. The transfer was soon made and the cars left the village with the ambulance leading.

Phillip paused at the desk where a nurse waited to accompany him to the room assigned Santiago.

"I'll be back to talk to you girls as soon as there is anything to tell you," Phillip told them and hastened on. The nurse who had preceded him opened the door and moved aside for his entrance. As he stepped in Chavelita arose from a chair near the window.

"Why, Doctor," he exclaimed, "what are you doing here?"

"I was told that you had an emergency and thought I'd stay and give you some expert advice. Who's your patient?" Then as the stretcher was brought in she ran to it.

"Papa, darling! What happened?"

Phillip explained as Santiago was lifted to his bed. Chavelita stood by, watching critically.

"You don't look as if you're comfortable, Papa," she said, bending over him. "I'm going to shift these pillows. Now, isn't that better?"

"I'm calling Dr. Barbosa in for consultation. And you'd better stay—I'm sure you'll want in on this case," Phillip said.

"Want in on it! What are you talking about? It's my case! You don't suppose I'm going to let anyone else take care of him, do you?"

Santiago smiled faintly. "There's nothing," he said, "like educating your own doctor."

"Well, since he's your patient I suppose you'll stay with him until I get back. I'm going to let my wife and Aunt Elodia in for a moment, but don't let Marquita get too emotional. She hasn't been feeling well."

"I'll take care of her."

The women were allowed in the room—but only for a moment; when Phillip returned with Dr. Barbosa they had to leave the room. They stood just outside the door until Elodia said, "I'm going down to arrange for a private room for the

163

duration of your father's illness. I'm not going to leave him, nor do I intend to spend my time standing in the hall." But Phillip had already provided for them, and they were shown to a room where Chavelita joined them.

"You'll stay with us for a while, won't you?" Marquita asked her.

"I won't leave Papa, you can be sure of that."

The morning passed, and Phillip came down at noon to take the women to lunch.

"We're running routine tests," he said, "and there are two nurses with him. There's nothing any of us can do now, so stop worrying and eat some lunch. Afterwards I want you to go to the apartment—you, too, Auntie; both of you must get some rest. I'm taking Chavelita with me. I'll come back later and take you to the hospital."

Phillip was dozing in the library when Marquita aroused and found him there that afternoon.

"How long have you been here, and how is Father?" she asked.

He looked at his watch. "I've been here for about an hour, and he was asleep when I left. Chavelita is with him. Now you and Aunt Elodia get dressed. I'm taking you to him for a few minutes; then I want you to go home."

"But Phillip, I don't want to leave him!"

"I know how you feel, but you can do nothing by staying. Come over here and sit down. I want to talk with you, and I don't want you getting excited. As far as we can determine, your father will be partially paralyzed. To just what extent, we don't know. I've chartered a plane and I'm taking him to Chicago to a doctor I know there. Chavelita will go with me; I'll leave her there so there'll always be one of the family with him. I don't want to be away from you

164

very long, so as soon as I have him settled and talk with Jim Reavis I'll come home. We leave here at seven in the morning and I want to know that you're safely at home before I go. I'll call you tonight at nine."

Phillip came home two weeks later.

"We can't tell yet," he said in answer to Marquita's question. "You know how long we had to wait before we were sure of Luis' mobility."

"How was Father feeling? Was he despondent?"

"No, he was quite cheerful. He sent his love and said you were not to worry. The doctors there don't think he is as bad as we had feared. They believe he will have the use of the upper part of his body, although he may never walk again. It's really too soon to be sure of anything."

"How soon will he be home?"

"I don't know. Chavelita doesn't want him to leave Chicago until they have exhausted every possibility of helping him. I look for them in a month or two."

People at both ends of the Valley were preparing for a fiesta. Paper streamers draped on wires were looped across the narrow streets. Tissue paper flowers bloomed on every tree not bearing its own blossoms. The men had been at work for a week erecting the towering frames for the fireworks display. The women were busy making tortillas and tamales. Booths were lined all around the plazas.

Two busloads of unexpected tourists descended on the scene.

"What's the occasion for all this?" one of the guides asked.

"*Papacito's* coming home tomorrow," they chorused.

Phillip had gone in to meet the plane, and early the next

morning the car rolled through Upper Valley to the garage. It was instantly surrounded by villagers who wanted to greet Santiago.

"If this is the sort of welcome that I get, I'll leave home more often," he said, his eyes misty. But other eyes misted, too, as a wheelchair was set up and Santiago lifted into it.

"Are you all right?" Phillip asked.

"Just fine. Where is the family?"

"Marquita said they would wait for you in the garden. She knew there would be a crowd out here."

"All right, Bob, you'll just have to push through this mob," Chavelita told the male nurse who accompanied them.

Phillip paused to speak to the villagers and assure them that Santiago would see at least a part of the celebration, then strode off after the wheelchair. They were held up again inside the gate where the family and Carlos waited. And as soon as they had welcomed Santiago the gardeners and house servants pressed forward.

"Who are these people?" Bob asked.

"They're employees. Some work inside, some out. This is an extensive estate and requires a large staff. I think we can move on, now."

"I'm glad you're in charge, Dr. Chavez." Carlos had dropped back beside the chair.

"Oh, I wouldn't trust him to anyone else. Have you met Papa's nurse? Bob Forest, Mr. Parmarez. As you have no doubt concluded, Bob, Mr. Parmarez is Dr. Phillip's father. Now let's push on through. I want to get Papa to bed. He's had a strenuous morning."

"Chavelita, we've arranged quarters for Father downstairs. Phillip thought he'd be happier if he could be where he can keep an eye on us. Here's his apartment. And Father, if you don't like it, we'll take you back upstairs."

"This is perfect, dear. I'll enjoy it."

166

"We'd better get out before Chavelita throws us out," Phillip said.

"I'll go with you and give Bob time to get him in bed. How do you think he looks, Phillip?"

"Very well. You've done wonders for him. I'm surprised that he has such good use of his hands."

"They're going to be all right. He's had massages night and morning. But his legs . . . I'm afraid."

"Chavelita," Marquita stopped and took Chavelita's hands in hers, "I wish there was some way we could repay you for what you've done."

"Teacher, this was all bought and paid for when you took a grimy little Indian girl in your arms and called her sister. As for Papa . . . here, I can't get maudlin, I'm sure Bob has him in bed by now and I have to go back in there." Santiago was stretched out comfortably when she got into his room.

"Feeling okay?" she asked.

"Wonderful! It's good to be home!"

"It is, Papa. There's no place like it."

Santiago looked at her wistfully. "How soon do you have to go?" he asked.

"Go where, Papa?"

"To Mexico . . . or wherever you're going to practice."

"I've arrived."

"I appreciate that, my dear, but it would be a waste of your talent to be tied to such a useless old log as I'm going to be."

"Papa!" she said sternly, "I will not have a patient of mine with that attitude! As for your being useless, if you never left your bed you'd be an inspiration to the entire Valley. My future is wherever you are, and I thank God that he has given me the ability to repay in a small part all the love and care you've given me."

Bob's entrance put an end to their conversation.

167

"Shall I take over, Doctor?"

"Yes, please. If you should need anything, the bell there will bring one of the maids."

The joy of coming home buoyed Santiago up for a few days, then the narrowness of his existence began to pall. Where once he had come and gone at will, now he had to be taken. The mountains he had loved to climb were off limits. His family and friends tried to interest him in the life of the Village but were unsuccessful. Even Father Clemente's best efforts failed to rouse him to an argument.

One day Marquita came upon him alone in the garden. "Where's Bob?" she asked.

"I sent him in. I'm weary of looking at him." Then as if ashamed of his outburst he added, "He had some letters to write."

"Are you terribly tired?"

"Now why should I be tired," he demanded irritably, "of anything but being tied down like a squash? Why do you ask?"

"Do you feel like painting some pictures for me?"

"That's a foolish question. You know that I haven't painted seriously since your mother died."

"Yes, I know that, but I think you owe it to me to do this. I want them for the girls' rooms. They have a birthday coming up, and I can't think of anything more appropriate to give them than pictures painted by their grandfather."

"You can buy better pictures than I can paint."

"Father, I'm disgusted with you! All my life you've preached the virtue of sharing with others. Here you have this wonderful talent and you've refused to use it for years. What about sharing it with your family?"

"I could use some for the hospital, too." Phillip had come up quietly.

Santiago looked from them to his hands resting on the arms of his chair. "I'm not sure, after all these years, that I have the touch. I would have to have special easels, too."

"I'll have them made," Phillip offered.

"What sort of pictures do you want?"

"Anything you want to do. The garden is full of subjects."

"The house is, too," Santiago said. "The patio seen through the open door, the old kitchen . . . you'd look a long time to find a better subject than that. When Carl comes in, send him to me. I'll need him to help me select my equipment."

Marquita kissed him soundly. "It was never your nature to be idle."

"Don't be too optimistic about the results. I'm almost afraid to think about it."

For a while Santiago's efforts were sporadic and indifferent, then as his interest grew he could be drawn away from his easel only when Father Clemente came over, and they became involved in heated arguments about the Bible.

One day after the priest had left, Marquita found her father busily ruling a sheet of paper into squares. "What are you doing?" she asked.

"I'm preparing to make digestion of the Bible more interesting to the children."

"What does that mean?"

"I'm plotting a Bible crossword puzzle. They sometimes get bored with the quizzes I've been giving them."

"Haven't you set yourself a tremendous task?"

"I have, but I think that by the time I've finished this I'll know a lot more about the book than I do now."

"No doubt, but I wonder if you can't buy these already made up."

"Perhaps, but buying one wouldn't help me much in my study, would it?"

"I'm surprised that the children have absorbed so much from the lessons you assign them. I don't think they get bored, but they're lazy about looking up your references. By the way, I came over here to look for Phillip. Have you seen him?"

"Yes, he came through here on his way to the library an hour ago."

"Thanks. I'll see if he's still there."

She found him at the desk, the open Bible before him.

"Now what are you doing?" she asked.

"Carl came to me last night for the answer to one of Father's questions, and since I am as blank about it as he is I came to headquarters for the solution. The trouble with this book is that you can never look up a reference and leave it. One verse leads to another, until before you know it you've spent hours without ever finding a place to stop. This brought me to a dead stand, and I've been trying for an hour to unravel it. Isaiah is speaking . . . isn't he the chap that had a lot to say about a lost book?"

"Yes, I think he was. What have you found now?"

"Listen to this, 'Woe to the land shadowing with wings, which is beyond the rivers of Ethiopia.' "

He paused and looked up. She leaned over his shoulder to study the words. After a moment she spoke. "Well, according to this some calamity is coming to Ethiopia."

"No, not to Ethiopia—to the land beyond. Where would that be?"

"Wouldn't that depend on where Isaiah was when he made the prediction?"

"You're right. Now where was he?"

170

"In Palestine?" Marquita suggested.

"I think it's reasonable to assume that he was. Let me get the large atlas." He wheeled the huge globe in close to the table, and both bent over it.

"Here's Palestine." Marquita put her finger on the spot.

"And here's Africa. Now, looking beyond that continent . . ." Phillip turned the globe slowly and studied his findings. "Why—that's the Americas!" he exclaimed. "Can that refer to us?" He turned back to the Bible. " 'The land shadowing with wings.' What can that mean?"

"Phillip, our national emblem has an eagle with outstretched wings. Could that apply?"

"I don't know. The eagle is also the national bird of the United States, and Guatemala has the quetzal for hers. Wings over the three countries. Is some calamity coming to us, or is it already past?"

"Are you two at the Bible again?" Elodia asked, pausing beside them.

"Yes, Auntie, we've found another prophecy that puzzles us."

"Well, you know enough not to ask me for an explanation. I know less than you do. Why can't we be satisfied with the Ten Commandments, the Lord's Prayer, the Beatitudes, and the Twenty-third Psalm? I used to read the Bible with great comfort. Now I find myself trying to analyze every passage, looking for a hidden meaning." And she passed through the room to her own apartment.

Father, shouldn't you rest awhile?" Marquita asked one evening several months later. "You've been bent over that easel most of the day."

"I want to finish this, then I'll quit," Santiago promised.

"That's sunset from the ledge at its very best," she said, watching his sure, swift strokes.

Bob came to stand beside her. "To someone like me who can hardly draw a straight line with a ruler, Mr. Salazar's skill is more than miraculous. Just look at how perfectly he blends those colors."

"I think I was born with a sense of color," Santiago said, "so I deserve no credit. In my thinking every person is endowed with some particular ability. If a man's endowment is creative, nothing human will prevent his creating. He'll paint it, write it, sing it, or find some way to express it. Your talent, Bob, is to be a good nurse, and you deserve as much commendation for that as Dickens does for being a great novelist or Shakespeare a playwright. . . . Marquita, I want the boy to have this if you ever hear from him. For years I've held onto the hope that he'd come home. I know now that I'll never see him again. But if he ever returns to the United States, Allan will know of it. I have the feeling that Allan will drop in on us soon. He wrote that he had sold all of the pictures he had taken from here the last time. Perhaps he can take this back with him. It isn't to be sold unless the boy wants to get rid of it." Santiago continued to work as he talked.

172

"Father, do you feel all right?"

"Yes, I feel fine."

"Well, I think you've been at this long enough." Marquita was alarmed and went to look for Phillip. She met Chavelita just returning from the hospital.

"I wish you'd go see Father, Chavelita. He's down by the lake."

"What's the matter? Isn't he feeling well?"

"He says he is, but I don't know. I'm worried."

Chavelita hurried over, slackening her pace as she drew near.

"Aren't you overdoing this, Papa?"

"I don't think so. Anyway, I'm through now. What do you think of it?"

Chavelita stood back to get a better view of the picture.

"That is the most beautiful thing you've ever done," she said softly. "It's the truest to the original that I've ever seen."

"Good. Then I haven't forgotten how the sunset looks from the ledge." He sat studying the painting for some time.

"Bob," he said at length, "give me a card, please. I want to label this. There's only one title for this picture; see that Allan gets the card when he takes the canvas. Perhaps when it's dry we can attach this to it. I'm ready to go in now. Won't you come with me?"

"After supper," Chavelita agreed.

"Come over and have supper with us," Phillip invited. He and Marquita had come up from behind and the doctor was looking intently at Santiago.

"I think the first thing for you to do, Father, is to rest."

"I am tired, a little. I'll rest until suppertime."

"What do you think, Phillip?" Marquita asked as the wheelchair disappeared down the path.

"I see nothing to be alarmed at, Marquita. He looks tired,

but I think a good night's rest will revive him. I'll check on him again in a little while. Where are the children?"

"They're supposed to be getting their lessons. They should be through soon."

"There they come now. I wonder if I was as noisy when I was a child."

"I know I wasn't. Aunt Elodia wouldn't allow it." Marquita made her way to the house, gathering flowers as she went.

"I'm going to put these in Father's room. He enjoys them."

"Fine. I'll go over to the hospital for a final check." Phillip held the door open for her, then turned to go back through the garden. But he hadn't gone far when an anguished cry from Marquita sent him charging into Santiago's room. Marquita had fainted and fallen across her father's inert form. Phillip lifted her and carried her out.

Chavelita and Bob reached the bed at the same time. After one look at the beloved face, Chavelita fell to her knees.

"Oh, no," she cried. "Not yet, dear God, not yet!"

Bob was drawing the sheet up over the body when Elodia came in.

"Bob, it isn't . . . my brother is not dead?"

"Yes, Mrs. Tobar, he is." Elodia crumpled to the floor. When the nurse lifted her, he found that she had joined in death the brother she had cherished in life.

A month later Marquita was in the room where Santiago's paintings had been stored when Father Clemente was announced.

"I hope I'm not here at an inopportune time, Marquita."

"You're always welcome, Father. . . . Our friend, Allan

Parker, whom I'm sure you've met, wants these canvases and I can't decide what to do about them. They mean so much to me now, but I know I can't keep them all—that would be selfish. Besides, Father was setting aside the money from his work for some new charity."

"I can appreciate your difficulty," the priest said, looking around at the picture-lined walls. "This, Marquita, is exquisite." He stopped before a picture still on its easel.

"That was his last. He finished it just a half hour before he died," Marquita said with trembling lips. "Do you suppose he had a premonition of his death, Father? He worked all day on that, and for the first time in years he talked of Romero."

"It may be. . . . I don't know. I am here on a mission, Marquita. The town council and some of the businessmen from both ends of the Valley came to see me last night. They want to put up a monument to your father's memory and came to me for advice. I suggested that you be consulted before anything like that is done."

"That is more than kind, but my humble father would not feel worthy. He would rather the money be used for some village need."

"I told them that, but they insist on some visible memorial."

Marquita was thoughtful for a moment, then said, "Since they want to remember him, let it be with a simple white shaft, and place it on the ledge where he used to stand to watch the sunset."

"And the inscription?"

"You choose that, Father."

"I have a suggestion—if I may paraphrase a line from the Bible. The original tribute was paid to a worthy woman, but it certainly applies to your father."

"Yes?"

" 'Let his own works praise him in the gates.' "

Everyone in the hotel lobby turned to watch him as he walked arrogantly past, seemingly oblivious of their interest and admiration. He waited impatiently at the desk until one of the clerks was free.

"Yes, sir?"

"You reserved a suite for me. The name is Sales, Rome Sales. I cabled you from Paris."

"Here you are, Sir. Will you register?"

The guest signed his name, giving a Cannes, France, address.

"My man will soon be here with my bags. Send him up when he comes."

As he turned to follow the boy with his apartment key, he ran into another guest. He was offering apologies when he suddenly recognized the man.

"Rome Sales!"

"Carter Ransom! How good to see a familiar face so soon after arriving! Come on up to my apartment so we can talk. Tell me what's happened since I left."

"That would take some telling. You've been away . . . how long?"

"Twelve years or so." The boy led the way from the elevator, unlocked the door, and made himself generally officious until he was dismissed with a tip.

176

"I'm sorry I can't offer you a drink from the bar, Carter, but I haven't had time to stock it. If you'll name it I'll have it sent up."

"Thanks, Rome, but I'm off the stuff. My wife doesn't approve. Bad example for the boys, you know."

"So you have a family. I should have known."

"You aren't married?"

"No, indeed! I can't conceive of giving up so much for so little. What business are you in, Carter? As I remember you gave up painting before I left."

"I'm on Wall Street. My artistic fever wasn't fatal. I'm still interested in good art, which reminds me that you're here in time to see a most interesting exhibit."

"You said the same thing once about one of mine."

"It was true, then, but if you'll permit some criticism, I was surprised and disappointed in some of your later work."

"Well, as you've heard many times, the artist paints what he feels; he sees different qualities and colors. He has a different perspective."

"Then all I can say from some of the things I've seen recently, the painter was either drunk or afflicted with astigmatism. I want to recognize what I'm looking at."

"You're a diehard. Don't you know that the day when a tree was made to look like a tree is past? A man would starve to death painting like that now."

"That's where you're wrong. Take, for example, the exhibit I mentioned."

"But who's looking at it?"

"Shall we try to get into the studio?"

They went down to the lobby, stopping occasionally to comment on the wall murals as they passed. Once outside they joined the crowd on the sidewalk.

"Seems strange to hear so much English spoken," Rome observed.

"From your accent, I'd assume that you've spent most of your time in France."

"Yes, or among French-speaking people. By the way, you didn't mention the name of this artist, or who's showing his work."

"Parker is handling it."

"And the artist?"

"An Indian named Salazar from a small village in Mexico."

Rome spun his friend so suddenly that passersby stopped, expecting a fight.

"Santiago Salazar! My grandfather! I'm Romero Salazar!"

"But your name?"

"I changed it when I came to New York. Come on, I've got to see this." But when they reached the gallery Romero stopped. "Carter, I don't want to go in now, with all these people around. I'll come back later. Mr. Parker will wait for me, I know. If Grandpa's in town—and I'm sure he is—he'll be here. I'd like to surprise him."

His friend looked at him in amazement. "Didn't you know? Salazar died a year ago."

Allan Parker admitted Romero to the gallery that evening after closing time.

"I appreciate your waiting for me, Mr. Parker."

"Glad to do it for Santiago . . . and you. You've changed a lot, yet I think I would have known you. We haven't heard from you for some time. What's the trouble, lose your brush?"

"I haven't had one in my hand in five years."

"Why?"

"Frankly, I don't know. I seem to have lost interest in almost everything."

178

"I see. Well, you wanted to see Santiago's canvases. I'm showing them in here. I'm sure you won't need a guide, but if you have any questions, I'll be in my office."

Romero walked slowly around the room pausing before each picture. Suddenly he was home again, not in Cannes but in Esperanza. There was the village church, its spire rising above the jacaranda tree whose purple blossoms drifted down onto its low roof. Then Father Clemente's house, its heavy door slightly ajar. In another he found himself facing the boy he once was, his arm encircling the neck of the donkey, Malevo. And there was the typical village house with its characteristic horizontal bands of color. An organ cactus fence confined a dejected horse and two stolid oxen, while in the shade of a pepper tree an emaciated dog listlessly scratched fleas. His own home came next, so perfectly portrayed that it seemed he could swing back the door and cross the *sala* to the patio.

He continued his slow pace around the studio, his mind traveling back over the years, and he realized that he was homesick.

"I'm going back," he said. As if conscious of his decision, Allan Parker returned.

"Well, what do you think of it?"

"My grandfather was a great artist. I never knew he had such skill. When did he do this? He was always such a restless person."

"All of us grow old, Rome. Time takes its toll and makes its demands. Santiago had a stroke which left him unable to walk, but his mind was alert and, with therapy, he regained the use of his hands. It was then that he began to paint again."

"Grandpa paralyzed?"

"Partially. It was certainly a personal tragedy, but the

179

world is richer for it. We would never have had all this beauty but for his affliction."

"It's hard for me to accept his death. I can't picture the Valley without him."

"The people there felt the same way. Come on back where we can talk in comfort." He placed a chair for Romero where the light fell on his face. "You're very much like your grandfather as I first knew him. You Salazars have always been a handsome lot. Have you produced any duplicates?"

"I've never married."

"No? What have you been doing all this time?"

"Frankly, not much of anything. I'm afraid I inherited my grandfather's restless spirit. I'm a wanderer. I've been in Africa the last few years. I left there to come back to the States."

"I note that you don't say 'home.' "

"No, my permanent address, if I have one, is Cannes, France."

"And you'll go back?"

"Oh, yes. I only came to see Grandpa. I'd hoped to persuade him to return to France with me."

"You never went back to Esperanza, did you?"

"I had no desire to."

"There have been many changes in the Valley since you left. It might interest you now."

"I doubt it."

"It has become an artist's mecca. I can understand that, for to me it's the most beautiful spot in a land filled with beauty."

"What ever attracted artists down there?"

"You saw your grandfather's pictures. That should answer your question. But what catapulted it onto the scene, I think, was Santiago's getting the Valley on the tourists' itinerary. After pictures of Esperanza were printed in one of

180

our magazines people began going down there. Then after Santiago took up the brush again he let me have some of his canvases, and soon other people were wanting to paint in the Valley."

"Did Grandpa realize what an artist he was?"

"He was a very humble man. He never quite reached the goal he set for himself—but then, who does? As to his being successful, success was nothing new to him. Did he ever tell you of his early life?"

"Not much, but from what he did tell me, I assumed that he was a sort of . . . hack artist."

"Far from it. He always had great talent, even as a small boy. My grandfather used to tell me how he met Santiago. He was putting the finishing touches to a picture when he was called into the next room for a moment. His studio was open to the street, and he often found a model among the people passing by. On this occasion he returned to find a little round-eyed Indian boy blending and applying colors like a professional. That boy was Santiago—he was seven years old at the time. Grandfather, recognizing genius when he saw it, persuaded your great-grandfather to let him give Santiago some lessons, and when the family returned to Virginia, he went, too. He lived in the Parker home until he went to college. That's how the Salazars and the Parkers got together. Your father came to my father for instruction, and Tony and I grew up like brothers."

"And following tradition, Grandpa brought me to you."

"Right."

"You spoke of Grandpa's success. It's odd that I never saw any of his painting until today, other than the little memorial things we used to do."

"You saw them, Romero, but you didn't recognize them. He was then known as 'Santos Sellers.' "

"Then the paintings I saw in your home were his?"

181

"All his."

"Why didn't he use his own name? Why did he change it?"

Allan leaned forward with a smile. "Why did you change yours?"

"So he was ashamed of being born an Indian, too."

"But he got over that. He became proud of his ancestry and was fiercely loyal to his people. He left a picture in my care, one he painted especially for you, in the event I ever heard from you again. He said you were to dispose of it as you wished. I'll bring it out."

Allan brought an easel and placed the picture in the light. Romero started forward, intent on the painting. Once again he was a boy. He saw himself climb to the top of the hill and heard his call, "Hurry up, Grandpa, or you'll miss the sunset."

He stood again on the pictured ledge, the Valley dark below him. Then in memory a few lamps were lit in the houses, and the pungent smoke smell from supper fires was wafted up on the still air. The Valley was filled with fireflies, and he recalled how their "lanterns" flickered like reflected fires on a restless wave. But the compelling force of the picture was the setting sun. The sky overhead was apple green, but the color changed and deepened as it neared the horizon, where between two mountain peaks it was a dazzling red. Starkly outlined against the crimson sky a single cactus stood. Romero leaned forward to read the title on an attached card: "A copy. Original by the Hand of God."

"Can you tell me how to get into the Valley?"

The boy questioned eyed the dazzling white car with awe.

"You can't drive in, señor. You will have to walk. Just drive your car to the store; we'll watch it for you."

"Well, get in and show me the way." The youngster hastened to obey and settled back proudly.

"What's your name?"

"I am Horatio Cantu."

"And your father keeps the village store."

"No, señor, he keeps the highway store. There are many small ones in the Valley, but my family has kept the big one for years. There it is."

"Why, it looks quite prosperous."

"You can leave your car here and then walk down the trail." The boy indicated a path at the back of the store.

"Oh, I won't block your entrance. I'll park around here."

Romero drove to the head of the trail and left the car. He paused to accustom himself to the changes. While there was ample space for a wider path, the old trail still existed and showed evidence of frequent use. The footpath down the hillside, however, boasted concrete steps, and as soon as he descended, a chorus of barks and growls greeted him. He looked about, picked up a heavy club, and continued. On entering the Valley he was immediately conscious of a barrage of stares directed upon him. Here and there a villager stood in a doorway, but most of them watched from curtained windows or from the dark recesses of their small homes. All this irritated Romero, and he longed for the oblivion of the city where he could pass the tenant in the next apartment every day for months without being recognized or even noticed. He had forgotten how quiet the village was.

"I hope my coming won't disturb Marquita too much. I suppose she must be feeling her age by now. I surely don't want to upset her routine. I'll just say 'hello' and go back to New York tomorrow," he mused.

It seemed a terribly long way to the old home, and the afternoon sun was hot. But at last it loomed before him and his heart beat faster at the sight.

"She may not live here anymore. I should have asked Allan. He wasn't too eager to discuss the family—except Grandpa. I wonder if Marquita is in need—she shouldn't be, but with Grandpa helping everyone in the area, it wouldn't surprise me if he left her nothing to live on." He rang the chimes and a maid answered the summons. She looked at him, and her eyes widened in fright. For a moment she stood staring, then turned and fled, screaming, "Señora, Señora, it's *Papacito*'s ghost!"

Marquita rose from her chair as Phillip came out of the den yawning.

"Why all the noise?" he demanded.

"Phillip, someone's at the door. Will you see who it is? And Josefa, stop that screaming and go on back to the kitchen."

The doctor crossed the hall and, seeing the figure through the grille, began apologizing before he reached the entrance.

"You must excuse our servant, Señor. She's quite excitable." He opened the door and stepped back as Romero came in. One look at his guest, and his eyes were as wide as Josefa's had been.

"You must be a Salazar! You look exactly like Father! Are you Romero?"

"Yes, and I'm looking for some of my family."

"Marquita!" But she was already in the room. She started to Romero, her arms extended, but before reaching him she fell forward. Both men rushed to her, but Aurora was before them.

"Get her smelling salts, Aurora," Phillip directed. He lifted her to a couch and cradled her in his arms.

"My wife has been ill and is still terribly nervous," he explained to Romero. "I forgot to introduce myself. I'm Phillip Parmarez. If you'll just find a chair we'll be with you in a moment." Aurora brought a small bottle and handed it to him. "Here, dear, take a whiff of this. Feel better?"

"I'll be all right in a minute." She borrowed Phillip's handkerchief and wiped the perspiration from her face. "I'm sorry, Romero, but this is such a surprise."

"I'm sure it's something of a shock. I should have written first, but I never thought of it. I didn't know of Grandpa's death until I got to Allan Parker's in New York. Where's Aunt Elodia?"

"Didn't Allan tell you? She and Father died the same day."

"No! Was Grandpa sick long?"

"He was paralyzed for years, but he died quietly without suffering. When Aunt Elodia came in and found him gone, she dropped beside him."

"I suppose it's the best way, but it must have been a horrible experience."

"I think it's the way they would have wanted it," Phillip said. "I might have lengthened her life a little. I had been giving her injections for her heart, but a week before her

185

death she refused to take any more. She was tired, and when she knew Father was dead, her heart just stopped."

"Then you're a doctor?"

"Yes, I'm the village doctor—one of them, that is. Now that we've brought you up-to-date, suppose you tell us about yourself," Phillip suggested.

"But you haven't told me everything yet. Allan wouldn't discuss the Valley. I think he wanted it to be a surprise. How long have you been married?"

"Twenty years," Marquita told him.

"No children?"

"Four—two boys and twin girls."

"Where are they? With four children, there should be some activity around here."

"They're at Woodwind, the estate in Guatemala. They spend a part of each year with Phillip's father who considers Esperanza on the very borders of civilization. He insists that they visit him to absorb a little culture," she explained.

"You know, Marquita, although you had suitors by the dozen, I can't picture you with a family."

"Well, I have one—a fine one, too."

"Now tell us about yourself, Romero," Phillip urged. "I've heard about you ever since I've been in the family. I'm glad you materialized. . . . I'd begun to think you were just a Salazar legend."

"No, I'm very substantial, but I'm so hungry for a home cooked meal!"

Phillip rang for Trinidad.

"If I'd only known you were coming, Romero, we could have had a proper meal for you," Marquita lamented. The cook came and received her instructions.

"Did you understand what I told her?"

"I wasn't really listening, but I doubt that I would. I haven't heard the dialect in years."

"That's right, you haven't. What have you been doing?"

"Very little," he confessed, then added, "very little but waste time. I've been over most of the world."

"And your painting?"

"I haven't done anything in years."

"What a pity!" Marquita sighed.

"Perhaps it is." Romero leaned forward, elbows on his knees, and examined his hands thoughtfully until Marquita roused him.

"Supper will soon be ready. If you want to wash up, you know the way to your room."

"Is Grandpa's door locked?"

"Oh, no."

"Do you mind if I look in for a minute?"

"Of course not."

A half hour passed before he returned. Supper was on the table so they were seated immediately.

"Marquita, does your cook still use the old brazier?"

"Almost exclusively. When Lupita cooks she sometimes uses the electric range, but Trinidad and Consuela are afraid of it."

"There used to be an old kitchen where we sometimes took our meals," Romero remembered.

"It's still there. When Phillip and I are alone and feeling nostalgic we eat there. But with four children we need more room." The conversation flowed smoothly on until they had finished the meal.

"I'm sorry to leave so soon after your arrival, Romero, but I have a patient I want to check on before bedtime. I'll see you later."

"We'll go for a walk after a while, Phillip. Maybe we'll meet you at the hospital."

"All right, but don't overdo it," Phillip cautioned.

"I'm glad you suggested a walk," Romero said. "After

that meal I need a hike. I don't think food ever tasted so good to me."

"I'm glad you enjoyed it. Let me get a wrap, and we'll go. Anna, bring my coat, please."

Romero took it from the maid and held it while Marquita slipped into it.

"Shall I make a confession?" he asked, fastening the collar under her chin.

"Only if you think you should."

"I don't know where I got the idea, but coming here today I pictured you as a rather frail, elderly lady. I was fearful of upsetting your routine and decided to make a hurried visit so I wouldn't agitate my aging aunt. And what do I find? You look as young as the day I left."

"Thank you, Romero."

"Do you know that you're an extremely beautiful woman?"

"Thank you again, but you're prejudiced, you know."

"No, I don't know. It seems that I remember something about your being judged the most beautiful in a contest once."

"That was years ago. I was still in school."

"Well, you're more attractive than ever."

"Phillip will be pleased that you agree with him. He says that being married to him has improved my appearance and my disposition. . . . I didn't realize it had grown so dark. We won't be able to see anything," Marquita said as they stepped outside.

"The village looked much as I remembered it when I came through this afternoon."

"No, I don't suppose there has been a great deal of change, except in the lives of the people, which is where it should be. We have a much larger school than we had, but there are still other improvements needed. Father always fretted over those who refused to help themselves. He did so much for so many. I used to try to comfort him with that, but he once told me that real success is not measurable by the schools built or teachers employed or in the economic advancement of the community, but in how many lives have been improved. The true test of any effort, he said, was in the quality of men and women it produced."

"From what Allan said he was quite successful in that area, too."

"There aren't many people in the Valley who aren't better for having known him. Romero, I promised Phillip we'd meet him at the hospital, and we're going in the opposite direction."

"My car is up on the highway unattended. I think I'd better check on it first. It seems there should be some way of driving into the village."

"We come in through the other end to the garages back of the garden. I'll walk up with you."

"It won't be too much for you? The doctor said for you to be careful."

"Phillip has an exaggerated idea of my fragility! I had surgery a few months ago, and he is being over-protective."

"There's no doubt about your marriage being a happy one. Where did you meet him?"

"In Mexico. He came here to lecture in the hospital, and we were married a year later. Father was very fond of Phillip.

"Where is Grandpa buried?"

"In the family plot near Mexico."

"I thought you might have buried him on the Point—he loved it so."

"No, he was against that. He said it was a place that every tourist to this part of the country should see, and no one should be depressed by the sight of a grave. However, the

189

villagers have put a monument there. . . . Well, here we are. Is this your car?"

"Yes, before I left Kenya I planned to buy this car and take Grandpa on his book-hunting trips. It seems ridiculous now, but I never thought of him as growing old. It seemed he would always be here."

The crowd of men and boys that had gathered around the car fell back at their approach. Marquita greeted them by name and inquired about the health of their families.

"This is my nephew, Romero Salazar." A few nodded. Romero offered his hand to those near.

"Can't we take some of them home?" Marquita suggested. "They live in Upper Valley."

"Sure, tell them to get in. They couldn't understand if I tried to tell them." Marquita spoke to them, and the back of the car was soon filled with laughing, chattering men.

"This is quite an event to them, Romero. They have never been in such a car."

"I can remember when it would have been an occasion in my life, too. Will they speak up when they want to get out?"

"Oh, they'll ride all the way to the garage and walk home. Slow down now and turn to the right."

"Ah! The lane has been paved. I can remember when this was covered with dust or mud, depending on the weather."

"Yes, we had to have it covered. We began using it a lot after we got our first car."

"Is that Upper Valley? That bright spot?"

"Quite a contrast, isn't it? It's modern here, but for the sake of the tourist business we've kept our end of the Valley almost primitive. The garage is just ahead. One of the men will open the door." When the car stopped Marquita spoke to those in the back, and several raced to press the button that sent the door sliding overhead.

"This is quite an innovation. How many cars do you have?"

"Just two, mine and Phillip's. And we house the ambulance here."

The passengers called out their *gracias* and left. Romero opened the door for Marquita and helped her out.

"Either you've shrunk or I've grown a lot," he said. "I used to look up into your face; now your head doesn't even reach my shoulder."

"You've done a lot of vertical expanding."

"Do you still teach?"

"Occasionally. Not as often as I used to, but once in a while someone wants a day or two off and I substitute. Now I've been doing all the talking. I want to hear about you. You haven't mentioned a family; does that mean you don't have one?"

"I never married. I've known a lot of women, and I've liked some of them, but not enough to want to spend my life with one of them."

"Obviously you haven't met the right girl yet. Just wait. When you do, one life won't be enough. . . . Here's our hospital."

Romero paused to read the name above the door, " 'La Casa de Esperanza.' Let me see if I can translate that—'The House of Hope.' Am I right?"

"You are. And it has been just that." Marquita led the way in. "There's someone you should remember."

"The nurse at the desk?"

"She isn't a nurse. She's a doctor, and one of the best. She's Phillip's right hand."

"I've never seen her before. She's beautiful. Who is she?"

"That's Dr. Chavelita Chavez."

"The name sounds vaguely familiar, but my memory of the Valley youngsters is that all the boys were leggy and

191

toothy and the girls were tall and thin or short and fat."

"Maturity brings changes in all of us, Romero." They stopped at the desk where Chavelita was studying a chart. She looked up as they paused before her.

"Hello, Mrs. Parmarez. Did you come to collect the doctor? He should be out in a moment. Are you having any trouble?"

"No, I feel fine. Chavelita, do you remember my nephew, Romero?"

She turned toward Romero, and her eyes widened with pleasure.

"When did you get here? The doctor didn't tell me you had come."

"I arrived in time for supper. And if I'd known you were a doctor I'd have pretended a serious illness so I could have called on you to attend me." The buzzer sounded, and Chavelita excused herself to answer it.

"Don't you keep a nurse at the desk to take these calls?" Romero resented the interruption.

"When one is available. We have a short staff at night. We've grown a lot, but we still have our limitations. I think we're very fortunate. I know of no other pueblo of our size that can boast of three doctors."

"How do you rate three? I remember when Grandpa couldn't get one."

"Do you remember Luis Mendoza?"

"I think I do. Wasn't he the boy who was always boasting of what he would do when he got his medical degree? As I recall, the other kids his age resented his bragging. Did he finally get his degree?"

"Yes, he got his degree; he also got polio. He's in a wheelchair or sometimes on crutches. He's a good pathologist, but his usefulness is necessarily limited. Chavelita . . . well, we couldn't operate without her. Phillip had to ease up

192

a bit, and this was home for Chavelita. From the day Father had his stroke she took care of him. Phillip was killing himself running all over the Valley and up in the mountains as well as manning the hospital. She has taken over a lot of that, and her being here makes it possible for Phillip to do some lecturing. I'd like for him to give up practicing entirely and concentrate on his writing and research."

Phillip appeared at the end of the hall. He'd been washing his hands, and they were still dripping as he walked toward Marquita and Romero.

"Chavelita just told me you were here. Have you waited long?"

"No, dear, we just got here. Can you leave now?"

"Yes, I think I've wrapped it up for tonight—my part of it, anyway. What do you think of our hospital, Romero?"

"It looks good to me, Uncle Phillip. I'm glad that Grandpa lived to see this dream fulfilled. I wish he could have found his book—if it exists."

"He was convinced that someday it would come to light and be an inspiration to our people."

"You say 'our people.' Are you also Indian?"

"Of course." Phillip finished drying his hands and gave the towel to an orderly. "Now shall we go?" With an arm around Marquita's shoulders he guided her through the door.

"Will you look at that moon!" Romero exclaimed as they left the shadow of the hospital. "And those mountains!" He turned slowly to scan the hills that rimmed the Valley. "It makes me eager to get at my easel again."

"That sounds as if you plan to stay awhile," Marquita said hopefully.

"I hardly know. It's too soon to decide. Tell me, Uncle Phillip, are you content in this quiet place?"

"Of course I am. I'm more than content. I'm happy."

"Marquita told me you had practiced in Mexico City for

193

a time. It seems to me that after the activity there this would bore you."

"Romero, I have everything I can possibly want right here—my wife, my children, my home, and a challenge to my professional skill. I didn't practice much in the city, but I had a lucrative clinic in Chicago. I came here as an instructor for a year. The night I arrived I met Marquita. She was the lure that brought me to the Valley. Then I got to know your grandfather. He taught me how to live. He convinced me that my family wealth wasn't to be spent selfishly to satisfy every whim but was entrusted to me to be used with discretion for my dependents and wisely and compassionately for those in need. He once said to me that our wealth placed us under moral obligations to help others."

"I don't agree with that. What is mine is mine—whether by inheritance or my own efforts," Romero said firmly.

"You remind me of my father. He used to argue with Santiago about his lavish contributions to charity. Your grandfather's reasoning was that a man had to provide sensibly for his own responsibilities, but after that it was immoral not to share with those who lacked. And that didn't apply only to material things—it included time, talent, and love."

"And what did he get out of it?"

"He didn't expect any return. He gave out of concern and compassion, and he had the love and respect of everyone who knew him. When he was buried we had to charter busses to take people to his funeral. If you climb to the Point any morning you'll find someone has been there and placed fresh flowers at the foot of the memorial shaft. And something else that is very peculiar to me: Your grandfather had always managed his business, and we knew nothing about it—at least I didn't. But we had to go over his records—and do you know what we learned? He had never lost money on any investment he ever made—and you'd be surprised at the extent of those investments."

"I can see he made a convert out of you."

"Yes, thank God. I had a certain degree of medical knowledge and skill, and he had a valley full of people in dire need of both. Of course his having a beautiful daughter didn't weigh against my decision to come here." They had reached the garden, and Marquita paused with her hand on the gate.

"Phillip, it's such a lovely evening, can't we extend our walk—or are you too tired?"

"I'm not tired, but I think you've had all the exercise you need. We still have quite a stroll through the garden ahead."

"This is paradise!" Romero exclaimed as he followed Marquita. Phillip turned the switch that flooded the garden with light. "I had forgotten it was so lovely."

"It is beautiful," Phillip agreed. "It's my favorite spot in all the world. This is where I proposed to my wife."

"You never proposed to me. You simply announced your intention of marrying me."

"It amounts to the same thing. Besides, you needed a firm hand. It's quite a romantic spot, Romero. Any time you want to bring the light of your life here, I'll see that you're not disturbed."

"Thanks, but I never expect to need your services."

"You can't tell. When I came to Mexico marriage was the last thing I was thinking of. And the night I got in here I looked up from my table in the hotel dining room and saw Marquita looking like a pink angel floating down the stairs. That marked the end of my bachelor freedom. I settled here, and I've never been sorry."

"It would be wonderful if you'd stay, married or single," Marquita said.

"At the moment I believe I could be content here for a while. But I don't know how I'll feel a week from now, or even in the morning. Sometimes I think I'm two people, each at war with the other. This unrest has kept me on the move. When I left Africa I hoped that I'd leave the conflict behind me, but I didn't."

"Well, come on to the patio, and we'll talk a bit before going to bed," Phillip suggested.

"I don't think I'm ready to settle down. Do you mind if I roam through the garden."

"No, indeed. If we go in before you get through your rambling, you know the way to your room."

"How do you feel this morning?" Marquita asked Romero at breakfast the next day.

"Fine. For years I've had trouble sleeping, but not last night. When I awoke the sun was shining through my window. Did I draw the curtains before I went to bed?"

"No, Phillip thought you might be too tense to relax and went to your room with a sedative. He said you were already asleep, so he put out your lights and drew the draperies to let in the air. Now today I'm going to show you over the Valley, so get into some comfortable walking shoes."

"Instead of touring the Valley, could we go to Grandpa's grave today?"

"Perhaps that's a better idea. It will give you time to get acclimated before we go on a hike. And while we're so near the city perhaps you'll want to get some materials and start painting again. Father's easels are in the studio, but you'll want your own brushes—and of course you'll need paints and oils."

"Right. After seeing the display in New York—especially after crossing the border—I've had an urge to put my impressions on canvas."

"What did you think of Father's work?"

"I had no idea he was that good. I never saw him do anything but those little memorial sketches—and he usually worked on those only when he wasn't looking for the book. Did he continue his search after I left?"

"No. I've often thought that he took you on those trips with the hope that you'd grow more content here in the Valley."

"I let him down, didn't I?"

"Will you have more coffee?" Marquita asked.

"No, thank you. I rather got out of the coffee habit." Romero began folding and unfolding his napkin. "Speaking of the book, I noticed last night that Uncle Phillip seemed sure of its existence. Where did he get his conviction—from Grandpa?"

"Partly. And Father got his from the Bible."

"From the Bible?"

"Yes, he found references to a book in the Bible and was convinced that they pointed to the book of our people."

"Grandpa read the Bible?"

"He did more than that. He made a systematic study of it."

Romero shook his head. "I can't picture that. I suppose, though, as you grow older your thoughts turn to religion. What was the remark someone made about religion being the solace of age and the opiate of the poor?"

"Neither condition would apply to Father. You certainly couldn't class him among the poor, and when he began his study he was as alert as you are. He was older, but just as active."

"I can remember that he used to sit and listen while Aunt Elodia told us Bible stories. I don't remember that he ever made any comment, though."

"That may be one reason why he tried to involve my children so early. He used to read them stories and then have them reproduce them on canvas. Later on he gave them quizzes and made crossword puzzles for them. He got all of us—Phillip, Auntie, and me—involved in trying to understand the book. It gave new meaning to our lives—a reason for living."

"A reason for living? Do we need one?"

"I think so."

"And that's how Grandpa spent his time after he quit looking for the book?"

"Not entirely. He worked harder than ever in both ends of the Valley and in the mountain areas. After I married he had a staunch supporter in Phillip. They lectured, showed slides, cajoled, threatened, and argued until they got deep wells dug and covered, schools built, and sanitary conditions improved. Father initiated Phillip even before we were married. He walked him all over the mountains every weekend until he would go back to Mexico exhausted."

"He was afraid you weren't lure enough to induce me to settle here, so he tried to arouse my sympathy," Phillip teased, locking his hands beneath her chin.

"How long have you been eavesdropping?"

"Long enough."

"How is your surgery case this morning, Phillip?"

"He's doing all right. I don't know why I keep patching him up. Eventually some hombre is going to carve his heart out and I won't be able to help him."

"A repeater?"

"I'll say he is. I can expect him at least once a month. We have two or three like that—born troublemakers. They go around looking for fights. If this one doesn't leave other men's women alone he's going to be irreparable—soon."

"We're driving into Mexico this morning, Phillip. Can you come with us?" Marquita asked.

"No, I'm afraid I can't make it. I need to go over the hospital accounts with Luis. What takes you to the City?"

"Romero wants to go to the cemetery. He also has some business there. We'll have lunch there but should be back in time for supper."

They rode into the City in silence and drove directly to the cemetery.

"The plot is nearly full," Marquita said as she knelt to arrange the flowers they had brought. "There is space for you and your family, which I devoutly hope you'll acquire."

"I never expect to have one. And chances are that by the time I need such accommodations I'll be thousands of miles from here. I surmise my bones will lie in France."

"I hate to hear you talk that way. It seems as if we as a family have failed you."

"The fault lies entirely with me."

Marquita arose and crossed the plot to a marble bench. He followed, and as they sat there Romero looked off over the forest of monuments.

"I suppose a cemetery is the only place in the world where there is perfect peace."

"I suppose so," she agreed thoughtfully.

"You know, I believe I got acquainted with myself for the first time as we drove in this morning." Marquita looked up.

"I've wanted to be on the move all my life, even as a child. I could hardly wait to get out of the Valley to Monterrey and from there to New York. And the minute I received my inheritance I sailed for Europe. I've been driven by the same restlessness ever since, and I've just learned the reason for it. It's remorse. I've been running from a feeling of guilt."

"Guilty of what, Romero?"

"Of almost everything. First, I was ashamed of being Indian . . . ashamed of Grandpa."

"Ashamed of Father? Why?"

"I was immature. You know how Grandpa always dressed like a peasant and expected the same of me. There were only rare occasions when we didn't look like the poor farmers around us, and I resented it."

"Father had a reason for doing that, Romero. We couldn't help these people if we didn't identify with them."

"If that was his motive, why didn't we live in a floorless cabin as most of the villagers did?"

"I suppose that does seem inconsistent, but I don't believe the people ever looked at it that way. We never held ourselves above them. We played with their children, and they were free to visit us any time. Of course, when El Jardin was built, Father didn't intend to become one of the villagers. I think he planned to dispense his bounty more as a patron. When he found that wouldn't work, he became friend and companion instead of benefactor. Why didn't you tell Father how you felt? I'm sure he would have arranged for you to live somewhere else."

"I never could talk to him about it. In my heart I loved him too much—but I hated him, too."

"Why, Romero! How could you come home feeling as you do?"

"I don't feel that way now, and I came home because I wanted to make amends. While I was in Kenya I had a sudden desire to see Grandpa. I decided to buy the best car I could and take him to look for his book. He once said he wanted me to continue to look for it if he failed to find it. I wish I could forget my flippant refusal. I shouldn't have gone into his room yesterday. I almost thought I'd see him sitting there at the window. I wish I could have seen him just once more."

He got to his feet restlessly.

200

"Shall we go?" he asked. He turned back to the grave, laid his hand for a moment on the monument at its head, then followed Marquita to the car.

Once under way Romero threw off his melancholy mood and began whistling.

"Romero, have you never been attracted to a woman? Have you never fallen in love?"

"As I told you before, not enough to make me contemplate marriage. I can't understand why a man wants to burden himself with a family. I like coming and going as I please. I don't have to consult anyone about anything I do. When I decide to move I just tell my man what my plans are and he takes it from there. I'm amazed at Uncle Phillip's being content to live in the Valley. He's an extremely handsome man and I surmise women are attracted to him . . . and from appearances he isn't lacking in money."

"Phillip is not a poor man," Marquita assured him. "It has never occurred to me that he wasn't happy, and as for other women—of course they admire him, but he has never given me any cause for jealousy. He came to the Valley because he fell in love with me; he stayed on after we were married because he was needed. He is content because he loves his family and is happily involved with the welfare of our people, just as Father was. We're a family, Romero, and we're concerned with one another and with our Valley."

"That's another snag in this man-woman relationship—children," Romero continued his line of thought. "I hate to disappoint you, but marriage just isn't on my schedule."

"I'm sorry that you have such an attitude. I've often thought of you through the years and hoped that you were happily settled down somewhere with a family."

"I'm happier without one."

"You don't know what happiness is. Don't you know that if you were content there'd be no need for this

201

restlessness? You're trying to find serenity and peace of mind, but you'll never succeed until you quit running. Life has to have meaning, Romero."

He laughed indulgently. "But I love the excitement of new places and new people."

"But do you make friends of these people you enjoy meeting?"

"Friends?" he considered the word for a moment. "No," he replied, "no lasting attachments, and what's more, my dear aunt, I don't want any. When you get friendly you get involved in all sorts of obligations. I don't want the responsibility that goes with friendship."

"That," said Marquita, "leaves me speechless."

"Let's go outside," Phillip said after supper. "I need some air. Besides, there's a beautiful moon." Marquita and Romero followed him to the patio.

"What kind of day did you have, Romero?" Phillip asked after they were seated.

"I think we accomplished what we set out to do, didn't we, Marquita?"

"Yes, and I bought some very pretty dresses in Miss Garcia's shop. The girls will look adorable in them."

"I'd like to see those boys and girls. As far as I know, they're my only relatives except for you."

"I've never known anything about your mother's family, Romero, but there are no Salazars. The name will die with you unless you marry and have sons."

"I have an idea that I'm the last of the line." Romero arose and walked restlessly to the fountain. Marquita followed him.

"What's troubling you, Romero? You haven't been yourself since we came home." He put an arm around her shoulders and hugged her to him.

Dusk had fallen in the Valley but in the west the mountains were flooded with moonlight. In this light Romero could see people moving about. A woman gathered in laundry that had been drying on bushes, trees, and a rock wall. A man sat in his lamplit doorway playing a guitar. In the opposite direction darkness had dropped like a curtain. Against this screen lighted windows gleamed like stars. Here and there flames from outdoor fires darted up, and children playing nearby were silhouetted against their brightness. As he stood there Romero sensed, rather than heard, the plaintive notes of a melody as some young singer came down the mountain. Silence followed his passing, and Romero was filled with an emotion he couldn't name.

"I don't know ... I just don't know!" he said at last answering Marquita's question. "I should never have come home, or perhaps I shouldn't have left. Now that I'm here, what shall I do? You and Uncle Phillip are accustomed to this quiet life, but I'm not, and I'm not sure I can stand it."

"I know how you feel, Romero." Phillip left the swing and joined them at the fountain. "When I first began coming here, if I hadn't been courting my wife I couldn't have endured it. When I'm away from it now, I can hardly wait to get back."

Phillip smiled at him. Then, reaching for Marquita's hand, he said, "See you in the morning." And they left him alone.

"Where's the head of the house?" Romero asked when he came down the next morning.

"Phillip had to leave early for Espada. They admitted three patients from there yesterday—all with the same symptoms. He's afraid of an epidemic of some sort and went up to check on sanitary conditions. In spite of his having two junior doctors, my husband is terribly overworked at times. I wish you'd consider his suggestion that you take charge of the habilitation program."

"I doubt that I'll be here long enough even to learn the routine. If I decide to stay I'll think about it."

"Well, I must get busy. Phillip asked me to look over an article he's written for publication. I know you can find something to do."

"Sure. I think I'll go over to the hospital and see if I can get a date with Dr. Chavez."

"You'll find her a charming companion, but don't be surprised if you have to wait your turn," Marquita warned him. "She's very popular and her free time is usually booked well in advance."

Marquita was right. It was a month before Chavelita agreed to a date. Romero called for her one evening at her small house near the hospital. He gave a long, low whistle of approval when she appeared, ready to go.

"I'll wager you're never able to dismiss a male patient," he said.

"I seldom treat men. Women and children are my specialty," she said as she preceded him down the steps. "What have you planned for the evening, Romero?"

"I haven't been here long enough to know what to suggest after dinner. Do you like to dance?"

"I'm too tired to dance. I'd rather sit, and the only place to do that without causing comment is the theater. The Mexican ballet is in town. Have you seen it?"

"Not since my return."

"Good. Let's settle on that. Here, will you carry my shoe bag? I can't walk to the garage in high heels so I'll have to change when we get there."

"It's a pity we can't get a car into the village."

"Oh, no, it isn't. Papa would never agree to widening the streets, and I'm glad he didn't. I like the quietness of the pueblo."

"I don't. I never walk out of the house that I don't feel as if I'm under a microscope. I'm always conscious of people peering at me from their doorways or peeping from behind their curtains. Give me the city where a person can live in the same suite for years without knowing the name of the tenants in the adjoining one."

"I wouldn't call that living," Chavelita commented as she picked her way over the cobbled street.

"Do you know I was beginning to think I'd never get a date with you?"

"I always welcome my time off. I anticipate sleeping late in the morning. Sometimes I wonder why I chose a profession that brings so many nights of broken rest."

"Why did you?"

"I'll take my shoes now," she said. Romero took the slippers from the bag and made the change for her. "Just put my walkers on the shelf."

He obeyed, helped her into the car, and backed it out of the garage.

"You asked me why I became a doctor. I think I was born to treat the sick just as you were born to paint."

"I haven't lived up to my calling, then. I haven't produced a thing in years."

"You haven't? With all that talent? What have you been doing?"

"Traveling . . . having a good time. At least I thought I was while I was at it. Oh, I've tried to get back to painting since I came here, but my heart isn't in it. I think I did it more to please Marquita than from my own inclination."

"She would be happy if you decided to stay and go on with your art."

"I know it, but I couldn't endure this for six months."

"Do you know what Papa used to say? 'Once you've breathed deeply of the pace of Esperanza you'll never be satisfied away from it.' "

"I suppose I'm an exception to the rule. Remember, I lived here for fourteen years and have been happy away from it for twenty."

Chavelita looked up with a smile. "Then why did you come back?"

"That was the most restless audience I have ever seen," Romero said as they started home three hours later. "There was more activity on the floor than on the stage. The man in front of us moved up and down the aisle constantly."

"That was Mr. Fierros, one of our lawyers."

"Why was he running around so? At first I thought he was going to the men's room, and from the frequency of his trips I expected him to call for a doctor."

"No, he brought his families to see the ballet. Society rules that his legal wife and her children take precedence over his other establishments. He sits with her and her children, but he's attentive to his other families, too. I've been trying to put this nicely. Bluntly, he has a legitimate wife and as many women as he can afford to keep."

"And this is socially accepted?"

"Let's say it's tolerated. There is no shame attached to the children of these unions. You must have known this when you were here."

"I may have, but I don't remember it. Now that's what I call an enlightened society. Man was never meant to be a monogamous creature. One woman can't satisfy him at all times. He needs variety—a woman for every mood."

"Are you out of your mind?"

"No, I mean it."

Chavelita had fought this custom in the Valley, and Romero's ready acceptance of it infuriated her. They argued

207

the subject all the way to Esperanza. At her door he paused to say, "Thanks for a pleasant evening, Doctor. Besides being beautiful, you have fire. I like your spirit."

"Well, I don't like your attitude or the way you live. I'm glad you changed your name."

"What do you know about how I live?" he demanded.

"A man with your principles is bound to put them into practice," she said and closed the door firmly behind her.

"The boy not down yet?" Phillip asked one morning several weeks later.

"No, he's sleeping late. He didn't get home until nearly daybreak. I'm worried about him, Phillip. I wish something would happen to stabilize his life. I thought he might become interested in Chavelita . . . but as far as I know they've had only that one date," Marquita said.

"Romero's a man, not a little boy. You can't hope to influence him after all these years."

"I know I shouldn't be concerned since he seems perfectly happy living his aimless existence."

"I don't think he's happy. He's pursuing happiness but he's not finding it. He doesn't know that it must be created day by day. I wish he could content himself somewhere. No man has a right to waste life. It's too precious a commodity. Here he comes, now."

"We were wondering if you were going to get up for breakfast," Marquita said. "You look as if you'd had a hard night."

"I did! I went to a party and drank too much. I have an idea some joker mixed my drink. I have a splitting headache as a result."

"We can get rid of that in a hurry. Eva, bring my bag, please. I think I left it in the den."

When the maid returned, Phillip took two pills from a box and handed them to Romero. "Here, take these and drink your coffee. You'll be feeling fine in minutes. Then how about riding up into the hills with me?"

"Thanks, but I must beg off this time."

"Well, I'm going over to the hospital now. If you change your mind while I'm gone, let me know." Marquita followed Phillip to the door and watched him swing down the path. Romero was sitting with his head in his hands when she returned.

"I wish you'd take better care of yourself," she said.

"Wine has never affected me this way before. It was a wild party."

"Did you drive home, or did Anastasia bring you?"

"I drove. Anastasia is too slow."

"He knows the danger of those sharp curves on the highway."

"Don't worry about me, Auntie. I'm a big boy now."

"Perhaps so, but you aren't so big that you can't profit by a little motherly advice."

He smiled. "Look, I've hunted lions in the Congo, wolves in Russia, water buffalo in India, and I came through unscathed. I can take care of myself."

Phillip came back before Romero had finished his breakfast.

"What's to see up in the mountains?" Romero asked.

"Magnificent scenery. I think you'd enjoy it. Better come with me."

"My headache is better—maybe I will."

"I thought you would, so I had a horse saddled for you."

It was late afternoon when they returned. Romero had argued the futility of trying to better the lot of the peasant.

"Marquita told me Grandpa spent forty years of his life and thousands of pesos on these people—and with what result? They're still living in huts, still cooking their food over outdoor fires, still getting their drinking water from a ditch."

"Romero, you speak of the few who resist change, not those who have accepted it. It's true, Father gave his life and spent hundreds of thousands of pesos on these people, but he didn't consider it wasted—nor do I. Perhaps the percentage helped is small, but I know of no greater satisfaction than seeing a young person receive his diploma or degree, and knowing that I have been a part of that accomplishment. Santiago often had the privilege of handing out these certificates, and I know the joy it gave him."

"He wasn't hard to please. But tell me, how can you enter those huts? I feel dirty just being near them."

"Here we are at the gate. Erasmo will take the horses, and you can dash in and wash away the contamination."

They found Marquita on the patio knitting. "Well, what did you think of the view, Romero?" she asked when they were seated.

"It's all Uncle Phillip claimed for it, but what a climb!" He sat watching her in silence for a few minutes, then said, "I've decided to take an apartment in Monterrey for a while. I think I'm going to see what I can do with my brush in that area."

"Can't you find inspiration here?"

"Perhaps if I looked for it; but let's face it, Esperanza isn't for me any more now than it was twenty years ago. I'm ill at ease here. I feel as if I'm on trial. Another thing, Grandpa's presence permeates the entire Valley, yet I can't see him or speak to him. It makes me uncomfortable. I'll be moving out tomorrow."

"If that's what you want, Romero," Marquita said, and offered no further argument.

210

The next morning she and the doctor walked him to the garage and watched him drive off.

"It's going to be lonely without him or the children," Marquita said. "Let's call Dad and have him send them home."

"Yes, I think it's time for them to get back. If they get too noisy for you, I'll calm them down."

"I think I'll welcome their chatter. I'll call them after a bit. First I must plan my approach. It's got to the point where they hate more and more to leave Woodwind after a visit."

"Dad turns everything over to them. I'm surprised he can keep a servant on the place. . . . Since we're so near, I'm going to stop by the hospital."

"I'll walk with you and see how Chavelita's getting along. She's refused all my dinner invitations recently, and she used to enjoy being with us."

"Perhaps Romero had something to do with her refusals."

"I hadn't thought of that. I'm sorry Romero got tired of being here so soon, but the children with their noise might have disturbed him."

They reached home an hour later just as the phone rang. Marquita took the call, but the connection was bad and she had trouble hearing the message. "It's Carl," she told Phillip. "He says something about going to college . . . wait, Dad is on now." Her eyes widened as she listened and made several unsuccessful attempts to break in. She finally gave Phillip the phone, but as he took the receiver his father hung up.

"What was it, dear? Dad hung up."

"I'm sure I'm mistaken, Phillip. It doesn't make sense. Dad says he has Carl enrolled in school in Guatemala City, a tutor for Ricky, and a governess for the girls. He says he's going to keep them the rest of the year."

"Why, that conniving old rascal. . . . No wonder he

wouldn't talk to me! He's going to put those kids on a plane. . . . I'll get him on the phone again. . . ."

"Now, Phillip, don't be impatient with him. He's never done this sort of thing before. Perhaps we'd better go down and see for ourselves. If you can't break away I'll take Aurora and go."

"You'll not go without me! I'll arrange to go with you, and Dad had better have a good reason for his piratical behavior."

"Now, Phillip, he's a lonely old man. . . ."

"He needn't be lonely. We've begged him to join us here."

"Well, let's reserve judgment until we've talked with him."

"How soon do we leave?"

"Tomorrow . . . if it's convenient for you."

"I'll go back to the hospital and get things lined up for our absence. How long do you think we'll be gone?"

"I don't know. If I can persuade Dad to move here, we'll stay and help him close Woodwind. If he's as stubborn as he usually is we'll be home very soon."

Marquita and Phillip had been at Woodwind two days before Carlos and the children appeared. Phillip was furious.

"Where have you been?" he demanded. "We got here day before yesterday, and no one knew where you were. Don't you tell any of the servants where you're going when you leave?"

"It's none of their business. Carl, see if you can get that shoe off without it killing me."

"Now, Dad," Marquita sat on the arm of his chair, "I want to know what all this nonsense is about."

"What nonsense?"

212

"About your keeping the children down here."

"No nonsense about it. There's no reason why they can't get out of that primitive valley and see a little of the world. I've enrolled Carl . . ."

"Now, Dad," Marquita began, but he waved her to silence.

"Get that look off your face, my dear. That's a Salazar look!"

"Well, after all, I was a Salazar long before I became a Parmarez."

"That's no excuse. Now let me finish what I started to say. I already have a governess engaged for the girls and a tutor for Rick."

"Don't you think you acted in a rather high-handed manner to take this on yourself without consulting their mother and me?" Phillip demanded.

"Son, you deprived me of my grandchildren until I was an old man. Are you going to deny me the pleasure of having them around now?"

"They have been here for weeks!" Marquita argued.

"What's that out of a lifetime?" he asked, then turned his attention to his grandson who had just entered the room.

"Why are you hopping around like a toad in a campfire, Ricky?"

"The Spindrift's here. She's already docked! Can we go now?"

"Sure. Carl, help me get these shoes on again. I don't know why we Indians ever started wearing them," he grumbled.

"What's the matter with your foot, Dad? Do you have the gout?" Phillip asked.

"No, I have an ingrown toenail."

"Let me see it. It may need to be cut out."

213

"You leave my toe alone. After we get back from our cruise I may let you look at it."

"Thanks, that will be a big treat! As for a cruise, we're going to take our brood and cruise home."

"Now, don't be hasty. . . ."

"We aren't being hasty. We'll finish the week with you, then take you back with us for good," Phillip said.

"And while we're here we can help you close the house. If you want to be with the children, you can make your home with us and have them underfoot all the time." Marquita turned to the children and said, "You'd better start sorting what you want to take with you."

At this the four raised an outcry and swarmed over their father. The girls each occupied a knee, the boys sat on the arms of his chair. "Please, Daddy, let's go out for just a little while!"

Phillip raised his hand and there was silence. "Look . . . I love you dearly, but you're driving me crazy. I don't know how your grandfather endures the noise!"

"Love it!" Carlos beamed.

"Now your mother and I have made a decision, and we won't discuss this any further. Agreed?"

"Yes, Daddy," they answered and turned to their grandfather with tragic faces.

"We'll have to wait until you come down again," he said, but one eyelid closed in a conspiratorial wink. "Since we aren't going anywhere, Phillip, perhaps you'd better take a look at my foot."

"Marquita, I wish you'd come with me and tell me what we've done wrong out here," Carlos proposed later that afternoon.

"Shouldn't you stay off your foot, Dad?"

"No, Phillip bandaged it. It's all right now. Come this way. I don't know why I'm having so much trouble with this one particular spot. Things just won't grow for me as they do for you."

"Nonsense, your garden's a showplace, and you know it."

"Well, unless I can correct this condition it won't be one for long. I want you to look at this shrub. I've tried repeatedly to get it started here, and look at it."

"It just needs more sun."

"Oh? I wonder the gardeners didn't think of that."

"I'll wager they did, but you bullied them into doing things your way."

He grinned sheepishly. "We had some words about it," he admitted.

"There are things that *will* grow here, but this is a sun-loving plant and can't take so much shade."

"Perhaps that's what is wrong with Phillip."

"What do you mean?"

"Well, does he get out much . . . I mean away from his business? He used to like deep-sea fishing. Does he ever break away for some sport?"

"No, he doesn't. He never has time for a real vacation, but he seems to feel well."

"It's probably my imagination, but I thought he looked rather pale. Now, here, Marquita," he walked ahead and pointed out an area with his cane. "What would you suggest that we plant here? How about going to the nursery with me in the morning and selecting what I should have?"

"I'd love it," she agreed readily.

As they walked back to the house they met Phillip.

"Why are you limping, Dad? Is your foot paining you again?"

"Yes, it is, Phillip. I think I'll go in and get off it."

"I told you to keep it elevated. I'll look at it as soon as we get in."

Marquita went directly to her apartment while Phillip followed Carlos. The doctor took a hassock near his father's chair and bared the sore foot.

"I can't understand why you let your toe get in this condition. You should have had this looked after weeks ago."

"Been too busy."

"Doing what? Amusing my kids?"

"Forget me and answer my question. Has Marquita recovered completely from her surgery?"

"I think so. Why?"

"She looks frail."

"Marquita has never been robust." Phillip adjusted the padding and began rebandaging the foot.

"I see her so seldom; in my anxiety I see symptoms that don't exist, I suppose."

"Symptoms of what?"

"That isn't the word I should have used. Just forget what I said. After all, you're a doctor. You should know if your wife is in good health."

Phillip looked up quickly. "Has Marquita complained of not feeling well?"

"No, of course not. There she is now."

"May I come in?" Marquita asked from the doorway.

"Of course . . . the house is yours," Carlos told her.

"Thank you, Dad. How is your foot?"

"It's all right."

"Phillip, Dad and I are going to work in the garden tomorrow. I think you'd better get out there with us and get some sun."

"I have a better idea. Since Dad has his heart set on a cruise, let's go with him. I think you need a change of scenery—not just a transfer from a garden in Mexico to one in Guatemala."

"I'd love it . . . and so will the children. They were heartbroken when I left them."

"Let them join us here, Marquita. Press that buzzer four times. That's our signal."

There was an instant clatter of feet down the stairs and the four arrived at the door. Carl raised his hand to knock, but Carlos called, "Come on in, you young buffaloes. Your mother and dad know by now that you don't stand on ceremony when they're not around."

"Why did you call us, Grandpa?"

"Well, your parents have consented to a short cruise, and . . ." But he didn't get to finish his sentence. The shouting and squealing lasted until Phillip spoke.

"I just can't believe these are ours, Marquita. Now calm down, children, your mother wants to speak."

They turned obediently to her.

"I started to say that we don't have suitable clothes for such a trip."

"Get what you and Phillip need, Marquita. I outfitted these wild Indians two weeks ago."

Two days later the girls raced their brothers to the boat landing. The adults followed more slowly. Before leaving, Carlos called his staff together for final instructions. "Remember, we're not to be disturbed. I have no business so pressing that it can't wait until I get back. And if anyone wants to know where we are you can truthfully say you don't know; neither do you know how we traveled. Is that clear? I'm depending on you, Saucedio."

"But, Dad," Phillip objected, "suppose I'm needed in the Valley?"

"Nonsense! You have two other doctors there. What could possibly happen that would require your attention?"

havelita stopped to break off a spray of bougainvillaea before going in. It had been a hard day. It seemed that every time Phillip left their admissions doubled. "Any mail, Maggie?" she asked.

"On your desk, Doctor."

"Hmm . . . from Guatemala. They've hardly had time to get settled there, and it seems they've been gone a month." She slipped her shoes off, leaned back, and lifted her feet to a hassock. The maid came in with a cup of coffee.

"Thanks, Maggie, I need this," she said, and began sipping as she read her letter. "I'm glad they're enjoying their visit, but we certainly need the doctor."

"Clarinda had her baby, didn't she?"

"Yes, and so did Sofia . . . just about an hour ago."

"Oh? So soon?"

"A little early, but she and the baby are all right."

"Well, it's good to get them both out of the way," Maggie consoled as she went back to the kitchen.

"Yes, we can take it easy for a while now unless some jealous hombre takes a shot at his rival. There's always that possibility." She closed her eyes wearily.

"Don't go to sleep now," Maggie cautioned. "Supper in ten minutes."

"Let's take trays to the patio. I want to watch the stars."

218

"You should be watching them with a husband, not an old woman," Maggie told her.

"And what man would put up with my hours?" she asked.

"You should be taking care of your own babies, not helping other women have theirs," Maggie said and left, determined to have the last word.

At three o'clock both women were aroused by a pounding on the front door. Maggie reached it first.

"Be quiet!" she scolded, "the doctor is trying to sleep!"

"I'm from the hospital. Call her at once," a voice spoke out of the darkness.

"I'm here, Marcos. What's the trouble? Another baby?"

"Oh, no, Doctor. There has been a terrible accident on the highway. Simon Cantu has called for the ambulance, and it's on the way back now. Eight people are injured. Dr. Mendoza says he can't handle them alone. He says to please hurry. It's bad, bad."

Chavelita hurried into housecoat and slippers. "Maggie, get my clothes together and follow with them as fast as you can. And come prepared to stay. We may need you. Here, Marcos, take my flashlight. Do you know how serious the injuries are?"

"It was a bus and car collision. There are two dead. Dr. Mendoza is trying to get Dr. Parmarez now."

"Oh, I don't think that will be necessary. We can get help from Mexico if we need it."

"I think we must have the doctor. One of the injured is Mrs. Parmarez's nephew."

"Mr. Salazar?"

"Yes, Simon said he had a head injury."

Chavelita ran the rest of the way.

"Down the hall in Five," the girl at the desk said as she dashed in.

At first she thought he was dead. He hadn't been touched since his admittance, and his handsome face was bruised and bleeding and covered with dirt. Chavelita tore off her robe and, forgetting her garb, set to work to determine the degree of his injuries. Maggie came with her professional clothes, but Chavelita didn't stop to change. Dr. Mendoza rolled in noiselessly.

"I haven't been able to contact Phillip yet, but I've asked Dr. Rolf to come out," he told her.

"You'd better get a brain man here, too. I'm afraid to touch his head."

"All right. There may be others who will need him also. As soon as you can leave here, will you look in on Three? Oh, if only I had the use of my legs," he lamented as he wheeled himself from the room.

A little later Chavelita left Maggie to watch while she checked on Luis' patient. The young woman was still unconscious, and the doctor left one of the aides with her. At the desk she found Luis making out a report.

"Another one just died," he said. "That's three out of ten."

"We must get some nurses from Mexico, but until they arrive we'll have to rely on local help. As soon as you can spare Ramon or Rudolf send them for Ann Lobo and Marie Rodriguez. Tell them we must have them at once. If you can think of others who can help, call on them. I'll be with Romero if you need me." As she turned to go back to her charge she met a nurse coming out of Three.

"She just died," she said, and hurried on to the desk to make her report.

For the next two weeks there was a grim battle for the lives of the remaining six victims, but in spite of their efforts,

220

three more died. Chavelita left the hospital only for a change of clothing. She slept when she could on a cot set up in Romero's room.

Dr. Peña, the brain surgeon, had given unstintingly of his time and skill to Romero, staying on a week after the operation.

Chavelita fretted constantly that they were unable to reach Phillip. It had taken hours to get the call through, and then she was able to learn only that the entire family was away, and no one knew where or for how long.

"Maggie," she said one day after checking Romero, "I wish you'd make me a cup of tea and some cinnamon toast. I'm going to lie here while you prepare it." She stretched out on the cot and was soon asleep.

"What are you doing in my room?" Chavelita started up as though a bomb had exploded under her. She was on her feet in an instant. Romero's voice was weak, but he regarded her with hostile eyes.

"I'm not in your room," she told him. "You are in one of mine. You're in the hospital in Esperanza."

"Why?"

"You were injured in a car accident. Here, put this under your tongue."

"I don't want it. Take it away."

"There are other ways of taking your temperature; if you won't cooperate we'll be forced to use one." Romero accepted the thermometer without further protest. He slept most of the next two days. On the third, Chavelita stepped into his room to read his chart while he was awake.

"Where is my uncle?"

"I wish I knew. He and Mrs. Parmarez went to Guatemala to bring the children home. We've been unable to locate them." She left as Dr. Mendoza entered.

"She's a wonderful woman," Luis said, looking after her, "as well as a fine doctor."

"I wouldn't know," Romero said wearily.

"No, you couldn't. You were unconscious all the time she lived in this room, never leaving it even to eat or sleep."

"Why couldn't you have attended me?"

"How I wish I could! But you know, Romero, I'm good only in the lab."

"How soon can I get out of here?"

"That rests entirely with Dr. Chavez, Mr. Salazar."

"It's been a wonderful trip, Dad, and I'm glad you tricked us into going," Marquita said as they prepared to leave the Spindrift.

"What do you mean 'tricked'?" he asked in an injured tone.

"Just what I said. You tricked us into going—telling me how worn Phillip looked and frightening him with your hints of my early decline! You should be ashamed of yourself."

Carlos only laughed. "You both talk too much," he said. "Come, girls."

"Mother, I wish we could sail on and on around the world," Marcia said. "Why can't we?"

"Because you have to go to school. You're already late in starting."

The children ran from the boat and along the sandy beach.

"How are we ever going to get them tamed down enough to fly them home?" Phillip asked, as he watched them race up the steps and into the house.

"Leave them with me," Carlos suggested.

"They've been here too long now, Dad. Another month

222

and we'd never be able to corral them. You spoil them too much."

"What are grandparents for? Besides, I like their noise. It's so quiet after they leave that I can hardly stand it. That's why I go to Florida after every one of their visits."

"Now that isn't good for you, Dad. We've told you dozens of times that your place is with us. Give up this museum and come home," Marquita insisted.

"I'm giving it some thought. Well, Saucedio, we're home again," Carlos said as his steward met him on the steps. "Everything run smoothly while we were away?"

"There have been several phone calls from Mexico for the doctor. He is to call the hospital as soon as he arrives."

"When did you get the first message?" Phillip asked.

"Right after you left."

"Get the operator, Saucedio, and call the doctor when you get through to Mexico," Carlos told him.

"Let's take a walk in the garden, Phillip. I'd like the feel of solid ground beneath my feet again," Marquita suggested.

"I'd better stay near the phone. Dad, why don't you go with her?"

"Phillip, it may take hours. Get on outside. I'll stay here and send for you the moment the phone rings."

But neither Marquita nor Phillip enjoyed the walk. He was preoccupied and made abrupt replies to her questions and comments.

"Phillip, why are you so worried? What could have happened? We have all the family here except Romero, and as he told me he's a big boy now and can take care of himself."

"I wonder if the house or the hospital could have burned," he worried.

"Since both are solid masonry I think it would be

223

difficult for fire to do a great deal of damage to either one of them."

"You're right, of course. I am disturbed because this is the first time they've ever called me when I was away."

"Hey, Daddy, your call's through!"

With an abrupt "Excuse me," Phillip ran to the house. Marquita hurried after him and reached his side in time to hear him ask, "How seriously?" He waited for a reply, then, "You think he's out of danger? Dr. Chavez? Sure, I'll wait."

"There was an accident," he explained to Marquita, then returned his attention to the phone call.

"Okay, let's have it straight without any frills." Again there was silence.

"How badly was he hurt? . . . You had Peña? . . . He says he's going to be all right? . . . Very well, we'll leave immediately."

"What happened, Phillip? What kind of accident?"

"A car and bus collision, dear." He put an arm around her shoulders and guided her to a seat. She looked up expectantly. "Romero was in the car."

She covered her trembling lips. "How is he?" she whispered.

"He's out of danger now."

"Are you keeping anything from me, Phillip?"

"Nothing concerning Romero. There were ten people involved. He was one of three survivors. As far as they can tell now, he will make a complete recovery. . . . We'll have to hurry if we get under way this afternoon." He looked around at the children who had gathered close to hear the news.

"Under the circumstances I think we'd better leave our brood here for the present, at least until we look the situation over. We'll have Romero in the house for some time, and I'm sure their clamor would drive him crazy." The girls hugged each other, and the boys turned handsprings across the hall and back.

"Dad, may we use the plane?"

"Of course. How soon do you want to leave?"

"Just as soon as Redfield can get the plane in condition to fly."

"She's never any other way. Saucedio, call the field and tell Redfield to be ready to take off in an hour."

Two hours passed, however, before they had clearance. Carlos and the children watched until the plane took to the air and was out of sight.

"Now make the most of the next three days," Carlos advised. "You start your studying on Monday."

"Oh, no, Grandpa, just one more week?" Marcia begged.

"Not another day! Do you want to grow up as ignorant as an Indian? Now get on with you," and he smiled fondly as they scampered to the car.

ncle Phillip . . . how long have you been here?" The doctor looked up from Romero's chart.

"About an hour. How do you feel?"

"All right. I want to get out of here."

"Not so fast! You had a close shave, and I have an idea you'll be our guest for quite a while. I hope you appreciate what Dr. Chavez has done for you. Dr. Mendoza gives her all the credit for your recovery."

"I'm sure she's very efficient, and I am grateful. Where is Marquita?"

"On my office couch, resting—I hope."

"Has she been in to see me?"

"Of course, but you were asleep. I want to check you over before I call her back. Now lie still. Don't exert yourself. I'll move you as I have need." Phillip examined him slowly and thoroughly.

"Well, it looks as if they've done a good job of putting you together again, including that handsome face of yours. And that, Luis says, is entirely due to Dr. Chavez's care."

"Again, I appreciate it, but she's so superior she gets on my nerves. Can't someone else do what has to be done in here? I'd rather she stayed out of the room."

"I'll take care of you from now on—and she'll be glad

because she's had to neglect other patients to give you the kind of care she thought you needed." Phillip turned and left the room abruptly. At the door he saw Chavelita a few steps ahead of him. He called, and she paused until he was beside her. One look at her face told him she had heard Romero's request.

For a month after his release from the hospital Romero spent most of his time lying in the hammock. As his strength returned he wandered through the Valley. But he was given to long periods of moodiness and became irritated over trivial things.

One morning two busses stopped on the highway, and their tourists began pouring into the village.

"I'm getting out of here, Marquita. I can't stand those gaping, gawking characters!" Romero exploded.

"They're our bread and butter," Marquita told him.

"Not mine, thank heaven!"

"Tourism has made the difference between living and existing. We couldn't get along without them. However, if they make you nervous perhaps you'd better get away . . . but not too far. One of the men will drive for you when you're ready to leave."

"I prefer being my own chauffeur."

"You certainly don't think you're strong enough to sit behind the wheel of a car!"

"I'll make it."

The next day he left. "I'll be in Mexico," he told Marquita.

Long before he reached there he realized he was not as strong as he had thought. He checked in at his hotel and went to bed. For the next week he never left his apartment but lay in bed staring at the ceiling. One morning his phone rang.

"Rome? I just learned that you were in town. Why are you hiding?" a gay voice demanded.

"Enrique! Come on up."

A little later the door opened to admit his caller.

"I'm glad to see you, old man! I've become bored with everything and myself. Mix yourself a drink and then come tell me what mischief you've been in since I saw you last."

"What's yours?" Enrique asked on his way to the bar.

"Nothing. I'm off the stuff."

"Aw, come on!"

"No, I mean it. I never did care for it. I've drunk to be sociable. If we hadn't all been drunk that night of the wreck those seven people would still be alive."

"But you weren't driving."

"Granted, but if I'd been sober I would never have let Leon take the wheel."

"Well, you're not responsible, so forget it and tell me why you're in retirement."

"I'm not. I drove up from my aunt's place before I had the strength. I've been resting, and as soon as I'm fit I'm going to head for the wilderness."

"What wilderness . . . and why?"

"I don't care where I go. I must get away for a while so I can think. I've got to decide whether to stay on here or go back to France."

"Can't you make that decision in a comfortable hotel room?"

"No, I can't. In fact, I think that's part of my trouble. I've always been too comfortable. I want to try roughing it."

"You? Rough it?" Enrique threw back his head and roared. "What do you consider roughing it? A safari outfitted with your personal servant, beaters, gun bearers, cooks, guides, and hunters?"

"I really hadn't thought about it. What does it mean to you?"

"A guide and a cook, a tent, a bedroll, and for food whatever the country offers—just the barest necessities."

"You think I can't take it?"

"I know you can't. It would be hard for me, but you—why, man, those mountains are killers."

"You forget that I lived in them for fourteen years. Besides that, I've climbed mountains in other countries— Mexico's can't be too different. I suppose the hotel can recommend a guide."

"No, let me get one for you. How long do you want to be gone?"

"Three months . . . maybe longer."

"Let me call and see if I can get this guide. Hand me your directory. . . . I'll see if he's available. If he isn't you'd better wait until he is. And let me tell you a little about this man, since you have such superior airs. This chap is anything but subservient, so be careful how you treat him. He's as proud as the devil."

"Why is he so superior?"

"Amigo, he's Indian. He's also well educated and has taught in a college somewhere in the States."

"Then why is he hiring out as a guide?"

"I asked him that once and he in turn asked me where else he could find employment that took him all over the country at another's expense. He gave as another reason, the fact that he doesn't like inside work. I think he's writing a book about the Indian."

"And he's a reliable guide?"

"The best. You'll be lucky if you can get him." Enrique dialed his number and when he had finished his conversation on the phone said, "I was afraid of that. He's with a party in Brazil now and won't be back in this area for two weeks. But you'd better stop here until he comes."

"What's this man's name?"

"Mucio Montoya. He's going to be rather aloof at first until he takes your measure. If he likes you he'll ask you to call him by his first name. Chances are by the time you return he'll be calling you by yours."

"In other words, you're telling me he isn't to be treated as a servant."

"You wouldn't dare! You'll find him good company around the campfire. I think he knows every legend of every tribe on both continents. You'll appreciate him more after you've been out a few weeks. With the ordinary guide's lack of conversational ability you'd be talking to the donkeys before sunrise the first day."

"Donkeys?"

"Yes, donkeys. Those little hidebound bundles of perversity. You certainly didn't expect to make the trip in that car of yours."

"No, but I assumed that Mexico still had some good horseflesh around."

"Mucio supplies the animals, and I'm sure you'll be astride a donkey."

"You're wrong! I gave that up when I was a kid. But I imagine you'd enjoy seeing me ride a donkey."

"With your distinctive elegance, you'd look like a prince! But you're right about the horses. Mucio has some fine ones and will furnish you with a good mount. Now . . . how about having dinner with me tonight?"

"I'd like to."

"Good, I'll pick you up here at eight."

Two weeks later the guide was announced.

"Show him in at once," Romero said, and a moment later Mucio stood before him. Involuntarily Romero arose and offered his hand.

"Mr. Montoya, I'm Rome Sales."

"Enrique Dominguez told me you needed a guide."

230

"Yes, he thinks I'll get lost without one."

"What is the purpose of the trip? Hunting? Fishing?"

"I don't care much for either. I've been after big game in Africa, so I doubt that hunting in the area would be very exciting."

"I believe Enrique said you were an artist."

"I used to be one. I may want to do some painting. I'll get my canvas and oils together. Enrique said you would attend to outfitting us."

"Collect what you want to take with you. I'll come and look at it so I'll know how many pack animals we'll need. I'd like to leave Friday if it's convenient for you."

Thursday evening Mucio called to say that he would be waiting at a point on the outskirts of the city at six the next morning and Enrique took Romero out to meet him.

"Is this it?" he asked when he saw the guide, a man he presumed to be the cook, three horses, and four donkeys.

"What did you expect? A couple of elephants with howdahs?"

"Hardly, but this seems a small train for an extended tour."

"You're going to live off the land, buying necessities only when and if you can get them. And you'll be surprised how few things are essential! You'll come back a wiser man." With a wicked grin Enrique watched him mount and ride off.

By midafternoon the third day Romero had to admit that he wasn't as fit for the trip as he had thought, and he began to wonder how long he could continue without a rest stop. Mucio noticed his fatigue and suggested a halt.

"There's a mountain stream where we can water the horses and refresh ourselves. I have some sandwiches and coffee we can have while we rest. I don't know how you feel about it, but I'm ready to eat. Turn down this canyon, Mr. Sales."

Romero followed directions and a little later reined his horse in while he looked around. Cliffs rose vertically above them, ending in jagged points. On the bare face of the precipice the rock was splotched faintly with tints of rose, green, and yellow.

"There must be minerals of some sort here. Have you noticed the color?" Romero asked.

"Yes," Mucio agreed, "there are, but not in quantity or quality to justify the expense of getting them out. . . . We'll wait here for Mike." Mucio turned his back and ignored Romero's difficulty in dismounting. He led his own animal to the river and waited patiently while he drank.

Romero struggled over the rough ground, for his legs and back were numb. He knelt and splashed water over his face while Mucio drank from a nearby spring.

"Men have tried everything from soft drinks to hard liquor as a refresher, but they've never concocted anything that equals good, cold water," he said.

"I feel as if I could drain the spring," Romero replied. They led their horses to the shade, and Mucio unsaddled his. When Romero tried to do the same for his, the guide saw his difficulty and took over.

"Mike's been doing this for me," Romero excused his awkwardness.

"I'll do it and show you how it's done. I've made it a rule that everyone I take on a trip of any duration learns all of the camp duties. You never know what may happen, and it's only sensible that every member of a group be able to take over any job if there should be an emergency. Here, take our mats over there in the shade of that grove. We'll sit on them and have our sandwiches."

"I hope I can sit," Romero said.

"Saddlesore or stiff?"

"Both."

"Well, you'll be broken to it before long. Here's your lunch."

The cook came up while they were eating. After watering his animals he found a small patch of shade, stretched out, and was soon asleep.

"Hasn't he any food?" Romero asked.

"Oh, yes, I gave him his when I bought our supply this morning. No doubt he ate it within the hour. And now, while the sun is hot, we'd better follow Mike's example." Romero watched the guide remove the larger stones from under his mat and stretch out with his sombrero over his face. For a while Romero continued to sit, looking at the mountains towering above them, then he, too, lay down and slept.

When he aroused long shadows stretched toward the east and the sun had invaded their camp. Mucio had the horses at the river again; the cook and pack animals were nowhere in sight. He arose as the guide returned.

"Feel better?" Mucio asked.

"Much better, thank you."

"Go to the river and douse your head in the water. It will put new life in you. And if you like, take time for a short swim. I did. I'll help you saddle when you get back."

When he returned to camp refreshed, as Mucio said he would be, he found they had a visitor. A young Indian boy had ridden up on the leanest donkey he had ever seen. The animal had shed its hair in spots so that it looked like a moth-eaten garment or a badly patched toy. A pad made of layers of rags sewn together covered its bony back. As Romero approached the boy dismounted and led the poor beast forward.

233

"What is he saying?" Romero asked when the lad paused after pouring forth a torrent of words.

"He says that you may ride his donkey for a peso."

"Ride his donkey! Why would I want to ride that flea-bitten animal? I'll gladly give him a peso, any number of them, but I won't get on that donkey."

"To him this is a fine animal. Many tourists, no doubt, pose on him for their home movies."

"Are we likely to encounter tourists here? I thought I'd made myself clear—I want to get away from people!"

"There is scarcely a place in Mexico where you won't find tourists. It is one of our most remunerative businesses. Sight-seeing busses don't come in here—the road is too narrow—but smaller cars bring individuals or groups of four or five on private tours. If we happen to meet any, you can ignore them." Romero sensed disapproval in his voice. Mucio spoke to the boy, handed him some money, and waved him off.

"Where's Mike?" Romero asked as he lifted his saddle onto his horse.

"I sent him on ahead. We still have some daylight left and we'll ride until sunset. Wait, you'll have to tighten that or your saddle will slip. There, that will hold. If you see anything you want to paint, speak up."

"So far there's been nothing very distinctive."

"Have you seen Copper Canyon?"

"No."

"See it before you leave Mexico."

"Why not see it now?"

"We're too far from it. It would take too long."

"I have plenty of time."

"I don't. I have other tours booked. Perhaps we can see it later."

Just before sunset they overtook the cook. Mike had set

up camp and started a fire. A blackened coffeepot balanced on three stones sent up savory steam.

Romero was hungry, and he found his dry tortilla wrapped around a strip of tough meat far from satisfying, but he ate it without comment. Later Mike rode off on a donkey and came back walking while the burro was almost hidden under a pannier piled high with hay.

"Where did he get that? I haven't seen a house all day," Romero said.

"Oh, there are *congregaciones* scattered all through here."

"I suppose that means a congregation of houses."

"Yes, too few to make a pueblo."

"That's interesting. I'd like to see one sometime."

"That's easily arranged. We pass them every day. I've avoided them because of your aversion to people. Bring your mat close to the fire. This will be a cold night." He added several sticks to the coals, and Mike came up with a fresh supply.

"Mr. Sales, I don't anticipate any accidents, but I always like to know whom to advise in the event there is one. The only trouble I've ever had has been minor illnesses, but there's always the chance something serious could happen."

"My aunt is my nearest relative. I'll give you my card and write her name and address on the back." Mucio offered his pen and studied the name when Romero handed the card to him.

"Parmarez? That name isn't common in Mexico. There's a Mr. Parmarez in Guatemala who's quite well known. I think his family somewhere along the line must have captured a Spanish galleon loaded with Indian gold and he inherited the lot."

"He's my aunt's father-in-law."

235

"He has a regular palace at Puerto Barrios. Mike, you've seen the place, haven't you?"

"The outside, Mucio, only the outside."

"Mr. Sales's aunt married the Parmarez son. Here, put this in that waterproof card case you carry."

Mike took the card and regarded it gravely as though he could read, then shrugged and buttoned it in his shirt pocket. "Plenty money," he said.

"I think we're going to have visitors tonight," Mucio observed. "I hear the murmur of voices."

Romero listened. "All I can hear is the wind."

Mike turned and motioned toward the slope above them and there a light moved, swinging back and forth, silhouetting the bare legs and feet of the men coming to join them at their campfire. They shook hands all around then crouched near the glowing coals.

News of the city was exchanged for that of local events. Then the conversation drifted to spirits, good and bad, of omens and methods of exorcism. One spoke of Juan Diego and the appearance of the Virgin and of the miraculous imprint of her image on his cape. They sighed, envying the fortunate Juan. After a while they arose, shook hands again, and wished the campers *buenas noches,* then disappeared up the trail.

Mucio established a routine. They arose before dawn, had coffee and a tortilla, and rode until the sun rose, when they repeated the menu. Or, if they had passed through a village and Mike had been lucky, a sweet roll replaced the tortilla. Each day took them higher into the mountains where the grandeur of the scenery aroused the artist in Romero. They frequently stopped and made camp while he painted some view that appealed to him.

"Do you realize, Mr. Montoya, that we haven't had a

visitor for a week?" Romero asked as they made camp one evening.

"Yes, we've been through some desolate country. No doubt we'll have company tonight. I saw the spire of a church about an hour ago, so the men will be coming down when they see our fire."

He was right. Romero had donned woolen shirt and trousers and would have shivered under his poncho except for the huge fire. He moved close to it as their self-invited guests straggled in with softly murmured greetings and found places near the bright blaze. They kept their sombreros on so that their dark faces were visible only as a darting flame illumined them.

"When I was a boy," Romero reminisced, "I often sat by a campfire like this with my grandfather and the men from nearby villages. He always encouraged them to talk of their legends."

"Would you like to hear them again?" Mucio asked.

"Yes, I would. I think I've forgotten all that I ever heard except one that Grandpa said he had been told over and over in every part of the country."

"Of the Fair God?"

"No, the one of four brothers who came from across the sea."

"Yes, that's a common one, too. The figure four must have had some connotation for it appears in so many of our legends. One tells us that the Great Spirit fashioned four men out of white and yellow corn. They were given wives and became our foreparents. In another the war god came to earth, struck the face of the mountain, and four hundred warriors sprang out of the cleft. Whenever I hear that one I am reminded that Moses was supposed to have struck a rock to get water for the thirsty Israelites. In still another, a great stone fell from heaven and shattered into four hundred pieces, and each piece became a man. You'll hear a different version from every tribe of what I believe was originally the same tale."

"Do you know where the first man came from?" one of the visitors asked.

"Tell us," Mucio said, then turned to Romero and asked, "Shall I translate this for you?"

"I'll first see how much of it I understand," and Romero urged the man to continue.

"Many years ago—too many to count—the Great God took some mud from the riverbed and started shaping it in his hands. After many trials he made the figure of a man and set it aside to dry. In time he came and blew on it, and it began to breathe. So he put the man in a beautiful garden and told him to dig a canal to water the beans and the corn. But the man was lonely, so one day while he was asleep God took a rib from his side and by saying some secret words he turned it into a woman. And that's how the world got started."

"Genesis with variations," Mucio said.

"I suppose they got these stories from the priests and twisted them to suit their fancy," Romero said.

"No, these legends were told long before the Spaniards got here. Sometime, in some way, our forefathers received a knowledge of the Bible. I'm sure of that. Perhaps the stories never have been written down but they have been told around campfires like this for centuries. The originals were bound to suffer with repetition. I've heard dozens of accounts of the creation, the flood, the confusion of tongues, and others."

"Will the señor tell us one?" another visitor asked.

Mucio shifted his position, then began. "According to our old people the world was made and destroyed many times. At the end of the last creation tigers came out of the forest

238

and ate all of the people except one man and one woman. They became our ancestors. There is another legend of four couples that peopled the earth. They were joined by other tribes who had lived in darkness and had a very peculiar language. Could that be the Tower of Babel story?" Mucio turned to Romero to ask. "I've often puzzled over that tale."

"I don't know. I can't understand a group of people living in darkness. If every legend has a basis—and my grandfather argued that it did—do you suppose these people lived underground and like fish found in cavern streams were born blind?"

"Perhaps they were culturally in the dark if, as you say, there is any foundation to the story," Mucio suggested.

"Once many years ago," another visitor began, "the earth was covered with pueblos. The ground grew plenty of beans and corn, but the people were very wicked and didn't thank God for his gifts. One night it began to rain and the people said, 'Now our fields will bear more. We'll have to build bigger barns to store our corn.' But it didn't stop raining; it kept on and on. There was a good man who said to his woman, 'The earth will soon be covered with water. Come, get into my boat; we'll go into the hills.' The woman took jars of corn and beans and put them in the boat. Then they rowed toward the hills. It rained for a long time, and when it stopped they were on the top of a mountain they had never seen before. One day a vulture came and brought them a bone. It was a sign of death, so they waited some more; then a dove brought them a flower. The man and the woman were very happy because this was a good sign. They went down into the valley and became the mother and father of all the people in the world."

"There's your Noah's Ark story, Rome. Thank you, señors, for entertaining us so well." Mucio stood—a sign that the travelers wanted to retire—so the group arose and left.

239

"You'd better bring your *petate* close to the fire, Rome. It's going to be another cold one," Mucio cautioned.

It was indeed cold, and one or another of the men was up every hour adding wood to the coals. When they arose at dawn they found the ground around them white with frost, and even the animals had a light sifting on their rough coats. The men drank their coffee close to the fire, warming their hands on the hot cups.

"I'd forgotten that it could be so cold in Mexico."

"The mountains always get snow. On the whole, I suppose you'd call our climate semitropical, but I've known winters when one of those Texas northers disregarded our national boundary and swept in as far as Mexico City. The poor in that part of the country are not prepared for such cold, and they really suffer."

"How do the people in those thatch huts survive?"

"Many of them don't. One year there was a report of eight hundred dead from exposure. I surmise the toll was much greater, for there's no way of knowing how many people live in the remote mountain areas. . . . Let's empty the coffeepot and get started. We'll be on the lower slopes by noon, and it won't be so cold."

Mike dumped the coffee grounds and added the pot to his pack, then started the burros down the trail.

"How old were you when you left Mexico, Rome?"

"Fourteen."

"A heedless age."

"And I was the most heedless. What a pity we don't have a second chance at life—an opportunity to correct our mistakes," Romero said.

"I doubt that we'd improve any. We'd make the same ones over again."

"I don't think I would. I have many regrets."

"No man is without them, Rome." They were silent until

240

the live coals were a heap of ashes. Mucio arose, kicked the last dying embers, and extinguished them.

"The horses will be glad for some exercise. They need warming up, too," Mucio observed. The sun topped the mountain as they left the shelter of the trees. The valley was filled with mist, and the peaks rising above it looked like ships at sea.

"This reminds me of a trip I once took with my grandfather. We stopped to watch the clouds drifting below us, only there was a church spire."

"There's your church, Rome. Look to your right. We'll be down by noon. It's a beautiful valley village . . . you may want to do some painting there."

"You've been here before?"

"Many times. I often bring hunters through here. I decided on this for you because of the beauty."

"How long have you been a guide?"

"Twenty-five years."

"Isn't it rather a strenuous life?"

"I don't find it so. We Indians are a hardy lot, or we wouldn't have survived the persecution we've had to endure."

"Enrique told me you were a college professor at one time."

"Enrique talks too much. Yes, I taught in a small college in California. Then came the war; I enlisted and was sent to France."

"Then you know France!"

"I know its cold and its slush, its dirt and discomforts, but I know nothing of the culture."

"I love France."

"You will go back?"

"I hope so. This trip will decide it."

"Then there is no woman to hold you here or draw you there."

241

"No . . . I'll never be burdened with a wife. When I want to go somewhere . . . and I usually do . . . I don't want a woman or a child clinging to me."

Mucio smiled. "I always pity the man who has never known the comfort of his wife's arms, or the joy of his child's kiss."

"Then you're married?"

"I was. My wife died twenty years ago."

"I'm sorry I spoke as I did," Romero began, but Mucio stopped him.

"No apology is necessary. You're a young man. I hope that you will someday meet a woman who will change your thinking. There's still time."

"That is not a kindly wish, Mucio. I've met hundreds of women—brilliant and drab, saints and sinners, but they all leave me cold when marriage is mentioned. Perhaps if I ever met a woman like my aunt I'd change my mind, but there isn't another one like her. She's thoroughly good and the most beautiful woman I've ever seen . . . and she seems totally unconscious of it."

"It would be refreshing to meet such a woman. Most of them are very much aware of their charms . . . we turn here."

"Where's Mike?"

"He's camped a little way beyond the village. I told him we'd have lunch here. I know a woman who serves good food, but we'll have to give her time to prepare it. While you're sight-seeing I'll go talk with her. I'd like you to see the church, and I'll ride over with you and say hello to Father Tranquiliano."

"Well, well, well, how is the pagan Mucio?" the priest asked when he came to the door.

"Still pagan, Father, and here's another one, Mr. Rome Sales from France. He's interested in our legends."

242

"I suppose you've been hearing fantastic tales about the Fair God."

"No, I haven't. Who was he?"

"Just a figment of someone's imagination. The story has been told so often that the poor Indians believe such a creature actually existed. Come, let me show you our church. We're doing some remodeling and repairing. These old churches need constant care or they'll crumble to bits."

"How old is the building?" Romero wanted to know.

"It was started in 1692."

"It's seen a lot of service, then. I see you're making some changes in your altar."

The dome of the altar was painted an intense blue, and from it a crescent moon and numbers of stars looked down on a veritable forest of white crosses.

"I've never seen one like this before," Mucio observed.

"Neither has anyone else." The priest was evidently not pleased with the alterations. "Our bishop believes that too much worship is directed to the Holy Mother and not enough to the Son. So to discourage too much Marian adoration he had the pictures and statues of the Blessed Virgin removed and crosses erected in their place. He thinks this will turn thoughts to the suffering Lord and center worship in him."

"He may have something there," Mucio agreed.

"Mr. Sales, I'll leave you here with Father while I arrange for our lunch."

"*Amigos*, you will eat with me."

"Oh, no, Father," Mucio began to object, but the priest cut him short.

"You will honor me by sharing my meal," he said.

"Well, since you put it that way. And don't look so disappointed, Rome. The padre does not set a frugal table."

"I sensed as much by the size of his girth."

"You're an observant young man. Follow me now. I

heard the bell as you rode up so I know lunch is ready."

Romero tried to introduce the story of the Fair God during the meal.

"Give it no heed, señor. A white man with fair hair and curling beard appears among the people, and in each hand is the imprint of a cross! Can you imagine anything more absurd?"

Romero would have pursued the subject further but for a warning look from Mucio.

That night around the campfire he brought the topic up again. "Why was the priest so unwilling to discuss it?"

"It's a sore point with some of the fathers. When the church sent her representatives in here they found the story widespread. A white man in flowing robes had mysteriously appeared among the people and instituted an order of worship similar to theirs. The Indians had a form of baptism, celebrated the Holy Communion, and used the cross in their services. Since they knew no priest had been here before them they concluded the devil must have introduced a false creed. They've been trying to stamp it out ever since. But you know these Indians don't forget. They've been taught all of their lives that this God-man did exist and will one day return."

"Why haven't some of our evening visitors mentioned this legend?"

"For one thing, the priests have forbidden them to discuss it. They have been ridiculed and persecuted because of their faith in this personage. And another reason, his name is sacred to them—he is their God. They talk only among themselves and those they feel they can trust."

"Was this personage the one known as Quetzalcoatl?"

"Yes, he is."

"Hmmm, that's interesting."

"The next time we have men drop in I'll introduce the

subject and try to start them talking. There are dozens of legends about him. They've always intrigued me."

"We're going to need shelter ... and very soon," Mucio said, looking off where dark clouds boiled and lightning flashed.

"It looks like a full-fledged storm, all right," Romero agreed, "but where will we find shelter in this wilderness?"

"We'll hunt a cave. These mountains are full of them if you know where to look. I'll go back and see if I can help Mike prod those donkeys into hurrying."

Romero reined his horse and sat watching the storm as it moved down the slopes. He heard a shout and looked back. Mike was herding the animals down a side trail, and Mucio motioned that they were to follow.

"Mike says there's a family living in a cave over there."

"I hope he knows what he's talking about."

"I think he does. He met the man when he was on a trip through here last year."

The donkeys, evidently sensing the approaching storm, broke into a trot, but none were quick enough. They were all thoroughly drenched before they reached their haven. A man stood under a palm-thatched roof that sheltered the entrance to his cave-home. He indicated that they were to bring their animals as well as themselves under this cover. He shook hands cordially when Mucio explained their presence. A woman and several children could be seen hovering in the gloom of the cavern. The man called, and when the woman came in answer he gave some orders. She retreated again and a moment later flames lit up the inside of the cave.

"You may as well unsaddle your horses, señores, and prepare to spend the night. This storm will not be over before dawn. Bring your packs in or they'll be soaked."

"They are already," Mucio said.

"Well, perhaps the warmth of the fire will dry them."

They unburdened the animals and carried the saddles and packs inside. Romero was blinded for a moment by the light from the fire built in a large brazier. The cave, he saw, was quite commodious, with a high ceiling. Directly overhead a maguey cord stretched across the room was festooned with strings of onions, garlic, herbs, and strips of meat drying in the smoke of the fire. The dirt floor was swept clean. A ledge cut in the cave wall served as pantry, wardrobe, and storage bin. The bed mats were rolled up and placed there. A jar of beans and a few squashes rested near. There were some clay pots, a wooden mixing bowl, and in a clay jug four or five tin spoons. A griddle, also of clay, was balanced on top of the brazier, and the woman began placing her flattened tortillas on this to bake.

An open-mouth pitcher containing drinking water was half buried in the dirt floor, and Romero winced when he saw a pig wander in and thrust his snout in for a drink.

Mike brought out his commissary and prepared their meal. The men sat down together and ate, and when they had finished the women and children had what was left.

The storm seemed to increase in fury and lightning flashed in solid sheets. Romero walked to the entrance to watch it, and Mucio and their host followed.

"It must have been on just such a night as this that the Fair God left the wicked city," Mucio said.

"Yes, it was a fearful time," the host agreed.

"Will you tell us the story?" Romero asked him.

"You would like to hear?"

"Indeed I would. Where did this God come from?"

The man dropped a curtain of woven palm leaves over the entrance to shut out the wind and the rain. Mats had been spread for them to sit on, and taking his place he lit a cigarette before replying.

"Who knows?" he asked in return. "From the east . . .

out of the sky . . . no one knows for sure. He just walked into the city one day with a big tiger beside him. The people began to run, for the tiger is a wicked beast, but this stranger motioned to them to come back. Then they saw in each of his hands a cross-shaped scar. His skin was white and his hair and beard were like gold. He taught the people how to harvest, how to make beautiful things out of metal and precious stones, but most of all he taught them about the one Great God and his love for men. One day he told them he must leave them for a while, but that he would come back.

"The people loved him very much and decided to build a temple for him, but the priests were jealous and began to say bad things about the stranger. They made some of the villagers believe them, and when they heard the fair stranger was coming back they hid along the way and threw stones and shot arrows at him. The Fair God didn't understand. He looked at those he had healed, and instead of love he saw only hate. He lifted his hands over his head and fire came down from heaven, just like tonight. The wicked priests and those who had tried to kill him were burned to ashes, but when the storm was ended the Fair God was still standing with his arms raised. He looked at them sadly and went away." For a moment there was silence, broken only by the heavy breathing of the children who had fallen asleep.

"Where did he go? Does anyone know?" Romero asked.

"No one, señor."

"That was extremely interesting. It's the first time I've been told about the Fair God." Romero arose and pulled aside the curtain that covered the doorway. Mucio joined him. The storm still raged.

"We'd better get some sleep," Mucio said. "Tomorrow will be a fine day for traveling."

Rome, when you want to turn back, say so."

"I'm not ready yet. Are you in a hurry?"

"No, the tour I had planned to guide has been canceled."

"Let's keep going."

So they continued their wandering. Word of their approach often preceded them, and they seldom failed to have a group of men and boys around their evening campfire. Romero told of his travels, but more often he encouraged them to talk of their tribal past.

When they reached a pueblo the day after a severe storm the people were still excited over the rush of wind and roll of thunder.

"I was so frightened that I fell on my face and said ten 'Hail Marys' before I knew I was praying. How I wished for Quetzalcoatl!" one man exclaimed.

"Why?" Romero asked.

"He is the ruler of the wind and the water. I've heard the old people tell of his power. He used to go all over the land teaching the people, then he would come back to see if they were doing what he told them to do. He returned one day to a city where the people had worshiped him, but they had become very wicked while he was away. When he tried to join them they told him to leave—they had their own gods and didn't need him. Then over his shoulder they saw a dark cloud coming, trailing a black tail. The priests told them to go hide in the caves from the anger of the Wind God, but Quetzalcoatl called them back. 'No harm can come to you,' he said, 'for my father holds the winds in his hands.' The people were terrified that he would defy the Wind God and stopped to see what would happen. The black cloud came nearer, and as the tail dipped down, almost upon the Fair God, he reached up and tossed it back. The cloud was blown away over the mountain."

"And what became of the Fair God?"

The storyteller shrugged his shoulders. "Who knows?" he said, and walked away.

"Well, Rome, we're in Yucatan. Would you like to see some of the ruins?"

"Perhaps later. Right now I'd like to get rid of this pain in my back."

"You've been in the saddle too long. I carry something in my bags for just such an emergency. I'll give you a good rubdown after we eat."

"I don't think I can ride tomorrow, Mucio. My back is really in bad shape. I thought for an hour I couldn't stay on that horse."

"Well, why didn't you say something? I don't mind stopping here for a while. This is a beautiful spot. Perhaps you'll want to do some painting. Mike, before you do anything else ride over to the village and get some hay for the horses, and see if you can buy a thick, wool blanket for Mr. Sales. The bare ground isn't the best bed in the world for someone with an aching back."

So that night Romero eased himself down on a pile of mats and a wool blanket. Mucio applied linament and rubbed vigorously, then had him lie with his back to the fire. He was in this position when visitors arrived. Mucio explained Romero's trouble, and they grunted their sympathy.

"How far are we from the ruins?" Romero asked by way of getting a story started.

"There are ruined cities all over Yucatan."

"Who built these cities?"

"No one knows for sure, señor. Some say that long ago a tribe of dwarfs built some of them. They were small but very strong. Their priests told them a great storm was coming and that it would flood their land. Those stupid people built boats of concrete, thinking that wooden boats couldn't last in such great flood water. When the rains came their boats sank, and they were all drowned."

"No, no," one of the others protested excitedly, "they were good people. When the white men came to destroy them they dug caves under the temple and are living there now. Someday they will return and finish building their city."

"Do you know why the city was never completed?" another asked. "I will tell you. A long time ago the people set out to build a tower tall enough to reach into heaven. But God didn't like that idea and said, 'I'll put a stop to that right now.' So the next morning when the men went to work they couldn't understand each other. They all spoke, but nobody knew what anybody else was saying. Those who were setting stones on top of the wall would ask for water and the men on the ground would send up sand. They began to quarrel and fight, so the tower was never built."

"There's your Tower of Babel story, Rome."

"You seem to know the Bible very well, Mucio."

"I should. I took the full course in college."

"Why?"

"Why? Because for one thing it's a very interesting piece of literature. And I don't consider a man well educated if he

250

doesn't know at least as much about that book as he does about Shakespeare or Dickens."

"Speaking of books, my grandfather spent years looking for one—a history of the Indian people."

"You are Indian?"

"Yes."

"But your name . . ."

"I changed it when I left Mexico. I was born Romero Salazar."

"I see." They were silent for a moment. Then Mucio asked, "Did your grandfather find the book?"

"No . . . I doubt that there ever was one."

"Your pardon, señor, I have heard my grandfather tell of the time when Kulkulcan walked the earth. . . ."

"When who walked the earth?" Romero asked.

"Kulkulcan. The Fair God was known here as Kulkulcan," Mucio explained, then he asked the guest, "Will you continue your story, señor?"

"Kulkulcan told the people of a time when strange men would come and make war with them, and when they saw these invaders they were to take all their records and treasures and hide them in caves in the forest."

"And did they hide them?"

"Oh, yes, señor. They were very carefully put away."

"Has no one taken them from their hiding place?"

"No one knows where they are."

"If Profilio dared look into the Stone of Light he could find them."

"What is this stone?" Romero wanted to know. The visitors were quiet while Mucio explained.

"According to legend there was once such a stone. It was said to reveal secrets to the high priest of the temple. Now the witch doctors claim to have duplicates; by looking into them they can see into the future and expose any secret."

"Have you ever seen one of them?"

"Yes, they're nothing but a piece of clear glass or a crystalline stone. However, they're treated with great respect. That's why I'm speaking to you in French, which I'm sure none of them understands."

"This is the first time I've heard of the stone." Romero tried unsuccessfully to turn over.

"Back still bothering you? I wish we were near a town that had a doctor. As soon as you're fit we'll head for one, perhaps Espinola. I'm stopping there for my mail. We can accomplish both tasks at the same time."

"I'd like to send my canvases to my aunt. I'm getting too many to carry around conveniently."

"I'll have them forwarded from there. Let me give your back another rub so perhaps you can sleep."

But Romero spent a restless night, and when he roused the next morning he found an old Indian woman crouched beside him.

"What is she doing here?" he demanded.

"One of the men who was here last night told her of your trouble, and she's here to relieve it."

"Nonsense! Send her away. I don't need her incantations."

"You'd better let her see what she can do. Let me turn you over. It can't do any harm to let her try."

"It won't do any good, either," Romero argued, but he let Mucio turn him over and take his shirt off. The woman ran her hands over his back, went over the area the second time, then spoke to Mucio.

"She says you've had a back injury. Is that true?"

"Yes, I was in a car wreck."

"Well, score one for her."

She continued her examination and at its conclusion reached into a wide-mouthed jar she had brought with her and drew out a number of leaves. She dipped these into a pot of hot water and plastered them to Romero's back. When she arose she again addressed Mucio, who translated. "She says you're to lie as you are until she returns in about an hour."

"Since I can scarcely move, I don't think I'll be changing positions very soon. How far are we from a doctor?"

"A day's riding should get us there, but we don't want to do anything that will interfere with this woman's treatment."

"You don't think this is going to help, do you?"

"It won't surprise me at all if this takes the pain away entirely. And now, since we're grounded for a few days," Mucio continued, "I'll repair my saddlebags. I noticed that your stirrups need mending too. There's nothing like enforced idleness to give you a chance to catch up on your odd jobs." Romero watched him bring the articles to be mended and sit down with his awl and strips of leather.

The woman returned before he had finished, removed the plaster of leaves from Romero's back, and applied a fresh one. She left with the same instructions.

"How long is this to go on?" he asked impatiently.

"All day, no doubt." Mucio arose and put his work away. "There's a good fishing hole a few kilometers away. I think I'll go over and try my luck. Mike will be around if you need anything." He went off through the trees whistling.

Mike was making coffee when the woman returned that afternoon. She removed the poultice and told Romero to get up. He moved cautiously.

"Hurry! Hurry!" she urged.

"But I don't want that pain coming back."

Mike explained Romero's reason for caution as he poured coffee for them all. The woman drained her cup and held it out for more, talking and gesturing all the time she was drinking it.

"She says the pain won't come back because she has drawn it out."

Romero stood, straightened his shoulders, and moved them about experimentally. "She's right! The pain *is* gone. Now where did she learn that those leaves had any medicinal value?"

Mike repeated Romero's question and relayed the woman's reply.

" 'Viracocha once came to the village of my people and lived with them a long time. He taught them how to use herbs, and that knowledge has come down from mother to daughter in every generation since.' " When she had finished her recital she arose, took the cigarette from Mike's lips, and ambled off smoking contentedly.

She hadn't been gone long when Mucio returned with a string of fish. He was welcomed with shouts of pleasure. Mike began at once to clean them, and in a short time the men leaned back, replete and happy.

"I wonder where our visitors are tonight," Romero said.

"There's a fiesta in town; I surmise they're all celebrating there." Mucio spread his sleeping mat and lay down. Mike tidied the camp and brought his bedroll to the fire. Seeing that he sat alone, Romero wrapped up in his blanket and followed their example. But he was wakeful. "I wonder what kind of leaves she used on my back. I'd like to pass that bit of information on to my doctor uncle."

"Why didn't you ask her?"

"I didn't think to. I did ask where she learned it, and she said Viracocha taught the women of her tribe generations ago."

"Well, at least you have another name for the Fair God."

"Do you think Viracocha was the same person?"

"According to their legends he was white, had light hair and beard, and wore the same flowing robe. The greatest similarity is in his philosophy."

"There is bound to have been such a person! We've heard of him everywhere we've traveled. Who could he have been?"

"Perhaps he's the man you Christians call Christ."

"What?" Romero bounced up. "What did you say, Mucio?"

"I said that perhaps Quetzalcoatl, Kulkulcan, Viracocha, Wakea, and Jesus Christ were all the same person."

"Oh." Romero lay back to consider this. After a moment he asked, "Mucio, aren't you Christian?"

"I am Indian," was the firm reply, and from his tone Romero knew the subject was closed.

Mucio reined in his horse on the crest of a hill, and Romero stopped beside him. The guide indicated a large village in the valley below.

"There's Espinola," he said.

"Is that an airplane I see?"

"Yes, it belongs to Senor Pentajos. He has a large hacienda near here. His holdings include an archaeological site. A few mounds have been uncovered, but there is nothing outstanding in the shards they've found. Our camp has been set up a little farther down the slope. We'll rest up tonight. In the morning I'll ride in early, so get your pictures together. I'll have them forwarded when I pick up the mail."

"This has been a long day. I'll be glad to rest."

"Better let me get that saddle off," Mucio suggested later when they had joined Mike. "We might not be so fortunate as to find another witch doctor."

"Witch doctor or not, she took that pain out of my back." Romero took their sleeping mats and spread them near the fire. Then he stretched out on one and sipped the hot coffee Mike had poured.

"Mucio, why are so many of the archaeological mounds left untouched? Superstition?"

"No, lack of money . . . and of interest to produce it. You've seen Palenque, Mitla, Kabah?"

"Yes, when I was a boy. My grandfather said the sight of those monuments should create a national pride in every Indian. It didn't have that effect on me."

"No doubt we had a great past."

"I think I'm beginning to understand, to a degree, why Grandpa was always puzzling over our origin, and why he hunted so diligently for a record that would answer the question."

"There have been numerous theories," Mucio said thoughtfully. "I read an interesting article recently in which the author claimed that this continent was colonized about three thousand years before Christ and that the descendants of this early group were joined later—somewhere around six hundred B.C.—by two smaller groups. And he said these last came from Israelite territory. He cited an account found in an early Guatemalan record of a voyage that reached the Continent 587 B.C."

"But that isn't proof."

"Not unquestionable proof, I'll admit, but many of the old accounts tell of a people coming across the sea. While it isn't actual proof, the legends are interesting."

"Grandpa wanted proof," Romero said stubbornly.

"That, Romero, will be difficult if not impossible to come by."

Romero waited with half-closed eyes for Mucio's morning call. The odor of boiling coffee roused him to full wakefulness and he turned to face the fire. Mike sat beside it, cup in hand. When he saw that Romero was awake, he reached for another, filled it, and handed it to him.

"Where's Mucio?"

"He went for the mail."

"Are we to join him, or is he coming back here?"

"We are to wait and have breakfast when he comes. He will be gone about an hour he said."

But Mucio returned much sooner—and with a grave face. "I'm sorry, Rome, we're going to have to cut this trip short. We'll have to get back to Mexico at once. You and I will go by plane, Sanchez will follow with the animals."

"I'm not ready to turn back," Romero objected.

"Then I must go alone. I found a message from my daughter waiting. My grandson was accidentally shot while out hunting. Little hope is held for his recovery. Are you willing to continue without me? As you've seen, Mike is entirely trustworthy and knows the route. If he had a better command of English he'd be as good a guide as I am. Do you want to go on with him?"

"If he's agreeable, I am."

"Then that's settled. I stopped in the village and learned that the Pentajos plane is leaving at noon. Under the circumstances he is willing for me to go out with it. The pilot will take me to an airport where I can get a flight to Mexico."

As soon as breakfast was eaten they broke camp and moved on down into the valley, and at noon Romero and Mike watched Mucio take off.

Romero did a little painting and wandered about the village, but he soon tired of the place.

"Mike, how do you feel about taking a plane to Guatemala? Have you ever been there?"

"Si, señor,"

"Can you leave the animals and equipment here until we come back?"

"My wife's cousin lives here. He'll take care of everything."

"All right, as soon as you can get ready we'll go."

A week later they stood on the banks of the Motagua

River. While Mike hunted for horses and pack animals to take the place of those left behind, Romero roamed about.

The river fascinated him, and he spent hours wandering along its banks. The native houses intrigued him, too. Some were roofed with tile, even though the walls were woven mats. Others had a coarse, shaggy covering of palm leaves, giving them the appearance of a thatch of uncombed hair.

One evening Mike came in with complete camping equipment, and the next morning they set out again.

"We'll follow the river for a while," Romero decided. So day after day they rode on, never beyond the sound of rushing water.

Their evening fires attracted visitors as before, but Romero had grown tired and didn't find their stories especially entertaining. It was Mucio who drew them out and made their legends live.

"I think we'll start back," he said abruptly one evening. "How far are we from an airfield?"

"About a day's ride, maybe a little more."

"All right, let's head for it. My back is giving me more trouble, and I'd like to get to a doctor. I want to turn this money belt over to you. It irritates me. Here, you wear it; it goes underneath your trouser belt."

"But there's money in it, señor!"

"Of course there's money in it! Why do you think I've been wearing it? Leave the money there. You buy the supplies, anyway." As he stretched out on his mat Romero felt a contentment he hadn't known since Mucio's departure. Mike had done his best, but it was Mucio who had made the trip worthwhile. No wonder he was in such demand as a guide.

The next morning Romero refused breakfast.

"My back hurts," was his excuse. "Let's go as soon as you've eaten."

"We're going to have a wet day for traveling," Mike said. "There's a storm brewing."

"Perhaps we can beat it to shelter." Romero helped with the packing and loading of the donkeys, then saddled his own mount.

"Better water them before we start, señor."

"I was thinking the same thing," Romero answered and rode on toward the river, Mike following. As they left the shelter of the grove Mike looked up. Dark clouds boiled overhead. He spurred his horse and yelled to the burros. They broke into a fast trot.

"Señor, make your horse move a little faster," he called. He could have saved his advice for a flash of lightning startled the animals and sent them racing toward the river. When Mike realized that he had lost control of his mount he jumped off and shouted for Romero to do the same. Romero kicked one foot free of the stirrup, then his head struck a low-hanging tree limb. The horse, more frightened than ever by his relaxed burden, plunged down the riverbank and into the stream. Mike saw Romero's body slump over the horse's head and the turbid water close over both.

With a cry he drew his knife and leaped in. He had no trouble finding Romero, for the fear-maddened animal was thrashing his way toward deeper water. With a quick thrust of his knife Mike loosed the shackled foot and began the superhuman task of towing Romero's inert body to shore.

His cries had attracted some village men hurrying home out of the storm. As soon as they understood the struggle, they drew a boat from under some sheltering vines, pushed it into the river, and rowed to the rescue.

When Romero revived he found himself lying on the dirt floor of a mud and wattle hut. He tried to rise, but someone pushed him down again. His throat and lungs felt as if they would burst. His head throbbed with pain, and his eyes and nose burned as if seared with a hot iron. He retched, and a woman turned his head, letting him get rid of a quantity of river water. Two days passed before he could speak, but during that time the woman was in constant attendance, bathing his face when nausea overcame him and keeping a pack on his bruised head. He had moments when he roused to see strange faces about him and to hear the low murmur of their voices.

One morning he awakened more alert and noticed that he was wearing a brilliant purple shirt and coarse cotton trousers. He motioned for Mike to come nearer.

"Why am I wearing these clothes, and where are mine?"

"Yours are still wet. Don't you hear the rain outside? It hasn't stopped since we came here." Romero listened and could hear the sweep of wind and water as it battered its way past the small house. "The new pants you have on Evilio bought for himself, but you needed them so he gave them to you. The shirt is very fine. Carmelita made it out of her Sunday petticoat."

"What happened, Mike?"

"The horses bolted and ran right into the river. Yours ran under a tree and you got a bad blow on the head. I went in after you, but it was Evilio and Gustafo who brought the boat and saved us both."

"How long have we been here?"

"Oh, seven, eight days. Everything is gone, señor, horses, donkeys, and all our supplies."

"It's unfortunate, Mike, but we can remedy that as soon as we get to a town. We'll buy what we need then."

"But Señor Sales," Mike's voice was apologetic, "we have no money."

"No money?"

"No, Señor; after cutting the stirrup strap to loosen your foot I tried to put my knife back in my scabbard so I could hold you with both hands. But I cut the money belt and my pants belt, too. I lost everything but my shirt in the river. I, too, am wearing borrowed pants."

Romero sighed. "Don't worry about it. When we get to a telephone I'll make a call. Everything will be all right as soon as my back quits hurting and we can travel again. I'll be fine in a day or two."

But instead of improving Romero grew worse. His stomach rebelled at the native food, and added to that, he developed a low, persistent fever. The village herb woman was called in, but her ministrations were futile. The witch doctor came and after consulting the spirits predicted Romero's death.

As the fever hung on he became delirious, and when Mike spoke to him he only stared vacantly, uttering French which was lost on them all. Then one day Mike recognized the name 'Parmarez' among his ramblings.

"Ah, Señor Magill, such a stupid donkey I have been! There has been so much happening that I forgot Mr. Sales has

262

an uncle living in this country. Have you heard the name 'Parmarez'?"

"Yes, yes, rich old man, big house and many servants. He lives in Puerto Barrios."

"I'm going to take him there."

"It's too far."

"I must try. Will you and Gustafo help me?"

Evilio was doubtful. He shook his head and called his son outside for a conference. After a lengthy absence they returned, bringing another man whom they introduced as Edelberto Hernandez. He became the spokesman.

"Señor Mike, to go by land to this place is impossible. Your friend could not stand the trip. I am going out in the morning with a boatload of bananas. I can take you as far as Ixtapal, which is a small village on the coast. There I am sure you can get a boat to take you on to Puerto Barrios."

It was the only solution, so the next morning Romero, unconscious, was carried on board the banana boat. The friendly villagers stood on the bank and watched it leave.

Where are you young limbs of Satan headed now?" Carlos sat at the top of the steps leading down to the beach.

"We're going to look at our boat, Grandpa. Can't we take it out? Carl is a good pilot."

"You may not! I'm responsible for you while you're here, and I intend to return you to Mexico intact. Is that understood?"

"Yes, Grandpa."

"If Harvey has time to take you, you may go. Otherwise, stay out of that boat!"

"Well, I don't know why you bought it for us if we can't use it! And I don't think it was very flattering to call it 'The Parmarez Perils,' " Macaria complained.

"That's exactly what you are, all four of you. Now go and leave me in peace."

"I suppose we can at least look at it," Marcia pouted as they ran down to the beach.

"What are you doing on that wall, Carl?" his grandfather called.

"Watching a boat. I thought it was going to tie up at the wharf, but it looks as if it's coming in to the breakwater."

The girls became interested too. "What in the world is that?" Marcia asked as a small boat was put out and a man lowered into it. The twins were frightened at the unusual event, but their curiosity overcame their fear. They stood rooted to the spot as the boat was beached, and one of the men approached them. When Carl saw this he jumped from the wall, shouting for his sisters to come back. Carlos, hearing his cries, sent one of his men to investigate. He and Carl reached the girls in time to hear the boatman say, "I've brought Mr. Parmarez's nephew. He's very sick."

"Mr. Parmarez's nephew?" Carl repeated.

"Yes, we left Mexico on a tour, only Mucio had to go back and he told me to bring Mr. Sales to his uncle."

Carl looked from the speaker to the boat. The sick man was being brought ashore. "I'll go talk to Grandpa," he said. "You stay here with the girls," and he loped off across the sand.

"Here is the card Mr. Sales gave to Mucio." Marcia reached out and took it.

"Look, it says 'my aunt,' and it has mother's name on it!" Then to the man, she said, "Bring him in."

Marcia followed Carl; the men with their burden walked close behind.

"Stuff and nonsense!" Carlos was saying testily when they arrived. "I have no nephew that I ever heard of! This is just another imposter! I'll get rid of him in a hurry! Saucidio! Francisco! Harvey! Where are those blockheads? Stop right where you are!" he roared to the strangers. "You can't foist some sick man off on me!"

To the guards he said, "What good are you if you can't keep such as this from landing on a private beach? One of you go inside and call the police!"

"No, Grandpa, don't do that!" Marcia cried. "This card has Mother's name and our address on it!"

"Let me see it." Carlos took the card and read aloud, " 'Rome Sales' . . . your mother has only one nephew, and his name is 'Salazar', not 'Sales.' But I suppose I'd better look into this. Have the man taken to one of the servant's empty houses. Francisco, show these men where to go. And Saucidio, get my son on the phone. Harvey, send Dr. Cordoba to see the sick man."

"Marquita, I really belong in the hospital. We can't spare a nurse to look after me, and I'll be too great a care for you."

"You are not going to the hospital, and that's final. Gilbert and I can do what's necessary. Chavelita says there are no broken bones, just strained ligaments. Fortunately this should keep you in bed for a month. You need a rest and will never get one any other way."

"Good for you. If he were at the hospital he would be listening for every buzzer, worrying for fear someone was not getting attention." Chavelita had come in unnoticed. "How do you feel, Doctor?"

"Like seven kinds of fool. Here I've ridden all over these mountains on a horse and now I let one throw me."

"Was that the phone?"

"I'll take it in the den," Marquita said. Both doctors listened.

"Who?" they heard her ask.

"Yes, Dad, he is. . . . That's his professional name. What about him?"

Chavelita and Phillip fretted over the one side of the conversation they heard.

"Something about Romero," Chavelita said.

"I wonder what Romero's done now and how he and Dad got together." They turned their attention again to Marquita.

"But Phillip can't go down, Dad. He's in bed with a back injury. Wait a minute."

"What's the matter, dear?" Phillip asked as Marquita came in crying.

"Romero's at Woodwind very seriously ill. Dad wants you down there at once."

"Perhaps I can make it. Here, give me a hand, will you?" He tried to get up, but Chavelita firmly prevented it.

"I'll do nothing of the kind! Do you want to become a cripple?"

"I have to go. Stand aside."

"I will not! I'll go in your place—that is, if you feel you can trust me."

"Of course we trust you," Marquita assured her.

"Now wait a minute, you two. I may be able to get a doctor from Mexico . . . no, they have just as good ones in Guatemala. Chavelita, are you sure you want to do this?"

"Of course! Evidently your father thinks some of the family should be there."

"I suppose you're right. Marquita, tell Dad to have the plane in Mexico City as soon as he can get it there, then have Navarro take Chavelita in. Of all the times for me to be laid up!" he fumed.

"Dr. Chavez, I'm sorry I couldn't meet the plane, but I didn't think it wise to leave the house. In fact, the doctor advised against it."

"That's quite all right, Mr. Parmarez. Where is Romero?"

"I'll go up with you."

"He isn't in a hospital?"

"No, I moved a hospital in here, and I've had the three best doctors in the state. Here we are; I'll wait outside."

Chavelita gave her coat to a maid and turned toward the sickroom. She hesitated at the door for a minute, then went in. The doctor in attendance came forward and introduced himself.

"I'm sorry Dr. Parmarez couldn't come. I understand he's an authority on tropical fevers."

"I'm Dr. Parmarez's assistant. What is your diagnosis?" Chavelita walked to the bed and took Romero's hand in hers.

"I've never had a case of this kind and neither have my colleagues. The man is so weak that . . ."

"Dr. Rossinni, what, exactly, do you think his chances are?"

"He'll be dead in forty-eight hours."

"Then shall I take over?"

"Please do. I stayed on only because Mr. Parmarez insisted that one of us be with him all the time. If you should want me, call."

Romero's forty-eight hours passed into sixty, then seventy-two. Chavelita had Dr. Rossinni called back. He was surprised that Romero had lived so long, had no suggestions, and left without extending any hope.

But Chavelita fought on, driving herself and the nurses. At times Romero lay inert, at others he was delirious and fought off the nurses. Then only Chavelita could quiet his restlessness.

A call went through to Phillip each day with a report. He suggested a new medication or a repetition of an old one.

At the end of the third week Dr. Rossinni stopped in again. Chavelita stood by for his opinion.

"I believe he has a chance," he admitted. "The tide seems to have turned in his favor."

"I feel it has. I'm glad that you agree."

Chavelita stood at the window looking down into the garden when a groan from the bed spun her around. Romero's eyes were open, and there was a fleeting flash of recognition when he saw her.

268

"Something hurt you?" she asked, her hand on his.

"Back," he whispered.

"Did you hurt it again?"

He nodded.

"Miss Nunez," she said to the nurse, "let's get a picture the first thing in the morning. Mr. Sales had a back injury about a year ago, and it seems to be giving him some more trouble." Chavelita moved aside to give the nurse her place and went back to the window. Romero's eyes followed her until she was out of range of his vision, and he began to mumble incoherently. She hurried to him again and, sitting beside his bed, took his hands in hers. It quieted him, but there was a question in his eyes.

"Dr. Phillip couldn't come," she told him. "His horse threw him, and he's in bed with a painful back, too. He sent me to take care of you." He seemed satisfied with her explanation and went to sleep.

"Romero," Chavelita said several weeks later, "I'm needed in the Valley, but your aunt doesn't want me to leave you. I've discussed this with Dr. Parmarez and Dr. Rossinni, and they think that by wearing a brace you can travel to Mexico in comfort. It's entirely your decision. If you prefer staying here you're welcome. Mr. Parmarez will assure you of that."

"I'd rather go home."

"Very well, I'm sure we can make your trip an easy one. We'll leave in the morning. I'll call Dr. Parmarez and tell him. He wants to meet you in Mexico."

With the help of his nurses Romero walked down the ramp to the wheelchair Phillip had waiting.

"Just see how thin he is. . . . He doesn't look as if he would weigh a hundred pounds!" Marquita cried.

"Don't appear concerned, dear," Phillip cautioned.

"Well, you made it! We're glad to have you home again. We'll have you climbing mountains before you know it." They walked slowly to the exit as Phillip talked.

"How is your back, Uncle Phillip?" Romero asked. "Chavelita said you'd taken a tumble."

"I feel fine as long as I wear this corset she put me in. Dr. Chavez, what have you planned for this chap?"

"I've arranged for him to go into the hospital here for a while. I'd rather he didn't attempt that long ride to the Valley right now. The main thing is for him to get his weight and strength back. You're going to look him over, of course."

"Yes, now that you're on hand I thought we'd stay here for the next two weeks. My wife doesn't want to leave Romero and I don't want to leave my wife."

"I'll be glad to get back into familiar harness," Chavelita said.

"Don't forget to leave his records with me."

"I have a complete report in my briefcase. It may give you another chapter for your book."

"Uncle Phillip, don't you think I could stay at my own apartment? I have these two chaps who have been taking care of me," Romero said as he was helped into the car.

"Dr. Chavez knows your condition better than I do, Romero. She prescribed the hospital, and we'd better do as she recommended."

When Chavelita checked in at the hospital on reaching the Valley and found she wasn't needed immediately, she went home and to bed.

"I missed you, Maggie! Lord, how I missed you!" she said on arousing.

Maggie was distressed at her loss of weight. "Didn't they feed you at all at that place?" she demanded indignantly. "The next time you leave, I'll go with you. Here, sit down while I get you some coffee."

She saw Chavelita settled, then went to the kitchen and called out the news as she worked.

Susan Perida had had twins, so very unattractive that they could be mistaken for monkeys. And small wonder, with a father like Jacob. Consuela Valdez was going to marry that worthless Encinal Varo. Well, she'd better hold on to her job at the ceramic works if she expected to continue eating. There had been a fire up on the mountain. One of those lazy farmers had set fire to some brush so he could plant his corn. He'd gone to sleep under a tree, the fire got out of control and burned four houses before it could be stopped.

Chavelita expressed her concern as Maggie came in with the tray. She had included a cup for herself and sat down companionably near.

"And, oh, yes, Doctor, the worst news of all . . . we have to get a new teacher."

"What's the matter with our old one?"

"Maria's husband has been transferred to Reynosa. He's going to leave the first of next month, and as soon as he gets settled she's going to join him."

"Now that *is* bad news! Maria will be hard to replace, especially now that the school year is so far advanced."

"Now tell me about *Papacito's* grandson," Maggie said.

"Well, he was very ill."

"But you saved him," Maggie said with satisfaction.

"I can't take all the credit. Three other doctors were also on his case, and I called Dr. Phillip each day for instructions."

"But he would have died if you hadn't been there," the maid insisted. "Where are the doctor and his wife?"

"They're staying in Mexico for a couple of weeks."

And in two weeks they were home again.

"We left Romero at his apartment with his friends, Mr. Montoya and Mr. Sanchez. He seemed quite content visiting with them. I said he was content, and he was more nearly so than I've ever seen him. Basically he's an unhappy man, and you can't do a thing for him even though you think you have the remedy for his discontent."

"What is the remedy, Doctor?"

"A very simple prescription—a goal in life, something to aim for. No man can be happy living like that grub there on your ivy. It spends its entire life trying to satisfy its appetite. That's the way Romero's living. But since I can't help him, I'd better get to work on someone I can. . . . Isn't this the day Eucebio Salinas was to come in for some more tests?" Phillip turned to the file, selected a card, and regarded it gravely. "Did Luis get the X rays I asked for?"

"Yes, he left them hanging up for you to see."

Phillip started for the laboratory then turned back. "Didn't I see Felicia Navidad leave? What is she here for?"

"Do you need to ask that, Doctor?"

"You mean she's pregnant again? After the lecture I gave her and Adolfo?"

"She is. It seems her one task in life is to produce her kind."

"Well, she's certainly constantly employed! Is there anything special I should know about?"

"No, everything is under control, I think. I'm going up on Trucas today, so I'll be away until evening."

"I'll be around."

What's on your mind, Rome?" Mucio, trailed by Mike, crossed the hall to join Romero in his sitting room. The two had frequently been called to relieve his loneliness during his convalescence, but now that he was up, Mucio had been surprised at the summons.

"I'm feeling stronger now," Romero replied, "so why can't we continue our adventure?"

"Because I think you've had enough of it for a while. Even though you've improved, you're not fit for any rough living yet. And I have a tour coming up in a month."

"Well, we couldn't get much excitement in a month. I'm bored with sitting around and keep wishing that we had spent a little time at some of the ruins. While my aunt was here she went out and bought me some books on archaeology. They're very interesting."

"I suggested once, when we were near Bonampak, that we go there," Mucio reminded him.

"I know, it was my fault that we didn't. Now I suddenly have an urge to see those places. I've been thinking a lot about my grandfather lately. . . . I suppose that inspired me."

"It has just occurred to me, Rome, now that you are interested—you haven't been to Teotihuacan since you came back, have you?"

"No."

"Well, we can see it daily for as long as it takes to satisfy you."

"That sounds good," Romero agreed.

"Then, if we have the time and you're of a mind, we'll take a plane to Poza Rica and get a car there to take us out to El Tajin. The pyramids there have a distinctive type of ornamentation."

"I'd like to see them. I hope you know their history, Mucio."

The guide laughed. "So do I. No Sherlock Holmes has ever been sleuth enough to unravel that mystery. And speaking of riddles, why not come out to my place and read some of my books on these Mexican and Central American riddles? I have a large library on the subject; some of the volumes are now out of print."

Romero looked up with surprise. "You mean stay at your place?"

"Sure, you've roughed it before."

"Why, Mucio, I'd like that."

"Very well, then. Have your man get your trappings together and we'll go out now. Bring him along, too. I have room for both of you."

As Mucio showed Romero to his bedroom that evening he said, "This doesn't compare with your hotel, but I think the change will be good for you. This is your domain, but we'll have to share the rest of the house. The library is just across the hall, and since the bug has bit you I have an idea you'll spend a lot of time there."

Mucio was right, for every free moment found Romero reading and making notes, and *Popol Vuh* was his bedroom companion. One day he and Mucio were discussing it.

"Do you understand it?" Romero asked.

"Not all of it." Mucio paused to light his pipe. "You have to dig through a hard shell to get to the kernel. I've read that repeatedly and get a new angle with each reading. Then you read a commentary and get an entirely new idea. You pick up another chap's explanation and it refutes the first. I've just about decided to stay with my own conclusions."

"Perhaps I shouldn't be too hasty in finding analogies between biblical events and legends of the Indians. For instance, *Popol Vuh* starts out with the creation of the world when there was no solid thing, only water and sky; as I read it I am reminded of the story of Genesis 'and the earth was without form and void, and darkness was on the face of the deep.' Then hidden within a welter of words is the story of the fall of man. A barren tree suddenly began producing fruit after the head of a male sacrifice was hung in it. The order was given that no one must pick the fruit. But the virgin daughter of a lord heard the marvelous story and determined to see the tree for herself. When she reached up to the fruit the head of the sacrifice spit in her hand and she became pregnant, and later bore two sons. You remember that Eve conceived after eating the forbidden fruit."

"Do you know the Bible well, Rome?"

"Not really. My great-aunt tried to drill it into me when I was small, but I remember only a little."

"There are many similarities between it and our legends. I'd give a lot to know where the ancients got all this. Some time in the past there was a book that contained the originals of these legends. It is said that when the Spaniards first got to Guatemala they were shown a book written in characters that resembled Hebrew letters. There are students of Indian folklore who believe that the *Popol Vuh* is the translation of an original book, and that it was written to replace this original which had been lost or destroyed."

"Perhaps my grandfather had good reason to believe in his book."

"I think he had. Now, if you feel equal to it, we'll take a run to Teotihuacan in the morning. You can't begin to see it all in one day, so don't try. We'll take our time."

"I miss the children," Phillip said one evening. "How soon will they be home?"

"In another two weeks. Because of Romero's illness they have been at Woodwind much longer than I anticipated. I thought Romero would be home before this and was afraid the children's noise would disturb him. Since it's near the end of school I thought they might as well finish the year there."

"I have an idea Dad presented that excuse for keeping them."

"You're right, but it's a legitimate reason for their staying on."

"My father can think up some good ones! Have you heard from Romero this week?"

"No, nor last. I hope we hear something soon."

Marquita's hope was realized the next day when she received a long letter from him. She read it, then hurried in search of Phillip, rereading part of it and trailing a length of white net she was embroidering.

"My dear, you're not looking where you're going," Phillip chided when he met her coming into the library. "You're going to get a nasty fall. What has you so excited?"

"This letter from Romero. I'm not sure I like it." She gave him the letter, then gathered up the net at her feet. "He says he's going to visit in Mucio's home."

"He's going to do what?" Phillip hastily scanned the letter. "I don't know why he would leave a comfortable apartment in the City to stay in a private home in a small

276

village. Perhaps I'd better drive in and check on him. He can't stand a recurrence of whatever he had, and he has to watch his diet. I think I'll go in . . . things are relatively quiet at the hospital now."

Phillip was back at the end of the week. Marquita met him at the garden gate.

"He's looking well and says he feels fine. The Montoya home is simple—strictly a man's *casa*—and Romero is comfortably situated. He's changed a lot since his illness."

"Maybe his experiences taught him a lesson."

"Perhaps. This is the first time I have thought he resembled his grandfather except in appearance. He and Mucio were at the ruins at Teotihuacan when I got there. He was so full of what he had seen that he was bubbling over with excitement, just as your father used to be when he returned from a visit to one of the sites."

"I wish he could become the man Father was."

"I doubt that anyone can do that. In his hopes and ambitions for the Indian, he was another Moses. He was a rock against which all their troubles and sorrows broke. He was a giant of a man."

Romero came home a month later. Marquita, trowel in hand, was busy in the garden when he arrived.

"Where's the fatted calf?" he demanded. "I don't see it being barbecued."

Marquita arose with an exclamation of surprise. "How good to have you home again, Romero. I thought you'd forgotten us." Marquita took off her gardening gloves and put them with the trowel on a bench. "Come over here and tell me what you've been doing—but first, how do you feel?"

"Never better."

"Well, what have you been doing?"

"Have you visited the sites of Mexico's ancient cities?"

"I think I've seen the major ones."

"They're all major. Did they excite you as much as they did me?"

"I found them very interesting." Marquita was not too enthusiastic.

"Interesting! Is that all you can say of them? They're intriguing, mystifying! At last I can understand Grandpa's infatuation with the country's early history. I know now why he was so determined to find the book."

"You too are convinced that there is one?"

"There has to be. The legends refer to it as the 'Book of God.' I'm going to continue Grandpa's search for it."

"Where will you look?"

"I don't know. I only know that I must try to find it. I've engaged Mucio to go with me as soon as he has filled his other commitments—which will be some time next year."

"I'm afraid you're going to waste a lot of time and suffer a lot of disappointments."

"Perhaps, but if I eventually find the book it will be worth it. Marquita, do you know there are white Indians?"

"No, but generations of intermarriage with white-skinned people would naturally produce lighter ones."

"They claim it's the other way round. They were all white at one time but have grown darker through mixing with dark people."

"I am amazed, Romero, that you've become so excited over this. I know you've seen these places before."

"Yes, Grandpa took me to them, but I was a young fool and couldn't see any good in Mexico. Now I wonder why our people are so slow to discover the beauty and mystery of their country."

"Then you're not going to rush back to Europe."

"I may never go back."

What's the matter with you, Romero? Are you having a relapse of the jungle fever—or whatever you had?"

"I feel fine, Uncle Phillip. I'm just restless."

"Well, come with me to the mountains. I have a patient up there I must see and you might as well come along for the fresh air and the exercise. Let's get a sombrero for you. We don't want you to add heat stroke to your other ailments. There's Albert; he can get your hat."

"You and Marquita worry too much. I feel great."

"Let's keep it that way." The horses were soon saddled, and they started out. They had barely left the stables when they saw Chavelita coming toward them. Romero's heart skipped a beat and he felt his face burn as she approached.

"She rides well." Romero tried to make his voice sound casual.

"She does most things well." They reined in their horses when they met.

"If you're going to see Victoria, you needn't. I made your call while I was in the neighborhood," she told Phillip.

"How is she?"

"I think she belongs in the hospital. I told Juliano to bring her in this evening. I'm discharging Beatrice so we'll have room for Victoria."

"You think it won't be necessary for me to see her now?"

"Not unless you want the ride. She'll be down in a few hours. Here's my report." Phillip tried to still his restless horse as he read.

"How are you feeling, Romero?"

"Quite well, thank you."

"You don't look it. You're flushed. Do you have a fever? Have you checked him today, Dr. Phillip?"

"Who? Him?" Phillip looked up. "No, I thought he looked a little puny, but he said he felt great." Phillip turned back to the report, as Chavelita spurred her horse to Romero's side and reached for his hand. She studied her watch as she counted his pulse.

"You'd better come over to the hospital and let us run some more tests."

"Do you suppose we haven't killed that bug, after all?" Phillip asked with concern.

"I don't know, but we'd better find out right now."

"Well, Romero, instead of a trip up the mountains let's go over to the hospital."

"You're going to a lot of needless trouble," Romero insisted.

"I hope so, but let's make sure."

Dr. Mendoza was busy with another patient when they reached the hospital.

"I'll take care of you," Phillip said. "Just go into the lab. I'll be with you in a minute."

"I didn't know you did this sort of thing," Romero said when the doctor returned.

"I did it all when I first came here—diagnosis, lab, and treatment."

"It must have kept you busy."

"I said I did it all . . . which isn't exactly true. My wife, even before she was my wife, and Aunt Elodia worked with me. I couldn't have done everything alone. Here, put this under your tongue. Dr. Chavez is disturbed over your rapid pulse. We'll see if an abnormal temperature is causing it. And we're going to check your blood again. Push up your left sleeve."

"Luis checked the lab tests," Phillip told Romero that evening. "No sign of the bug."

Romero leaned back in his chair, hands behind his head, and stared at the ceiling. Phillip watched him for a moment and a teasing light flashed in his eyes.

"Do you know, Romero, that I've just now diagnosed your affliction?"

Romero transferred his gaze to the doctor's face. "You have?"

"Yes, I think you're in love."

"I know . . . I found it out this afternoon."

"Then why aren't you over there doing something about it?"

"She's on duty. And besides that, I don't have a chance. She has every reason to hate me."

"I know it. I know, too, that women are wonderful, unpredictable creatures. There are poor things here in the Valley that put up with all manner of abuse from their husbands just because they love the rats. And don't get the idea that I think that Chavelita loves you. I wouldn't even venture a guess. Now, since you can't see her tonight, let's have a game of chess."

Dr. Chavez was hurrying down the lane to the hospital, her attention on the flowers that bordered the road, when she became aware of a pair of masculine feet barring her way.

She looked up, ready with a reprimand, and found herself face to face with Romero.

"Where are you going in such a hurry?"

"I have to relieve Dr. Mendoza in exactly twenty minutes."

"Every time I see you you're moving as if you're racing the fire department to the scene of the blaze."

"A doctor's life isn't noted for its leisurely pace," she replied. He turned and walked beside her. "Luis told me that your tests were all negative."

"So Uncle Phillip said."

"During your illness you talked constantly of going back to Guatemala. I hope that when you do you will be careful of your diet."

"I was careful—that is until we lost our supplies. The natives who took me in shared their food, and I wasn't accustomed to it. I surmise that's where I picked up the 'bug.' Mucio and I went back down there just before I came home. I was unconscious when I left, and I wanted to thank the people for their kindness. Chavelita, their poverty was appalling! I'm going to do something that will make a permanent improvement in their lives."

"Now you sound like Papa!" They stopped before the hospital.

"Must you go in now? I haven't begun what I came to say. There's so much I want to tell you. When may I see you?"

"I'll be free tomorrow evening."

"May I call then about seven?"

Chavelita agreed.

Romero presented himself shortly before that time, and Maggie admitted him grudgingly. She had sensed Chavelita's

282

unhappiness and suspected that *Papacito*'s handsome grandson was in some way responsible.

"You're to wait in the garden," she told him and went back to her work in the kitchen.

He found his way outside. The moon was full, and its light flooded the small yard. He took the path toward the back of the enclosure where he saw a table and some chairs. The mingled perfume of the flowers lay over the garden like a fragrant blanket. A branch of a mimosa tree brushed his face, spreading its cloud-like pink blossoms before him like an offering. He started as Chavelita spoke.

"I know you're thinking that my entire garden is scarcely as large as one of your aunt's flower beds."

"It's lovely . . . what I've seen of it."

"Thank you. Shall we sit over here? I'm tired tonight."

"Perhaps I should come some other time, but you're always busy. Besides, I don't know how much longer I'll be here."

"Oh? Does the doctor approve of your leaving?"

"I haven't discussed it with him, but the tests prove that I'm all right." He leaned forward, elbows on his knees, one hand cupped in the other. Chavelita reached overhead and broke off a cluster of gardenia blossoms, waiting for him to speak. At length he began.

"I don't know how I had the courage to ask you to see me after what has happened. Before I forget it again, I haven't received a statement from you. . . ."

"You won't. There is no charge."

"Yes, there is. Considering the heel I was you'd have been justified if you'd given me poison."

"We aren't permitted to dispose of our patients that way, no matter how uncooperative they are," she replied, smiling. Romero didn't see the smile, for his gaze was focused on the ground.

283

"Not only did you take care of me here but you went all the way to Guatemala to look after me there."

"Romero, let me speak, then we won't ever discuss this again. No matter how hard I try, I can never repay Papa for all he did for me—not only in giving me an education and a profession but for his love and wonderful understanding."

"I'm sure Grandpa never expected any return."

"I know he didn't, but I'd like to pass on to others some of the kindness he showed me. And as long as one of his needs me I'll go to him if I have to crawl! Now let's forget it."

Romero was so quiet following that that she thought he had gone to sleep. At last he stirred.

"I've tried all day to analyze myself, to learn why I have acted toward you as I have. When I first came here I thought you'd be someone to flirt with, date a few times, then forget. But I couldn't forget. Beautiful women have always attracted me, and next to my aunt you're the loveliest I have ever seen. But I didn't want to be drawn to you. I suppose that's why I struck out at you as I did. When you came to me at Puerto Barrios I began to understand. Your life was filled with useful activity; mine with wasted opportunity. You've been a reproach to me ever since I came home. You've gigged my conscience, you've kept me in inner turmoil, yet you've drawn me to you as a magnet does steel. I didn't know the reason for this attraction until I made the startling discovery that I love you. And I'm dazed over it. I've boasted that it could never happen to me, and now that it has I'm completely unhinged." He clasped and loosed his hands nervously. Chavelita sat silent and still, afraid that if she moved she would shatter that moment of enchantment.

"I'm not such a fool as to think that after the way I have acted you can do less than hate me. I've given you no reason to feel otherwise. Besides, your life is complete. You have your career; you don't need anyone."

"Romero, stop thinking of me as a doctor! I'm also a woman. Just because I happen to know that the heart isn't shaped like a valentine doesn't signify that mine doesn't pulse with as much love as yours." For a moment he sat looking at her, arose, and drew her to her feet.

"You mean that after all you do care?"

"I mean that I love you so much I've been in agony ever since you came home." His arms went around her and held her close.

"I just don't believe this is happening!"

She stifled her sobs and moved away from him. "It's happening, all right, but when I think of all those weeks in Puerto Barrios! I've fought for the life of many a patient, but that was the only time I've ever taken one in my arms and willed him to live through the love that was in my heart."

"I've been such a blind, stupid fool! You should have operated on my head while you had the chance. How soon can we be married?"

"I don't know. I'm stunned. You'll have to give me time to absorb this."

"Don't make me wait too long . . . I'm just now beginning to feel like a whole person. You'll have to marry me to keep me in one piece. Isn't it the Chinese who believe that a person becomes responsible for one whose life he saves? You've done that for me twice, so you're doubly committed."

"Romero, from now on I'm going to shrug off all responsibility. I'm never going to make another decision. I'm tired of being a strong, dependable character. From now on I'm going to be a helpless, docile woman."

"Good! I'll enjoy being the boss. Come on, let's go over

285

and tell Marquita and Phillip. He offered me the use of the garden for my romancing."

The big house loomed white in the moonlight, and the intricate design of the gate cast its shadow on the tiled entrance. Marquita met them at the door and opened her arms to Chavelita.

"I'm so very happy!" she cried.

"You knew?"

"Of course I knew! Why do you think he moved out of his comfortable home here into a suite first in Mexico, then Monterrey, then Guadalajara? Why did he chase all over Central and South America? Like all men, when he realized that the matrimonial noose was whirling over his head he tried to outrun it."

"Marquita, if you knew so much why didn't you tell me and save us both a lot of misery?"

"Because you wouldn't have listened to me. You said that you would never be tied down by a woman and children. You've had this coming to you for a long time, and I'm glad I'm here to see it happen. Phillip," she turned to call through the door. The doctor came in, a finger marking his place in his magazine. He dropped it when he saw Romero's face.

"Uncle Phillip, she's agreed to marry me!" Romero said.

Phillip grasped his hand. "You know you don't deserve her, but I'm glad she's accepted you. I can relax now. I was afraid she was going to marry one of those persistent medics from Mexico and I'd lose my favorite doctor."

"You will anyway. She isn't going to continue her practice."

"Oh, yes I am! Papa didn't educate me for such a short term of service. He doesn't expect me to give up my career just because I'm marrying his grandson."

"Wait a minute. I thought I was going to make all the decisions."

"Not this one. I worked too long and too hard for my degree not to use it."

"And what am I to do while you're running up and down the mountains dosing the sick and delivering babies all over the Valley?"

"You," she said after a moment's hesitation, "are going to teach school."

"Me? Teach school?"

"Yes, I thought when I saw you drifting idly by yesterday what a perfect replacement you'd make for Mary. It doesn't look as if we'll ever get anyone to complete the term when she leaves."

Romero waited with a dazed expression. "What do I have here, Uncle Phillip?"

"Don't look at me. There's simply no knowing women. I've been married to one of the gorgeous creatures for more than twenty years and I still don't understand her—thank the Lord. We're not supposed to. We're just to love them to the limit, enjoy them to the fullest, and be glad we lost a rib."

"But it hasn't been a half hour since she told me what a submissive wife she was going to be. Now she's assigning me to a job that I'm not fitted for, do not want, and will not accept."

"You'll love it, Romero, once you get into it," Chavelita assured him. Then she turned to Phillip and said, "I want to talk with him privately, and he says you offered him the use of the garden. Do you mind?"

"It's all yours," Phillip told her. "Mrs. Parmarez, do you suppose we dare sit outside again?"

"Of course. They'll want more privacy than they would have out here." And she led the way to the patio.

"Why don't you finish reading your article to me?"

"Are you interested in that or are you trying to feed my vanity?"

"I'm interested in anything that concerns you."

"Lucky, lucky me," Phillip said and took up his medical journal. But before he was launched into the subject Chavelita and Romero returned.

"How can they change so quickly?" he demanded of Phillip. "Less than an hour ago this woman, who will soon promise to love and obey me, I hope, voluntarily assured me of her docility . . . that was her word, docile. Now she's as stubborn as a donkey. She insists that I take over that class. If I ever have to work—Lord forbid—it will not be to teach grimy little kids."

"Poor boy," Phillip sympathized, "he has a lot to learn. Volumes have been written about the meek, retiring woman of Mexico who sits behind a cactus fence while her lord goes forth to spend his time and pesos at the cantina. But no one has said anything about her scheming and plotting to get her own way once the master comes home. If you're wise, Romero, you'll get those textbooks and start boning up, because next week you'll be taking Mary's classes."

And he was right. On Monday morning Marquita and Romero went to school together, and after a briefing on the day's program he was left to carry on.

Rain had forced Marquita indoors. She was sitting at a window overlooking the garden when Phillip came in.

"I see that the mail has arrived," she observed. "It looks as if you have a lot of it."

"About the usual." He singled out a letter. "Do you remember Dr. Bertaldo?"

Marquita shook her head. "The name doesn't register."

"You met him at the hospital. He joined the staff just before we were married. I have a note from him. He has a son who has been studying medicine and will soon finish his internship. He wants to know if we can use him here for a year or two."

"You mean he wants his son to start under you? With Chavelita leaving that would be a good arrangement, wouldn't it?"

"Yes, extremely convenient for me. I'll be glad to have someone take over the mountain pueblos. Chavelita has looked after them for so long I'd find it difficult to go back to it again. Can we put the chap up here for a while?"

"Of course, Phillip. Was there any mail for me?"

"A letter from Carl. We didn't achieve our purpose after all, did we? We insisted that Dad leave Woodwind and come up here, and he doesn't do a thing but talk us into letting him take the boys into Mexico for their schooling."

"Well, at least he's closer now than he was in Puerto Barrios."

Ben Bertaldo arrived a month before he was expected. He was taken to the guest room but was soon downstairs again, eager to get to the hospital.

"I've heard of what you are doing, and I want to become a part of it. If I can learn how you started perhaps some day I can set up a similar operation in another area," he told Phillip on their way to the hospital.

"I can't take credit for what's been done here. My father-in-law had a dream and he put that dream to work. He began the program more than forty years ago. Here's our little infirmary."

" 'House of Hope'—what a significant name!"

"I trust you will like working with us. Here's Dr. Chavez, whom you're to replace."

"A woman doctor?"

"One of the best!"

Chavelita welcomed the young man graciously.

"Dr. Chavez is to be married very soon to my wife's nephew."

"Will you continue to practice?" Ben asked her.

"In a limited way," she answered. "I expect to have a family, and that will take precedence over everything else."

"Now, if you'll come with me, Dr. Bertaldo, I'll show you our laboratory and introduce you to Dr. Mendoza, who has charge of it. Luis is handicapped, but he's an excellent lab man."

"With three junior doctors on the staff I feel like a gentleman of leisure," Phillip told Marquita.

"You'd better make the most of it for you won't have three very much longer. Chavelita's wedding day isn't far off. And that fact brings up a question—what's troubling Romero?"

"I don't know. He seems very absentminded."

"I thought his approaching marriage would tend to settle him down, but he seems more restless than ever."

"Perhaps that's why he's restless," Phillip suggested.

"He's made three trips into Mexico within the last two weeks. Why?"

"That, my dear, is his business."

Marquita had to admit that he was right.

His abstraction had also troubled Chavelita. They had been arranging their furniture for over an hour.

"Cherie, you've had that chair moved a dozen times, I'm sure," Romero chided.

"I know." Chavelita pinched her lips thoughtfully. "I think I'll leave it where it is, but I'm still not sure about the couch. Does it look better there under the window, or here in the center as a sort of room divider with the wing chairs and the lamp?"

"Do you have to decide right now? Can't you tell better after we've lived here for a while?"

"Yes, of course," she sighed. "It's just the submerged housewife triumphing over the doctor."

"Well, I'm rooting for the housewife, but I have something I want to discuss with you."

"All right. Shall we sit here?"

"No, let's go to Grandpa's old room. During the past weeks I've felt that he was very near me, almost as if I could reach out and touch him. I've seen him waiting for me at every turn in a garden path, and I've felt him beside me as I've walked through the village, trying to decide what to do with my life—what there is left of it. I think I've reached a conclusion, provided you approve."

"Let's sit in Papa's chair. There's room for both of us. I wonder why he wanted such a big one?"

"So he could cuddle all the children in the Valley when they swarmed over him."

"I know, I was one of them. Now tell me what's on your mind. You've been very serious lately."

"I've been thinking." She moved to make room for him and turned in anticipation.

"You know of my interest in pre-Hispanic Mexico. It's more than that . . . it's an urgency. It's almost . . . well, if I were a student of divinity I'd say it's a religious fervor. I think it was at Monte Alban that I became convinced that we Indians have a destiny. Do you realize that we don't even have a name of our own? We're called 'Indians' because of a sailor's nautical miscalculations! The condition of our people today is shocking, but we'll climb out of it. From the ruined cities and monuments of the past I know we were once a people to be reckoned with, and we will be again."

"Romero, you get more like Papa all the time."

"And I find myself with his goals and ambitions. I had intended continuing his search for the book next year, but I've changed my mind. As I said, I've sensed Grandpa near me almost constantly, and the feeling given me by his presence is that finding the book is not my task any more than it was his. It will be found, I know, but I'm impressed with the knowledge that our people cannot benefit by any advantage offered them by this history as long as they remain illiterate. They will have to be educated. I've talked to you about those people who took Mike and me in after we were washed out. I want to do something for them—not just for that family but for the entire area." He paused and looked down into the garden where Ricky was chasing the twins, threatening them with a lizard. "Until we went back after my recovery I didn't know how poor their house was. I'll never forget it. Like so many of them, it was made of mud and straw. The rains had washed a lot of the soil away leaving straw ends sticking out like a beard on an unshaven chin. I'll always remember that Mike risked his life to save mine. And I can never forget that Josie killed her one chicken to feed me, or that Ester gave me the last tortilla she had in her house. Carmelita took her Sunday petticoat and made a shirt for me, and Evelio gave me the trousers he had bought to wear to the fiesta. I can't remember all their kindnesses. I must do something for them in return."

"I thought you'd provided for them."

"Temporarily, yes. While we were there we took all the people into the village and outfitted them from head to toe. We saw to it that they had food in their houses, pigs and goats, chickens and turkeys in their yards. They have been helped over a present difficulty, but with their lack of education and guidance they no doubt will be back in the slough before the year's end. They must be taught to help themselves."

"I get the message, Santiago Salazar. You want us to start an Esperanza down there."

"Is it asking too much?"

"No, I'll be proud to be a part of the plan. Tell me more about the place. Is the village about like Esperanza?"

"Oh, no. It's probably like Esperanza was when Grandpa first came here. I didn't go into any of the homes except Evelio's. But from the outside they looked very much alike. Some of them had only one room. Evelio's had three, but he shared it with his married son and his wife and an unmarried daughter. The rooms were divided by walls only breast high, and the floors were dirt. They didn't even have a brazier, which to me is the most primitive of furnishings—at least it

293

was until I saw Josie balance her bean pot on three blackened stones. They barely had enough dishes for the family, so our coming was a problem until we went into town and bought more. As soon as we get back from Europe we'll go there and figure out what problems we have to solve before we can begin operations. Then we'll come back here for a year or so and learn how Grandpa got this thing rolling. That will give Phillip time to get another doctor. Perhaps Ben will stay." Romero's eyes shone with anticipation.

"Let's go tell Marquita." Chavelita preceded him from the room and into the hall.

"Why, there's another tour!" she said. "I don't think this one was expected. I didn't notice any activity of getting ready when I came from the hospital." They paused at the foot of the stairs.

"It won't take long to prepare . . . haul a few looms outside and build fires under some braziers. There goes Adelina to the fountain with her pitcher balanced on her shoulder. That never fails to bring out the cameras." They stopped to look through the door, then went on to the garden.

"There's Marquita coming to meet us."

"You look as if you're bursting with news. Have you postponed the wedding?"

"What a horrible thought!" Romero grimaced. "No, we're not putting it off a day. We do have some news though, and we want to share it. When we come back from our trip we're going to try to build an Esperanza in Guatemala in that poor area where I was stranded—that is, if we'll be permitted."

Marquita's eyes widened with surprise. "You're serious about this?"

"I'm so convinced it's what I want to do that I'd like to grab my girl and start out right now."

"And you, Chavelita?"

"It's a case of 'whither he goest,' Marquita. But aside from my love for him, I think Papa would be pleased with the idea. To me, Romero and I are ideally suited for the work. First, we have the dream, the zeal and determination, and while he teaches I can work with the sick."

"I don't think anything would have pleased Father more," Marquita said. "I wish he could know. Next to finding the book, this program for the people was nearest his heart, and in his later years it came first."

"Grandpa wanted me to look for the book," Romero remembered. "Who knows . . . perhaps we'll find it down there."

I don't think I ever saw so many tours during one season," Chavelita said as she and Marquita were coming through the village a few days later.

"Yes, we've had as many as five here at one time. It's been pretty crowded. Perhaps it's just as well that Romero was away this week."

"I suppose so, but I surely miss him."

"I'm eager to see him, too, but for a different reason. I'm tired of teaching."

"You've certainly been a faithful substitute all these years," Chavelita observed. "Well, here's my *casa,* so I'll leave you. If Romero should call, will you send someone for me?"

"Speak of the devil . . ." Marquita began. Chavelita looked up and saw Romero leaving the big house. She hurried toward him as fast as decorum would permit.

"What kept you so long?" she demanded.

"Oh, just finishing up odds and ends. I also discussed our project in Guatemala with some of the authorities."

"Will there be any difficulty?"

"I doubt it. We'll talk about it again after we come back."

Maggie unlocked the door and let them in.

"Now am I invited to supper, or do I go home to a cold snack?" Romero inquired.

"Let me see what we're having . . . perhaps you'd better go home—I know the sort of cold snack Marquita sets before you."

"Are you insinuating that it's too good or not good enough? All that concerns me is the quantity—I'm a very hungry man. While I think of it, has Ben spoken to you about renting the house while we're gone? He reminded me when I passed the hospital a moment ago that he'd like to have it."

"My goodness, the man is eager. Yes, he asked me about it, and I told him I'd have to discuss it with you."

"You do as you please, cherie, but if you really want my opinion it seems to me that you can't do better than having him as a tenant. After all, we won't be living here when we come back anyway."

"That's what I thought. And it will be a place for Maggie while we're away. . . . I see she's set a plate for you, so you're invited."

"Good, I'm starving." He held Chavelita's chair for her then took the one opposite.

"There was a lot of activity in Upper Valley as I came through. I understand they didn't have room to accommodate all the tourists this past week."

"That's right. Phillip says we'll have to add to the motel or build a new one. There's an artist in the group who wants to stay on for a while. He has asked for a room in this end of the Valley . . . wants to do some painting here."

"I wonder who he is."

"I didn't catch his name. Lucy told me about him when she came on duty last night. Now let's take Maggie and go up to see the fireworks."

"What are the fireworks for?"

"I can't tell you that, my love. Maggie, do you know what's being celebrated?"

"It's the mayor's Saint's Day, Doctor."

"That explains the lavish display of paper flowers. Let's stop and get the girls. Marquita never lets them go into a crowd alone. Of course they may have gone with one of the maids."

"I doubt that, Romero. The twins ignore the maids—who are afraid to cross them."

But when they got to the big house the girls had gone with Dr. Bertaldo and Ricky, and Phillip was fuming about it.

"You know they're perfectly safe, Phillip! I would never have let them leave the place if there'd been any danger."

"I'm not thinking of danger in that respect, my dear. I just don't want my daughters going anywhere without an older woman with them."

"They're with Ricky and Ben!"

"That's just it! Ben can't keep his eyes off Macaria. I know . . . I've watched him!"

Marquita gave a short laugh of exasperation. "Phillip, don't be ridiculous! Ben is a grown man, and Macaria is a little girl."

"There's twelve years difference in their ages—exactly the same as in ours!"

"Oh, my goodness!" Marquita cried when she caught the implication, "I'm going after them."

"Wait," Chavelita said, "I doubt that we can find them in that mob, but we'll look for them. I think you're both being very foolish. Ben is one of nine children, and I'm sure he looks on the girls as his own sisters."

"Quit worrying. You can't blame Ben for enjoying their company. After all, they're as cute as they are beautiful, and they're fun to be with," Romero added his reassurance.

"I wonder if you two are going to be as calm when you have daughters of your own," Phillip observed grimly.

"When you put it that way, no. Come on. Let's find the twins," Romero said and took Chavelita by the arm.

Romero paused beside the easel of the visiting artist and watched him work, then turned to look at a painting in an open portfolio. There was something familiar about it, so he bent to examine it more closely.

"I hope you don't mind my intrusion," he began.

The man looked up. "Not at all."

"This picture looks like one of the ruins south of here."

"Monte Alban."

"But this figure in white descending—from the halo I would conclude that you're suggesting one of the saints . . ."

"It's the Lord."

"But these figures all have Indian faces and dress."

"They *are* Indian. The drawing is my concept of Christ's appearance to the people on this continent."

"Then you think they knew the Christ?"

"Of course. Your own legends tell you that. The culture developed under his favor and destroyed itself when it forgot him."

"You're quitting?" Romero asked as the artist began cleaning his brushes. "I hope my interruption isn't the cause."

"No, I've lost the light. It changes so rapidly this time of day. . . . I'll try again tomorrow."

"Where are you staying? I don't remember seeing you before."

"I came in with a tour last week, but when I saw this place I couldn't leave. I'm staying with the Garcia family."

"Which Garcia? That name's as common in Mexico as Smith is in New York."

"I don't have the vaguest idea, nor where the house is—they're all so much alike. When I got ready to go last night I wandered around until one of the children claimed me. And if I'm to get any supper I'd better start walking."

"Here, let me help you. You have quite a load. I forgot to introduce myself. I'm Romero Salazar, another name common in Mexico."

"I'm Rod Bates." They shook hands, then the artist looked up sharply. "Salazar," he repeated. "Are you the patron saint of this area?"

"No, that was my grandfather. Give me your easel. We'll go to my home for supper. Your drawing interests me. I'd like to talk with you about your subject. I was south several months ago and heard numerous legends about a Fair God. He had a dozen names, more or less, but the same appearance and philosophy. My guide suggested that the being the Indians called Quetzalcoatl, Kulkulcan, Viracocha, we know as Christ." Romero took the easel and they set out. They hadn't gone far before Rod was stopped.

"Here they are," he said. "I'll just send these things home by Juan and Pedro . . . or is it Herlindo and Raul?"

"Henry and Bill, señor."

"Henry and Bill it is, then. Just set them in my room so they won't fall. I want the portfolio. Be careful of this canvas . . . it's still wet."

"I know how to hold it, señor. I used to help *Papacito.*" He lifted the unfinished painting to the top of his head and

300

held it in balance with his hands firmly pressed against the wooden framework.

"That Henry is quite a chap. He says he's going to be a druggist," Romero said. "He'll make a good one. Now Bill has no leaning in that direction—says he wants to be a farmer. He likes animals and hopes to have his own riding horse someday. I don't know him as well as I do his brother. Henry is in one of my classes."

"You're a schoolteacher? You don't look like one."

Romero laughed. "How should a teacher look?"

"Oh, sort of academic, I suppose. You look more like a gentleman of leisure."

"My grandfather had a theory that if you had something your neighbor needed it was your duty to share it with him. I've had an education so I'm trying to pass some of it on. This was a very poor, illiterate group when Grandpa came here. He and my great-aunt were the first teachers, and as soon as their pupils learned to read and write they were sent out to teach others while at the same time continuing to learn."

"Your grandfather must have been a remarkable man. Everyone here speaks of him with love and respect."

"Yes, Grandpa *was* Esperanza. Without him there would have been no Valley of Hope. But here we are at Bello Jardin, which means, if you need a translation, Beautiful Garden. My aunt and uncle own it, but they have taken me in. Come on out to the garden. This is where we live, weather permitting—and it usually does."

Walking up to where Marquita and Phillip were seated, Romero said, "I met Mr. Bates in the village and brought him home to have supper with us. My aunt, Mrs. Parmarez, and my uncle, the doctor."

"Sit down, Mr. Bates, and tell us how you like our Valley," Phillip invited.

301

"I'm fascinated by it, Dr. Parmarez. There's something familiar about it; I feel as if I've been here before. And this garden . . . wait a minute, your grandfather was the artist?"

Romero nodded his agreement.

"Do you know, I've stood before his paintings for hours. I've tried to imitate him, but I've failed. I simply don't have his touch."

"No one has," Marquita said. "Father loved the Valley and its people. That, I think, was the secret of his success as an artist and as a person. He had unlimited love. He saw beauty where no one else could. When Romero used to chafe to get away to find inspiration for his painting, Father would say, 'The boy is sitting on a gold mine of subjects but he can't see them for the New York skyscrapers straddling his nose.' "

"Then you are also an artist?"

"I used to paint."

"I don't know your work."

"I used another name—'Rome Sales.' "

"That name is familiar . . . and you wanted to see my paintings!"

"I did, and I do. And I want my aunt and uncle to see them, too."

"Let's wait until after supper. I operated today and had to skip my noon meal. There's the bell now; shall we go in?" Phillip offered Marquita his arm.

After the meal Phillip went to the hospital to check on his surgery case and returned with Chavelita. Rod was just opening his portfolio.

"This is what attracted me this afternoon," Romero said as the picture of the pyramid at Monte Alban was shown. "Do you remember I told you Mucio suggested that the Fair God of the various tribes was the Christ? Look at this figure."

302

"And here," Rod said, producing another picture, "is Jesus calling his twelve disciples. And here is our Lord blessing the children. They had a marvelous experience that day."

"Are you trying to parallel or duplicate biblical events here in Mexico?" Marquita asked critically.

"Oh, no, this actually happened. These pictures of mine are merely my idea of the events. Christ came to this continent soon after his resurrection."

"It seems to me, Mr. Bates, that you're taking a lot for granted. What basis do you have for this belief of yours?" Phillip asked.

"Well, Doctor, I know you're familiar with your own legends."

"You refer to the bearded stranger, I suppose."

"That's one. It would take a long time to recount them all. I don't believe there's an Indian tribe in your country or mine that doesn't have a legend of the White God. They give him the same appearance and character. He taught them the gospel of love and forgiveness, performed miracles of healing, and when he left he promised to return."

"Are these stories the foundation of your argument?" Phillip challenged.

"No indeed. My church had evidence of this long before much thought was given to the Indian or his legends. You see, there is a book . . ." Marquita clapped her hand over her mouth, and her eyes widened in amazement. Romero and Phillip also showed their astonishment as they echoed in unison, "There *is* a book?"

"Did I say something I shouldn't have?" Rod looked from one to the other.

"No, but I've heard my father utter those same words so often!" Marquita was the first to recover from her surprise.

303

"And I spent my vacations from school trailing all over the country with him looking for it," Romero said.

"What is the name of this book?"

"The Book of Mormon."

"The Book of Mormon?" Phillip exclaimed. "So you're one of those people."

"Yes, I believe that God never left any nation without the message of salvation. I believe that it was preached to every generation beginning with Adam until men chose darkness rather than truth. I believe that God was as deeply concerned with the inhabitants in this part of his world as with those in the East. This book tells of the coming of Christ to America. He is the theme throughout, although there is a very interesting history of the people, beginning with their leaving their homeland in the East, their arrival on this continent, their development, and their final destruction." Rod felt the tension rising so began collecting his drawings and repacking his portfolio.

Regretting his remark almost as soon as he made it, Phillip hastened to apologize. "Please, Mr. Bates, don't put those away yet. I'm sorry I spoke as I did. I was thoughtless and rude. But you have no idea what a shock this is to us. Father was always so sure that somewhere there was a record of the Indian people. There have been so many tales of records hidden in caves that he was certain some day it would come to light. For years he hunted among the older people, thinking he could find a clue as to where the book was concealed. Then rather late in life, he changed his thinking. While studying the Bible he read a prophecy by Isaiah relating to a mysterious book."

Rod smiled. "Twenty-ninth chapter . . . 'the words of the book that is sealed,' " Rod quoted. "This is the book."

"That's fantastic!" Marquita exclaimed. "How long since it was published?"

"Over a hundred years."

"I wish Father could have had it. He read everything he could find on the subject, but from the title you'd never suspect that this had anything to do with our people."

"Where can I get a copy, or is it out of print?" Romero asked.

"I have a copy, Mr. Salazar. I'll be glad to leave it with you."

"May I have it tonight?"

"Of course. And now I'd better be going. Thank you for a very pleasant evening."

"May I go with you and get the book?"

"Certainly. I'll need you to show me the way to my boarding place."

"Do you want to go, cherie?"

"No, Romero, I've had no supper. I'm going to forage in the kitchen . . . with Marquita's permission."

"Forgive me. . . . I didn't think to ask you when you came in."

"Think nothing of it, I'll just help myself." Chavelita and the girls turned toward the kitchen. Marquita and Phillip arose with their guest.

"Mr. Bates, you have a standing invitation to supper every evening as long as you're here," Phillip told him. "We'd like to hear more about the book."

"Thank you, I'll be glad to come and discuss it with you."

Romero waited outside the Garcia home while Rod went in to get the book.

"I'm wide awake now and there is such a glorious moon I think I'll take a walk," Rod said on returning.

"I'm in the same mood, so I'll walk with you if you don't

object. I must know more about this history before I go to bed, so start talking, please."

They walked around the plaza several times and on into Upper Esperanza, Rod talking, Romero listening and asking questions. It was near midnight when they ended their stroll.

"I'll take good care of this and return it as soon as I've read it," Romero promised on parting.

"I'm giving it to you, Mr. Salazar. One reading won't satisfy you."

Romero moved noiselessly through the darkened *sala* and up to his own apartment. The window curtains had been drawn and a square of unfettered moonlight brightened the floor. His talk with Rod had left him excited and restless. He was not ready to go to bed and stepped out onto his balcony. The moon, like a ship at sea, was riding a billow of clouds. The garden below was flooded with its brilliance. The mountains were gray shadows, but he could outline an occasional small village in the dusk, the little houses light smudges, the church spire pointing a white finger to the sky.

"Just think," he whispered, "He and his followers may have wandered over these mountains. Perhaps He rested here." He was elated by the thought and turned back into his room and to the book.

"I wonder what's keeping Romero. He isn't usually so late," Marquita said at breakfast the next morning.

"Maria, go see if Mr. Salazar is awake."

The maid returned a moment later. "He does not answer, Señora."

"Did you knock hard? He was out late; perhaps he's sleeping."

"I knocked and I called," she insisted.

"I'll run up and see what's wrong," Phillip volunteered.

"I'm going, too; he may be ill," Marquita said and followed.

Phillip knocked, then called, but there was no response. He opened the door gently and looked in. Romero was sitting beneath the lighted lamp reading, heedless of the sunlight pouring in through the windows.

"Romero, are you all right?"

Romero raised his eyes from the book and looked at the two in the doorway. It took a moment to break from the past. "What? Is something wrong?"

"That's why we're here. You didn't come down to breakfast or open to Marie's knock. We thought you might be ill."

"No, I'm all right. I've been reading."

"All night?"

Romero glanced toward the window. "Yes, it seems that I have."

"Well, come on down to breakfast."

"I want to finish this. I'll be down later," and he dismissed them by returning to his book.

Marquita and Phillip went back to the breakfast room.

"I'm eager to see that book," Marquita said.

"So am I. It must be exceptional to keep him awake all night."

The family didn't see Romero until he came down to early supper.

"You look as if you'd seen a ghost," was Phillip's greeting.

"I've been walking with them!" Romero placed the book on the table. "This is the most extraordinary piece of literature I've ever read. I've spent the night with people who walked this continent before Christ was born."

"Now don't get carried away. All you know is what some stranger has told you," the doctor cautioned.

"I have read the book," Romero defended himself simply. He took his cup of coffee and set it down beside his plate. "All the time I was in the south I was told of buried records, of books hidden in caves, and on one occasion of a magic stone that permitted the tribal priest to see into the future. The original of this book was engraved on metal plates. These, with a pair of lenses, were found in a stone box buried in the earth." He sat stirring his coffee until Marquita roused him.

"You aren't eating, Romero, and you've had nothing all day."

"I'm not hungry . . . later perhaps. Now, if you'll excuse me." He arose, took the book, and left the room. A little later they heard the gate close behind him.

"I wish he'd given us a chance to see that book," Marcia lamented.

"He has to return it to Mr. Bates. We'll buy a copy for ourselves," Marquita told her.

The family left the table, the children to their pursuits in the garden, Phillip to make his hospital calls. Marquita walked with him to the door, then turned and crossed the *sala* to the patio. The young people's voices came in muted tones from different parts of the garden.

Marquita halted uncertainly at the fountain. What Romero had said about the book filled her with unrest, and she walked nervously down the path toward the lake. She stopped midway, remembering Rod Bates and his conversation. Where did he get his assurance? There didn't seem to be any doubt in his mind. But Christ in America?

"I'm going to borrow that book from Mr. Bates. I can't wait to order one. I must know now!" she said aloud.

In the meantime Romero hastened down the cobbled

street and crossed the plaza. He didn't stop at the Garcia home, nor yet at Chavelita's house. For a time he was lost in the crowd, but he pressed on. He climbed the hill to Lookout Point for the first time since his return. He paused beside the monument and for a moment his hand caressed the white shaft that had been raised to honor his grandfather. Then, clasping the book in both hands, he turned to face the west where, in his memory, a lone cactus stood outlined against a crimson sky.